PENGUIN METRO READS
LIFE SWITCH

Madhuri Banerjee is the author of nine books, a columnist with *Maxim, Asian Age* and *Cosmopolitan*, and has her own blog with CNN-News18 called Chastity Belt as well as her personal blog on Blogspot. She was an editor with Star Bharat and produced 300 episodes of a daily crime show called *Savdhaan India* with multiple producers. Madhuri was an executive producer with Hotstar Originals and worked on several original films with Saregama Yoodlee Films for the platform. She has written the screenplay for the Bollywood film *Hate Story 2* and worked with stalwarts like Vikram Bhatt, Kaizad Gustad and Subhash Ghai. She won a National Award for a documentary called *Between Dualities*. Currently, Madhuri is developing a web series for an OTT platform under her production house Aria Entertainment House.

Life Switch

It's Your Life. Until It's Not.

MADHURI BANERJEE

Penguin
metro reads

An imprint of Penguin Random House

PENGUIN METRO READS

USA | Canada | UK | Ireland | Australia
New Zealand | India | South Africa | China

Penguin Metro Reads is part of the Penguin Random House group of companies
whose addresses can be found at global.penguinrandomhouse.com

Published by Penguin Random House India Pvt. Ltd
4th Floor, Capital Tower 1, MG Road,
Gurugram 122 002, Haryana, India

First published in Penguin Metro Reads by Penguin Random House India 2023

Copyright © Madhuri Banerjee 2023

ISBN 9780143459194

Typeset in Bembo by MAP Systems, Bengaluru, India
Printed at Replika Press Pvt. Ltd, India

www.penguin.co.in

For Ariaana
For being such an incredible, special, talented child and becoming a brilliant, responsible, mature teenager, and supporting me through the pandemic and much more

One

Nandita

How to Seduce Your Husband

I read the article once again. Tonight, was the night. It had been six months since Abhay had been intimate with me. I was dying to be touched. I needed my husband to desire me. What the hell had gone wrong with him? Or was it me? I'd been trying to be a good wife for so long that it may have altered his thoughts from being passionate to being passive. After all, he told me once that he believed all romance dies after a year anyway, then it was all duty. But he was very sleepy then. And I'm sure he didn't mean it. Or did he? I was determined to bring the spark back into my marriage and prove that romance doesn't die with each *phera*.

I read the checklist in the article to make sure I was doing everything correctly.

1. *Look the part.* I glanced at myself in the mirror. I'd blow-dried my shoulder-length dark brown hair, put on smoky eye make-up to make my dark black eyes pop, and applied

a light lip gloss that helped me pout just like they showed in the magazines. I wished I were sexier. More confident. I wished that I could demand what I wanted from Abhay in bed. But I've never been the type to assert myself or be overtly sensual. I was always nervous around too many people. I sprayed on some perfume. I looked good and always felt better after I put on some perfume. Check.

2. *Wear slightly revealing clothes*. I was wearing purple satin boxers and a singlet that would be casual and yet flirty. I refused to buy expensive lingerie that Abhay wouldn't notice. At the beginning of the marriage, he used to be so eager to get every piece of clothing off me. But then he struggled, and it became a chore for him. He grumbled at the hooks and lost his mojo by the time I was naked. The point of lingerie was completely lost. But sexy nightwear? Check.

3. *Create the mood*. I know about this one. My friend Diya gave me sound advice on how to spice up my sex life because she said she still had a roaring sex life. But I'm not sure I could do all the things she does. It seems like a lot of work. But the intimacy with Abhay had been dwindling over the last year. And with it, my self-esteem. I know. I know. I am a self-made woman. I like a lot of things in life—plants, swimming and reading books. But I've always wanted companionship. I hate being alone. And lately, Abhay has been spending more time playing tennis and hanging out with his friends than coming home to me.

'Nandita,' Abhay shouted as he entered the house. 'Where are you? Ma? Papa?'

'In our room, Abhay,' I call out. I lay on the bed, pretending to read.

4. *Don't seem over-eager.* Over-eager? Just the thought of being touched made me horny. God, it had been so long! When had the magic died exactly? Probably when I started wearing boring, cotton flowery nighties to bed. No, it was when we got the Netflix account. Maybe it had already been dwindling. I can't remember. But I was going to keep it casual. Just by the way. Check.

Abhay entered to see a variety of candles lit across the room and me sprawled on our large king-size bed with white satin sheets. 'Whoa, what's all this?' He dropped his laptop bag on the chair by the door, took out his nose drops from his jeans pocket, tilted his head back and put two drops in his nostrils.

Yeah, he was ready. Check!

I got up slowly and touched my hair seductively. 'I thought we could have some alone time.'

Abhay nodded slowly, comprehending the scenario. 'Nice!' He put his phone down on the dressing table and sneezed. 'What's that smell?'

I looked at the dozen candles I had lit to 'set the mood'. The store had been out of plain candles, so I bought all the fragrant ones. And lit each one of them. I sniffed to see which one was giving out the strongest smell. 'Lavender . . . I think. Or vanilla. Or green tea.'

Abhay sneezed again. 'God! Can we put them out?' he coughed. 'I think they're giving me an asthma attack. Or maybe throw all of them out and open a window?' He entered the bathroom to get away from the smell. And maybe me.

'Oh shit. Yeah, yeah,' I blew out all the candles and opened the window for the smell to find its way out.

'Where are my parents?' he asked from inside the bathroom.

'They've gone for a party,' I answered as I put on the fan and got back to lying on the bed alluringly. Fine if there were no candles. The mood wasn't dead. Yet.

5. *Don't let anything distract you.* Men tend to talk about trivial things because they believe sharing information is romantic. It's not. It's boring and they need to shut up. Bringing up parents did kill the mood, but I was going to focus on my desire and not the image of my in-laws. Check.

And then it struck me. The bug of self-doubt. Why was making love such hard work? Wasn't it supposed to happen regularly after you got married? I thought that, after I got married, I would be having sex all the time. And from once a day it became once a week and then once a month. And now . . . never mind.

He came out wearing faded denim shorts and an old college T-shirt. I hated him in these ugly clothes, which made him look like a schoolboy. He's twenty-eight years old, for god's sake. He works with his dad in the jewellery business. But he wears dowdy clothes that his mother bought for him ages ago, and if I buy anything different, he rarely puts it on, saying he's not comfortable.

'Oh god, I'm so tired.' Abhay said as he sat on the bed and rearranged the multiple pillows that I felt were essential for the ambience. His long legs flopped on the bed and he rubbed his angular jaw as if a mosquito had bitten him. 'I think I'm getting a rash,' he scratched his hand, looking irritated already.

How romantic.

I was not the kind of person who was direct. Trying to set the mood was the most I had done in years. And it was only because Diya had insisted I try to seduce him that I had done all this. I gave it one last try as I sat up to face him.

'Abhay, can we . . . um . . .?' I asked flat out. 'Would you like to . . .?' I raised my eyebrows and waved my hands down my body.

'Nandy, you randy!' Abhay pulled me towards him and gave me a long, hard . . . hug. 'You're taking the initiative. Wow. It's so unlike you . . .'

I closed my eyes and leaned in. His arms wrapped around my midriff and he gave me a peck on my cheeks. Then he pulled back and took a long breath as if to prepare himself for something more. I thought he would lift me up and throw me on the bed. But his phone rang.

'Just ignore it,' I murmured as I pulled him closer and kissed him. But I opened one eye and he was looking at his phone while his lips were stuck to mine. I pulled away.

'Um . . . one sec . . .'

'Seriously, Abhay!' I muttered to myself as I sat back with my arms folded.

'Sorry, I have to take this.' He promptly picked up his phone to chat with his boss. When he ended the call ten minutes later, my mood was dead.

'Sorry, babe. Maybe on the weekend, huh? Let's plan this better . . . maybe.'

I understood. It was the middle of the week. But there wasn't a set time to having sex, was there?

'It's been five months since we've had sex,' I spoke quietly as if reason or time was going to get him excited.

'That long? I don't think so! You're just overthinking. Relax.' He put on the crime show he had been watching for the past few days.

'The last time we had sex was when you had a cold.'

'Well, I do get horny when I'm sick,' he smiled. Babe, I'm tired today and I really just want to finish this season.'

I stood up from the bed, went to the bathroom and pulled out cotton pyjamas. I left our room to go to the drawing room. I hated crime shows.

As I walked out of the room, I saw the open article I was reading earlier lying on the chair. I picked up the magazine and threw it in the trash.

It was no use. He had some excuse or the other not to sleep with me. I had begun to wonder if he had truly lost his libido or was having an affair. My best friend Diya told me to check his phone, but that was sneaky and an invasion of privacy. If he chose to have an affair, I didn't want to find out by spying on him. Whatever it was, I wasn't getting any intimacy or love from my husband.

I plonked myself in the large living room of our joint-family flat that my mother-in-law had decorated with ugly brown leather furniture. I tried to calm myself yet again. Abhay didn't come after me to check if I was angry. He'd stopped doing that too. I went to the kitchen and took out the bottle of wine I had chilled for the evening to have post coitus. Maybe I should have offered him wine when he came home, to set the mood. Ugghh. I knew I was overthinking this as usual. I took a sip straight out of the bottle.

Is this what happens in marriages? The lust dies and spouses are supposed to be happy with the companionship that marriage offers? But after four years of marriage, I knew it was more than lust that had died. Abhay had stopped loving me completely. I might as well be the furniture in the house for all he cared. But then I wondered, had he ever loved me at all?

All I knew was that I'd been lonely in this marriage for too long. A marriage I'd never wanted to be in, in the first place because I was in love with someone else. But then, eventually, I decided I would make this marriage perfect for both of us. And eventually, I fell in love with my husband, Abhay. But for four years now, I knew for a fact that he didn't love me back. Sure, he cared for me and did things for me. But our marriage wasn't based on a functional give-and-take. It was based on emotions. But I was doing all the emoting and he was stonewalling me.

I was slowly giving up hope that anything would change. But I had to try one last time to make this marriage work. After all, I didn't have anything else in my life.

Surprisingly, after four years of marriage, Abhay still didn't know me at all. He didn't know I wasn't ready to be a mother and kept insisting that if I got pregnant it would give me 'something to do', as if sex with him was a project I could let go of once I had given birth. He didn't know I wasn't into athletics and insisted I try different sports all the time, but he judged me when I played badly in tennis, badminton and squash. But he hated swimming and refused to come with me to the pool whenever I went. He didn't know my favourite poet (T.S. Eliot) or any of my favourite books (*Anxious People, Siddhartha, Home Fire, The Storm*). Or that I loved going to the theatre to watch plays instead of watching films or shows on TV. Or that I loved talking to strangers. He always judged me when I chatted with the help about their lives commenting, 'Why are you asking them about their lives? They'll only tell you a sob story and ask for more money.'

And I knew one thing for sure. He certainly wasn't Mark, my ex-boyfriend, whom I was in love with in the US where

I studied for four years. But he had ditched me as well and I thought the best way to heal my broken heart was to get married. Sadly, I was mistaken.

Diya messaged: 'How did it go?'

I ignored her text as I raised the bottle to my lips. I whispered to myself, 'Cheers to my love life.'

Once I finished the bottle of wine, I scrolled through my Instagram feed and only saw happy couples, which made my mood worse.

What did I need to do to get my husband to love me?

Maybe I needed a miracle.

Two

Nandita

How to Find Your Talents

All our life is about the choices we make every day. Would you choose to marry someone if you knew they didn't love you but would always give you the peace you desired? Would you choose to be with someone who loved you but chose never to marry you?

My choice then was to get married. I believed in the noble institution that two people can belong to each other and fight all of life's battles together.

Marriage, as I have learnt, is just two people fighting with each other most of the time, so much so that the outside battles at work or with other friends and family seem to be a relief.

Abhay and I had an arranged marriage. It was because the person I had wanted to marry for love had declared he didn't want to get married. Ever. So I broke up with him and came back to India. And in a fit of rage agreed to an arranged marriage. Stupid? Yes. But people with heartbreaks don't always make smart choices. Not that age gives any wisdom either. Evident from the fact that there are far more people in their forties still looking for love and marriage on dating apps today than ever before.

I'd just finished my graduation from Yale and had come back with a heartbreak that I didn't tell anyone about. I was unable to do anything. My parents thought I did not have anything to do. So they felt a wedding would be 'interesting'.

'There will be some singing and dancing at least,' my mother had insisted as a good enough reason for me to agree to the match. 'You're always so morose. Sitting in your room. Reading away your life. You'll age quickly and then no one will marry you.'

'I'm just twenty-four,' I had said to my mother.

'Exactly. And before you know it, you'll be thirty-four.'

'So?'

'So no one wants to marry a rigid, over-smart, thirty-four-year-old woman.'

'Why not?'

'Because you won't be . . .'

'What?'

My mother raised her eyebrows and stared at me. My teenage sister, Samaira, who spent most of her time in the bathroom applying make-up and making videos of it, said loudly what my mother could not, 'Because you won't be a virgin at thirty-four. She thinks you're a virgin!'

'Maybe you should get *her* married,' I remarked to my mother. 'She might lose her virginity before me.'

'Don't talk nonsense. She's just fourteen. She doesn't have a boyfriend.' My mother slapped the back of my head while Samaira winked at me. 'We are going to meet Hitesh and

Kamini Patel tomorrow. You'll love Abhay, their son. He's a good boy.'

I guess I got married to get away from my mother. I'm not sure if most women do that, but it's a pretty believable reason to move into another household if your mom nags the fuck out of you daily.

When I had met Abhay in an arranged-marriage setting, he was kind, gentle, sweet, loving. Abhay gave me space. But I knew for sure that he wasn't *in love* with me. He allowed me to do everything I wanted, except find a job. Maybe he thought I would become too independent to look after him and his parents if I took up a job. That I wouldn't care for his needs. But he gave me freedom in other ways. I didn't need to take permission like a few women I knew, to go out for lunch or buy anything I liked. He didn't care about those things. And people thought that it was a wonderful quality in a man. But was it enough? There was occasional sex, but no passion. We made love every few weeks in the morning when he felt aroused. Quick kisses, a little mutual action, a few thrusts and it was all over for him. Then he'd head for a shower and work. I'd tried to slow it down and say what I liked, but he would get exasperated and give up. Then another two weeks would pass. The romance was dead. It was nothing compared to what I had experienced with Mark.

But I had tried hard to put my past behind me. And I believed that if I could make Abhay fall in love with me, the passion would come. But all we did was argue over small things. He wanted a child. I didn't. He wanted me to play sports. I hated sweating.

'Come play tennis with me? We can play doubles with Arun and Kiara,' he would suggest. But I knew they played competitively and when I had tried to play, Abhay had only screamed at me for not moving properly on the court.

'I'm not a tennis player,' I had argued several times.

'Just try harder. It'll be fun once you get the hang of it.'

But it wasn't fun. I felt bad that I was not athletic enough and worse, after he scolded me, I sulked. My ego was hurt and he never apologized for screaming in front of his friends.

I would recommend that we go to a book launch or a play or an art therapy session for couples. He would yawn the first ten minutes we were there, and we'd leave in half an hour. He'd take me to a fancy dinner place and call another couple who would join us. Then he'd say, 'See, isn't this better than that boring thing? Good food, good friends, great times!'

My friend Diya said it was just a phase all married couples go through. The plateau. Where everything you do is boring to the other person, the romance is dead, and you're trying to find your identity again, wondering if you made the right decision to get married to *this person*.

Her advice was, 'Just find a new hobby or a new man. An affair always livens things up.' But I knew that wasn't the answer. It never is.

Something needed to change before I went completely mad. I knew I needed to make this marriage work or find something else to do with my life.

'Nandita!' Abhay screamed from the dining room. 'Come quickly. See what Ma has made for you.' My head throbbed. I shouldn't have finished the entire bottle of wine last night.

I just wanted to sleep today.

I'd always been a late riser as compared to the entire family who woke up at the crack of dawn. The 5 a.m. club. Being productive was their motto. Workout, run, work on jewellery designs, chat with people, whatever. But do something before the world wakes up. Whereas I would be in the 9 a.m. club, if there was one. The one that preferred tea in bed and no chirpy 'good mornings', if I could have my way.

At first, I had tried to adjust to that as well, but when I fell asleep doing yoga and embarrassed my mother-in-law in front of her yoga teacher, they just let me sleep till eight o'clock when they all had breakfast and insisted I join them all fresh and ready because I had had 'enough time' by then, according to them, to be bright and up.

'Nandu,' Abhay called again. God that man and his ever-changing terms of endearment! Why couldn't he realize I needed some time alone sometimes? Was he so daft? My head throbbed. Maybe eating some toast would help.

I slowly tried to get out of bed, but I felt dizzy.

Hari, my trusted help, knocked and entered my room with a cup of masala chai and some toast. He had been with me since I was fifteen years old. And I'd only agreed to get married if Hari came with me to look after me. Hari knew what food I liked and what mood I was in. And even though we rarely said anything personal, he would always help me with some piece of advice or a dish I loved to eat.

'Shall I tell them you're unwell?' he asked.

I suddenly remembered that I had left the empty bottle of wine in the drawing room. I muttered with a dry mouth, 'The bottle.'

'Cleared,' he shook his head as if to say, 'Don't worry about it.' He was a gem I cherished in my life and I would not have survived the lockdown if it hadn't been for the oil head massages he gave me while he told me about the latest Hindi movie he had watched on an online platform.

Hari wanted to be in the films. He wanted to join Bollywood and was waiting for a chance when he could leave this domesticity behind and walk the red carpet. But with a face like his, I encouraged him to open a restaurant because he had better skills in cooking than he had a chance at acting.

'Nandyji . . .' he started as he looked sheepishly at me.

'*Bolo*,' I took a sip of tea. It cleared my head immediately.

'There's an audition this afternoon. I don't know how long it will take. I've cooked lunch already but won't be here to serve it.' Hari clearly wasn't the one to give up.

'Ya, ya, go, Hari,' I said, trying to make him happy.

He smiled so gratefully but stood there as I waited for him to leave so I could freshen up and get dressed. There was something else he wasn't saying . . . 'How much do you need?'

'Just one thousand, Nandyji. You can cut it from my salary,' he said excitedly.

I reached over my bed to my purse that was on the dresser and took out my wallet. I handed him two thousand rupees. 'It won't be cut. All the best. Go be a hero, Hari!'

He gave me a wide grin as he left whistling a tune.

I changed into a pink kurta that was a little crumpled, which I thought would go with my black night pyjamas and went to the dining room to see what the excitement was all about.

'Cheese omelette with mushrooms!' Abhay declared proudly. Honestly, that man would eat anything his mother would make even if he didn't like mushrooms. He never opposed his mother and had requested that I shouldn't either, to keep the 'peace in the house', as he put it.

'I'm not hungry.'

'Why isn't this ironed?' My mother-in-law asked, looking at my kurta and then turning her head slightly to scream, 'Honestly, Hari needs to iron clothes better.'

'Won't help, Ma. Nans just stuffs everything into her cupboard. Even if it's been ironed,' Abhay teased me.

'Hari doesn't iron clothes. He cooks and looks after us,' I muttered to Abhay, which went unnoticed as he pretended not to hear me as usual and continued to stuff his mouth with omelette. I hated eggs and, with this hangover, I couldn't even bear to smell them.

'Are you feeling all right?' my mother-in-law asked, seeing me sigh. 'Is there some good news?' She seemed hopeful and looked at Abhay and me.

Abhay shook his head.

She sipped her coffee. 'When will you people have a child?'

'When there's nothing to watch on Netflix, I guess,' I replied with a wry smile. Abhay glared at me.

Kamini held Abhay's cheek and squeezed it fondly as if she was protecting him from me. 'If only I could have had more kids, but I have this prized one here at least.'

Abhay was not in the mood to hear about baby conversations and reprimanded his mother ever so gently, 'Ma, please. You told me I ruined your career.'

'That's not true. I was most happy being your mother.'

'You said no one gave you a modelling assignment after your maternity leave,' I remembered. My mother-in-law used to be a supermodel in the seventies, gracing magazine covers and had featured in TV ads as well. But once she had Abhay, her career was over.

She ignored me and looked at Abhay, 'I sacrificed everything to have you. The least you can do is give me grandkids.'

'Oh god, Ma,' Abhay groaned. 'What blackmail.'

Hitesh, Abhay's father, laughed at this mother-son exchange. He piped in, 'Your mother was the most stunning model when I met her.'

Abhay shook his head and tried to cover his ears. 'I don't need to hear this story again.'

'She swept me off my feet and all I could think about was being with her day in and day out,' he lovingly reached out for Kamini to hold his hand as they stared at each other for a moment.

I smiled. My in-laws were really in love with each other and had a love marriage even though their age difference was almost a decade. I had wanted a love like that to develop between Abhay and me. But Abhay was the most unromantic person I knew. Of all the husbands in the world, I was stuck with one who hated romance and didn't believe in love. For him, marriage was a duty and a wife was a responsibility.

'Actually, I wanted to say something,' I said hesitatingly, after I had finished my cup of tea. 'I have applied for a job.'

'What kind of job?' Abhay asked.

'It's a counsellor's position in a Montessori school. I'll be helping teenagers in secondary school.'

Kamini looked at me intently before responding. 'I thought you did economics? Hitesh?' She asked as she looked towards her husband to check if they had picked the right girl to marry into their family. 'Your father told us you had done economics.'

I shook my head. 'No. I did psychology. And then I did NLP to be certified as a life coach for students. Remember, I finished getting my degree in 2020?'

'But why apply now?' Abhay asked. 'You don't need the money.'

I wondered how we had been married for so long when he understood me so little. 'A woman doesn't work only for money, Abhay. She works because she wants to, and she can and it gives her purpose. Anyway, I haven't heard back from them so I don't know yet. Just thought I'd tell everyone.'

'You know what I think you'd be good at?' Abhay seemed pleased with his idea. 'You should do your plants videos on

YouTube. Begin that again. Maybe start a YouTube channel on gardening and stuff. You were good at that.'

I had been keeping myself occupied through the pandemic putting up videos on how to make kitchen gardens and look after indoor plants. 'I don't want to do it any more. I'm bored. I've said everything I needed to once.' I sulked, unable to understand the resistance from him about me working.

'Let's talk about it later, okay?' Abhay said as everyone got up from the table while I sipped the fresh cup of masala chai that Hari placed in front of me. 'I'll be late tonight,' Abhay added. 'I'm practising for the tennis tournament on Sunday.'

I looked up. 'Today is Thursday. It's my last night before I leave for the retreat tomorrow afternoon. Then I'm gone for a week!'

Abhay looked surprised as if this was the first time I had said anything to him about this even though I had mentioned it several times when we were alone.

'Where?'

I was quiet before I spoke. 'To the Abhaynanda resort in Kerala. I've told you about it.' Anger rose within me and I tried to tame it as I had done since I was young.

He kissed me on my forehead as if I was a child. 'That place is horrible. You should be careful with this coronavirus still around.' The waves of frustration came back. *How was he so insensitive to what I needed?* I controlled myself by taking a sip of water and counting to ten.

'I had the virus three months ago. I have antibodies! I made a booking two weeks ago. I told you about it several times. We've had this discussion.'

'You waste too much money, Nandita,' Abhay said as he looked at his parents who ignored him, not wanting to get into their son and daughter-in-law's squabble. 'We just went to Goa. Why would you need another vacation?' *To get away from you all? To get away from the mushroom omelette and the crumpled kurta jibes?*

Abhay always made me feel guilty about spending money on myself. If it was anything for the family, he would approve. And, truth be told, I was getting a bit too tired of this idea that I needed his approval. That's why I needed my own money.

'Why do you need so much tennis coaching? It's not as if you're going to be Federer.' I said quietly. This shut him up.

'Fine. I'll see you when you get back,' he said, his mouth stretched into a line as he left the house. Any expectations I had of him changing his plans for me and saying a romantic goodbye flew out of the window. I was left disappointed.

Marriage was feeling tedious already. But I knew that every marriage has phases and it was important to allow one space to grow differently before one could come together again. And maybe this spa vacation would allow me to grow so Abhay would realize how much he missed me and would finally fall in love with me.

You know what they say, all wives are a bit delusional. But it's their husbands who have made them so.

Three

Nandita

How to Have More Courage

The Kerala Abhaynanda resort was one of the most beautiful spas I had been to, and I was glad I was spending a chunk of Abhay's money on my solo vacation here. He had got bored the first time we were here. Lately, I had felt we were such different human beings, and I was the only one trying to make this marriage work. I thought maybe this time apart would help him realize he was missing me and he'd want to come and be with me soon.

It was a beautiful room that overlooked a vast expanse of the backwaters and a mini beach dotted with swaying coconut trees. I took a deep breath and closed my eyes. For the first time in months, I felt a sense of peace washing over me.

I made myself some coffee and flipped through the spa treatments in the brochure. I recalled my previous evening when I'd met Diya for a drink before I left.

'Smile,' she said as she took a selfie of both of us with our drinks. 'Wait . . . one more.'

'Seriously, how many photos do you need to be an Insta influencer?'

'It's really hard work,' she insisted. 'Especially since I have a full-time job anyway. And a husband.'

'Then why are you doing it?'

'It's my side hustle!'

I rolled my eyes and laughed. 'All of you guys trying this side hustle . . . let me tell you, it doesn't work.'

She raised her glass. 'Cheers.'

'Cheers to you reading a book,' I said as I took a sip from my margarita.

'You always do that.'

'What?'

'You add "Cheers" *to* something.'

'Well, plain cheers is just an email sign-off. You need to raise a toast to something. Otherwise, how else can you ask the universe for all that you want?' I said.

Diya and I were school friends. We had always sat at the back of the class together finishing each other's tiffin in the first period itself and dozing off after lunch. Her confidence was amazing and even when she was complaining about being overweight, I would have to remind her that with her dark eyes and lustrous hair she could give any actress a run for their money though she had chosen to do an MBA and had a prominent job in a bank.

Diya put her arms on the table, 'Tell me what happened? Did you finally . . .?'

I shook my head and looked out of the window. 'Let's talk about something else.'

A waiter came to our table with nachos. I hated nachos. But it was the only thing Diya loved and we always ordered it.

'You should just have an affair to get over this dry spell,' she said as she picked up a nacho and popped it into her mouth. As if an affair were *that* easy.

'Oh yeah? Where shall I find someone to do this?' I asked. Our dates were predictable. Me complaining about the lack of love from Abhay, physical or otherwise. And she encouraging me to find other men to satisfy my desires.

'At your new workplace. Once you get a job, you'll have an affair with your boss or colleague. Once another man desires you, Abhay will realize what he's missing and fall madly in love with you,' she said as I laughed at her absurd suggestion. She always found ways to cheer me up and support me in all I did.

My thoughts came back to the present moment as my phone pinged. It was an email from the Montessori school. I felt excited and nervous. I opened the mail.

'Dear Ms Patel,

We are impressed with your credentials. Unfortunately, we are looking for someone more experienced to . . .'

I didn't read the rest of the mail. This was the third job I had applied for that had sent me a rejection letter. I felt like a failure. My in-laws didn't think I could get a job. Abhay didn't think I needed it. And, apparently, the job market didn't think I was worthy of having one!

I felt so desolate. I opened the minibar to have a drink but realized that the resort did not serve alcohol. Everything was organic and natural here. I felt miserable. I wasn't good enough for a marriage. I wasn't good enough for a job.

I decided to go for a walk instead of moping in my room. There was a restaurant across the resort that served alcohol and ice cream. Maybe I would grab both. Life suddenly seemed depressing and long. I grabbed my purse and room key and went to the elevator. I was so distracted by the thoughts that were reeling in my head that I didn't realize when the elevator stopped. I stepped out and I bumped into a woman.

'I'm sorry,' we both said in unison looking down at our phones.

When I finally looked up, my jaw dropped. There in front of me was a woman who looked exactly like me! From the hair to the colour of her eyes to the mole on her right cheek. It was like staring into a mirror. I could only say, 'What the . . .'

But she completed my thought and my sentence, 'Fuck.'

Four

Annie

How to Live with Idiots

Annie cleared her throat as she flicked her long brown hair back. She took her time with the presentation that she had been working on for a month. When she showed her final slide, she felt confident it had worked. She smiled a cute smile. 'After a series of montages of married life, the end result will be the couple enjoying a cup of tea in the rains while their laundry is drying in the new washer dryer!'

Mr Bhatt, the head client, yawned. Ranjana, Annie's boss, noticed this. She glared at Annie to wrap it up quickly. Annie gave her an imperceptible nod.

'The whole campaign is about growing in a relationship. From a young couple to an old one where the washing machine lasts the length of time of a long marriage because it is durable and thus affordable.'

Annie's boss Ranjana clapped, 'What do you think, Mr Bhatt?"

'What else? What else?' Mr Bhatt asked as he drummed his fingers impatiently and looked around. His team of four sitting and checking their phones looked up briefly and exasperatedly.

Ranjana ran her fingers through her short hair which was dyed blonde and gelled around the nape of her neck. It was a telltale sign that she was getting agitated. She glared at Annie with kohl-rimmed dark eyes as she mouthed, 'What happened?'

Annie shrugged. She stood there feeling horrible. She had worked on this with her team who declared they would all buy this product after her passionate speech. The bastards. They were all lying. After working in this advertising agency for six years, her boss, Ranjana, should have had the faith to back up her idea in this meeting. But Ranjana was the kind of boss who would mould her stance according to the person paying her.

'There's one more idea,' Sahil spoke confidently as he got up from his seat. Sahil was Annie's competition for the managing director position at the advertising agency, Bright Communications.

Mr Bhatt raised his hands and said, 'By all means . . . '

Sahil stood up saying, 'Picture this . . .'

Sahil went on talking about some nonsensical idea that was stereotypical and patriarchal. Annie scoffed at it. She knew Ranjana wouldn't buy it. She had been here long enough to know that this agency stood for the progressive values that Annie presented, on which she had climbed the ladder to become the youngest executive in the company.

When Sahil finished, Annie smiled. She couldn't wait to hear Ranjana trash the idea. Sahil had walked right into it!

But it was she who had read the room wrong. Mr Bhatt smiled and asked a few questions. Immediately, Ranjana started adding to Sahil's impromptu idea.

Annie scowled. She cleared her throat, 'Well, that's been done before though, hasn't it, Sahil?'

Sahil smirked and looked at Mr Bhatt, 'But consumers nowadays have had enough of the new, changing times. They want something familiar. Something real.'

Annie could see her presentation fall apart like a car crash in slow motion. They all got up to exit the boardroom when the client turned to Annie and spoke, 'Hey, by the way, I like your plants videos.'

'Excuse me?' Annie replied, feeling annoyed. They hadn't accepted her idea and now he was mocking her by talking about plants? Who was this bald, fat Bengali man?

'Plant Light it's called, isn't it? On YouTube? I have a wonderful kitchen garden thanks to you—the wife felt inspired!' he said with a smile, or was that a smirk?

Annie looked confused but faked a smile.

Sahil too smirked at Annie as they exited the boardroom. 'You and plants? Ha ha.'

'Shut up, Sahil!' Annie hissed as she headed to the washroom to take a moment for herself. She couldn't let anyone see the tears in her eyes. She had worked so hard and that was the third client who had not liked her presentation. She knew she needed a 'win' to refer to at the board meeting for the managing director in a few months. And this might have been her last shot.

She took a deep breath and gave herself a pep talk looking into the mirror, but no words came out. She went back to her cabin to see where she could have gone wrong with the presentation.

A very pregnant Ranjana came into Annie's cabin to sit down and fold her hands over her enormous belly. 'Well, Annie? That went off badly.' The Ranjana she knew never minced her words.

'What was wrong with it?' Annie threw her hands in the air in desperation.

'Seriously? You don't know?'

Annie shook her head, 'It was sharp, funny and showed a modern, equal relationship.'

'It's not relatable!' Ranjana said, throwing her hands up.

'You think Sahil's idea was relatable?' Her voice rose.

'It's the third idea of yours that has bombed. We can't afford to lose clients.'

Annie kept quiet, unable to respond.

'So what is your plan now?'

'Move on and get to the next presentation,' Annie sat back down. Her motto in life was to not lose sleep over the past but move on quickly to the next thing and succeed there.

'If you don't think about what went wrong, you'll keep making the same mistakes, Annie.'

'Mistakes?'

'Yes. Your ideas aren't working. Maybe you need to take some time to figure out what wasn't connecting with the client! Otherwise, how will you stand in front of the board without a win?'

'Ranjana, I've been here six years. I know everything about this company,' Annie started protesting. 'I am your next managing director.'

Ranjana raised her hand. 'Vijay doesn't see it like that.'

'Fuck Vijay!' Annie muttered under her breath as Ranjana raised an eyebrow. She hated Ranjana's boss who seemed to have the final say in the vote for the next managing director. She was appalled that Ranjana hadn't supported her when she needed it the most. She believed in female solidarity and would have done that for any woman who needed help. But she never got the support back. And she felt all alone in her professional life, which made her seem hard and cruel. Her thoughts turned to Vijay. When she first met him, he had stared at her and asked her some personal questions about where she was from and how old she was. She thought he was a creep and ignored meeting him after that. But she didn't want to believe Sahil would have schmoozed him enough that Vijay would choose a man over a competent leader like herself.

'How are your parents?' Ranjana asked. 'How's the restaurant doing?'

Annie glared at her. She knew where Ranjana was going with this line of thought.

'I'm not joining them, Ranjana. And you can't give the position to Sahil. He's a fucking asshole who will ruin everything you have built over the last two decades here.'

'Life is not about leaving a legacy all the time, Annie, remember that. It's also about family.'

Annie nodded, hearing what Ranjana was saying.

'So come up with a plan if you want to be managing director. Because he's going to use the fact that he's turned around more profit than you in the last six months.' She tried to get up but the low sofa made her waddle. 'Help me up, please.'

'Be careful,' Annie said as Ranjana held on to the edge of the desk.

'I'm a forty-eight-year-old woman having her first baby. Of course, I'm going to be careful, Annie,' said Ranjana grouchily. 'Sorry. Hormones. Also, please be a little gentle with your team. After the pandemic, they're all a little shaken.'

'They've been at home getting paid for doing nothing for two years. Can't I expect them to come to the office on time and work harder?' Annie asked. 'Everyone is vaccinated. We get tested often. Now it's time to work!'

'Sahil allows them to come in late and work flexi hours,' Ranjana winked before she left.

Annie looked at her team members from the transparent window of her cabin. They were on their phones or chatting in groups. Useless bunch of incompetent people! she thought.

Sahil smirked at Annie from outside. Annie smirked back. His job was secure. He had buttered Ranjana up well, bringing her presents for the baby and had sweet-talked Ranjana's boss, Vijay, during the annual agency party where they had bonded over the IPL. He would never get fired. Only she was required to upgrade her skills. Why was it always a woman who needed to improve herself in a corporate atmosphere whereas men were absolved of any need to improve and given far more headroom to make mistakes?

Annie felt frustrated and anxious. She opened her laptop. And Sahil entered her room. 'Wassup?' he said cockily.

Annie didn't want to engage in a verbal dispute with him. 'Is there something I can help you with? I have a lot of work to do.'

'Actually, since you're also single,' he raised his eyebrows to confirm this, 'I wondered if you could help me set up my Busybee account. I want to use it before I present to the clients.'

Annie felt a slight knot form in her stomach. 'Busybee?'

'Didn't Ranjana tell you? Maybe she forgot. Busybee is a new dating app. They want to launch an ad campaign in India. Ranjana asked me to make the presentation.'

Annie felt horrible that Ranjana had not told her about it. After all, she was the prime candidate to present this properly, a single woman who could be on the dating app.

'Aren't you married?'

'Hell, no. I've never been married.'

'But you're like fifty years old.'

'Ha ha. You're funny.'

'No one will want to date you, Sahil. Now leave. I have work to do.'

Sahil got up, grabbed an apple that was kept on Annie's desk and took a bite out of it. 'Pretty soon you won't have a job, so why work, Annie? Maybe you should make an account and look for a man to marry. That's all you'll be good for.'

Annie scowled. He'd taken her snack and left her seething. She couldn't have him become managing director. She needed a plan.

But as she tried to come up with a campaign idea for Busybee, she felt her head exploding. Nothing was working out. Her brain felt as if it had melted and she couldn't breathe. She started taking deep breaths, but they came out shallow. Her chest tightened and she tried to scream, but nothing came out of her mouth. She grabbed her purse and walked out of the office. She was having a heart attack.

She hailed a taxi, 'Emergency room,' she muttered as she collapsed in the back seat.

Five

Annie

How to Train a Puppy

Annie could see herself as she looked into Nandita's eyes. They circled each other to see if they were looking into a mirror. They were both the same height with dark eyes and a sharp nose. But even though they looked exactly alike, Annie wore her clothes more stylishly than Nandita. Annie had a Sabyasachi scarf draped around her neck with gold hoops and a Kate Spade bag casually draped over her arm. Nandita wore a casual kurta and jeans that were ill-fitting and crushed, and a sling bag across her body that cut her in half.

Annie recovered first. 'What the fuck!' Her voice was husky and loud.

Nandita could immediately make out the difference as she spoke softly and could only reply, 'How?'

'Oh my god! You look . . .' Annie was in complete shock.

'Exactly like me.'

'This is not possible.'

30

'Are we related?'

Annie and Nandita stood outside the elevator and looked at each carefully—now for their differences. *How could this be?* Nandita had a diamond nose ring that Annie didn't. Nandita had shorter hair and Annie had a long ponytail. But apart from that, their appearance was exactly alike.

'I'm shocked,' Nandita spoke. 'I've never met someone who was my doppelganger.'

'Well, you know what they say. There are seven people in the world who look exactly like you.'

'Who says that?'

'People. I read it somewhere. I don't know,' Annie smiled. 'Hi. I'm Annie.'

'I'm Nandita. This is really strange!' Nandita hesitated and then asked, 'Well, I was going for lunch. Do you want to join me?'

'I'd like that. But here?'

'There's a restaurant I was going to across the street. They have alcohol.'

'I think I'll need it.'

Annie remembered how the doctor believed that she had had a panic attack and needed a vacation. She had insisted she didn't want one until Ranjana asked her to take some time off as well. And miraculously this resort had popped up in her Instagram feed and she had thought it might be a sign. Now, on meeting her lookalike, it seemed it most definitely was.

As soon as they sat down and ordered, they began questioning each other. They were born in different years to different mothers. They weren't twins or cloned. They just looked exactly alike. But Annie's voice was deeper and she didn't look after her hands and feet as much as Nandita did when they started examining each other up close.

'No time for mani-pedis,' Annie confessed, following her gaze, 'Plus, waste of time when you can cut your own nails.'

Nandita didn't mention how she loved being pampered at the salon. It was her favourite pastime with her friend Diya. 'I can't believe we've never crossed paths when we live in the same city.'

'I know,' Annie replied. 'Although I think a few times when I was making out with a man, I got strange glances from people.'

'Well, maybe they thought you were me and you were not kissing my husband Abhay,' Nandita laughed.

'See, and I was kissing a random stranger. So . . . they might have judged you!' she teased Nandita. 'So you're married?' Annie asked.

'Yes, yes . . . Married for almost four years. No kids!'

'Thank god!'

'I've never understood why everyone wants to get married and have children immediately. My in-laws remind me constantly.'

'As if it is only on you, right?'

'Well, Abhay, my husband, wants kids . . .' Nandita hesitated before the next sentence. 'But I don't. It seems as if all wives are judged by the children they have. It seems to be the sole purpose of getting married nowadays. Otherwise, why would anyone commit to it for an eternity, right? I wish women who have no corporate jobs or kids were taken more seriously. We have other purposes in life, you know?'

Annie raised her glass of water, 'Cheers to that.'

'Cheers to no kids,' Nandita replied.

Nandita felt a kindred spirit in Annie. 'Tell me about you.'

'Born and raised in Delhi. My parents own a mithai shop-cum-restaurant there. I came to Bombay six years ago and started working in this advertising agency called Bright Communications. I've been there . . . for like donkey's years.'

'You're not married?'

'Hell, no!' Annie threw her head back and laughed. 'Marriage is too tiring. I've seen loads and no one seems happy. Sorry, not referring to . . .'

'No issues.' Nandita smiled. 'I didn't want to get married either but my parents forced me.'

'What?'

'Yeah. Had an arranged marriage. At twenty-four.'

'Why did you agree to it?'

'Bored parents.'

Annie laughed, understanding. Most Indian parents aren't happy with the dating scene nowadays. There was a niggling feeling in her that she hadn't had in quite some time. This was a sign. Then, as if on cue, her brain began to formulate a plan. But she shushed the voice as she pretended to be nonchalant and curious, discussing various topics and getting to know Nandita better.

'How was lockdown for you?' asked Annie. 'I overworked when it wasn't needed . . . Nothing was working . . . I guess I deserve this break, huh?' Annie shrugged, trying to believe it herself. She hadn't taken a break in several years and had made 'working from home' a pattern on weekends well before the lockdown.

'We all deserve a break. I made plant videos to keep busy. I'm so sick of them now.'

'Plant videos?'

Nandita nodded. 'Kitchen garden, keeping plants alive, etc. Plant Light is my YouTube channel.'

Now it made sense, Annie thought to herself. The client was the first person who had got their identities wrong!

The food came and they ate in silence for a while. Annie felt she needed to share a little more of herself for Nandita to open up too. 'I have this guy in the office, Sahil. He's always trying to upstage me. Makes me so mad. Even when we didn't need to have meetings, he would schedule one.'

'My husband says stupid things too,' Nandita confessed as she sipped on her third mojito, realizing she was speaking her truth after a really long time. 'Like . . . "Try harder, Nandu, maybe you'll like it if you didn't give up so often."' Nandita began to feel the rage she had suppressed for so long in her marriage. 'I have tried. But it's all the things he likes to do. Tennis, jewellery design, hanging out with the same group of friends. Has he tried to do things I like?'

Annie shook her head. 'I hear you. I was in a relationship where all I did was compromise. Until I gave it up and just focused on my career. And here too it feels, only I am compromising. Sahil is acing it, doing nothing. Women have to work so hard to make anything a success.'

'Makes me so mad!' Nandita said, finally revealing her true feelings.

Annie raised her wine glass to make a toast. 'To women, because we will always help each other. And to no longer compromising on what we want,' Annie said as they clinked their glasses. They chatted for some time after that but Nandita felt exhausted after a while looking at an image of herself who was so different from her. However, for the moment she wanted to just lie down after the long flight. Annie got the check, saying she would charge it to the company. Nandita had a moment of envy. She only had a joint account with Abhay. She was using his add-on credit card and wished she had a job where she could charge her expenses to the company instead of letting him know where she had spent 'their' money.

They went back to their respective rooms to rest. By now, Annie's plan had formulated fully in her head. And it was because of the phone call she had had with Ranjana just before she had left for the resort.

'You need a strategy, Annie,' Ranjana had been on her evening walk when she spoke to Annie, huffing and puffing. 'Otherwise, I won't be able to say anything to the board. And Vijay, who has the most influence with everyone, will appoint Sahil.'

Annie had panicked then. 'Fuck, Ranjana. Sahil has only been here for a minute. I've built this company for six years!' Annie's voice rose in frustration. 'Men will just give jobs to other men no matter how qualified women are for the same position. They'll overlook men's mistakes but burn the woman at the stake.'

Ranjana ignored Annie's rant and gave her some advice instead. 'Well, that's why most women in jobs turn out to be ruthless instead of using their gentleness to succeed. It's a complicated world, Annie. But the next few campaigns are right up your alley. Busybee is a dating app for single women.'

'I hate dating apps,' Annie said but didn't tell Ranjana that she had been on several dates through dating apps and fixed up through friends since she was sixteen years old. She was tired of the dating scene and the men she had invested in. They all seemed the same after a while—insecure, unsure, immature.

'Which is your favourite dating app?' Ranjana asked.

'None.'

'Then how . . .?'

'I have friends who talk about the apps.'

'You have friends?' Ranjana sparred with Annie, who laughed.

Annie loved the relationship Ranjana had with her. More of a mentor than a boss, she had helped groom and promote Annie in the beginning and that's why Annie had stayed. But lately, Ranjana was more concerned about her health and the baby than Annie's career and it had left Annie unnerved, unhinged, unmoored. And Annie needed some security from somewhere.

Ranjana put on her serious tone. 'Well, I have meetings with some clients coming up and a few new products are being launched for married women.'

'I'm not married.'

'You need to get into the head of the consumer. And you need a winning campaign.'

'How has life become only about campaigns? I thought the company was also about strategy and expansion. I'm a strategist, not just a creative lead. And Sahil isn't anything!' Annie was sure that her qualifications would give her the edge in a job. She had seniority, experience and the qualifications to become the next managing director.

'If you focus less on Sahil and more on having a winning campaign . . . well, then you could use all your strategy talent at the board meeting and convince them. Clear your head.'

Annie had no plan or strategy in mind then. Not until she had met Nandita. Desperate times called for desperate measures! Meeting Nandita had triggered an idea in her head to switch places so she could observe the life of a married woman and come up with insights that Sahil would never get. He was a forty-something-old man who had never been married. She would have the upper edge at the board meeting when she would tell them about the adventure of a life switch. People loved stories and women with spunk. Vijay would give her the job in a heartbeat. And then her parents would feel more 'settled' with her in a secure position. She would be able to support her father's restaurant through any lockdown or crisis.

She looked at herself in the mirror as she spoke confidently, 'Annie Singh. Managing director, Bright Communications. And you, Sahil . . . are fired!'

She laughed loudly, knowing everything was falling into place. It had to.

Six

Nandita

How to Manipulate a Friend

I was feeling overwhelmed for the next two days after I met Annie for lunch and dinner. We looked alike, but we had nothing in common. So I took a break one afternoon, skipped lunch and went for a massage. My thoughts swirled in my head and I wondered if I should call Diya to tell her. *How did I meet someone who looked so much like me?* I was so wrapped up in my thoughts that I didn't even notice when the massage ended and the gentle masseuse asked me to wake up.

After a hot steam and shower, I decided to go for a walk to sunset point. I came down to the lobby when a young girl came up to me. 'Miss Annie. Here's your PAN card.'

I turned to her, 'I'm not Annie. She's in room 415.'

The young girl thought I was pranking her. 'Excuse me?'

I repeated myself.

The young girl smiled, 'Ma'am, I checked you in. Don't you remember? When I came up to return your PAN card, you weren't in your room.'

I sighed and took it from her, 'Yes. Thank you. Now I remember.' Annie and I looked so alike that people were starting to confuse us!

When I reached sunset point, Annie was already there having a drink.

'Oh hi,' she turned towards me. 'Want to have a glass of house wine? It's free.'

I declined. 'I just want some chai.' I found a man from the hotel behind a small counter serving tea in small *kulhads*.

We clinked our kulhad and glass and found a bench to sit on and listen to the band that was playing near the pool.

I handed over her PAN card. 'The girl at the reception thought you were me.'

'I'm not surprised. We do look quite alike.'

I looked out into the horizon at the sun setting. My body felt relaxed until I heard the next sentence. Annie laughed, 'You know what would be funny?'

I shook my head.

'If we actually switched places.'

'I'm not giving up my suite!'

'No. I wouldn't want you to. I meant here . . . in these public places. We can try pranking a few more people. Just for fun. We'll never get this opportunity again. And after two massages, one gets bored here, right? And I have a whole week off from work.'

'But I don't like fooling people.' I wondered why she thought doing something so uncomfortable was 'fun'.

'Okay. I guess I'll see you around then.' She finished her glass of wine and kept it on one of the round tables where people left their empty glasses. Then she turned to me and asked once again, 'Do you think our families would be able to tell the difference?'

'I guess so. They know us well enough.'

'You're right,' she nodded and turned. But a thought entered my head. *Would Abhay really be able to tell the difference? Did he really know the real me?*

'Maybe . . .' I started speaking as she turned to me. 'Maybe . . . we can try the theory out.'

'Seriously?'

I nodded. 'Why not?'

'Okay.'

We went back to my room where we had more wine that Annie had bought from a local liquor store. We hatched a plan to see if pretending to be each other would work on a phone call.

'I don't think it would work.' I knew for a fact that people weren't as dumb as we thought. 'We don't sound alike. We may look alike but our mannerisms are so different. I don't exercise. I don't cook. You love all those things. I write. You hate opening the Word document on your laptop.'

'You'd be surprised, actually,' Annie started pacing across the room. 'People aren't as observant as you think they are.' She paused for a few seconds. 'You know what? Let's try it now.'

'What?'

'Let's do a video call with them to see if they would recognize us!' Before I could change my mind, she picked up her phone. 'Okay, I'll go first. I'll call my boss, Ranjana. But don't say anything that could upset her. Just be casual and agree with her.'

'I thought we'd do it in a few days . . . I barely know . . .' I tried to protest but Annie had dialled the number and handed me the phone. Ranjana her boss came on the line. She blurted out, 'What, Annie? What happened? Why are you calling me at nine-thirty? It's my bedtime.'

I smiled to see that Annie had forgotten to tell me that her boss was a woman in her late forties and heavily pregnant. I spoke nervously, 'I just wanted you to know . . .' My mind went blank. I looked up as Annie guided me about something, but I couldn't understand the words.

'What? You just what?'

'I, um . . . just wanted to ask how you're feeling.'

Ranjana paused for a minute and I thought I had been caught. It wasn't easy to be someone else. I grinned and was about to tell her that I wasn't Annie when she said, 'I wasn't feeling too well today. How did you know?'

'I had a feeling . . .' I realized that all pregnant women need to hear the same things regularly and I suddenly remembered a brochure I had seen earlier at the spa I had crossed on the way to the lawns. 'Also, at the resort, they were selling some lovely oils that help pregnant women calm their minds. I'll get you some. You'll be okay. Just don't worry too much.'

She paused to blink a few times. 'Thanks, Annie. Good night.'

'Good night.' I hung up. We both looked shocked for a second before we burst into giggles. 'It worked!'

'My turn,' Annie gave me my phone. 'Call your husband.'

I felt nervous to call Abhay. A part of me wanted to know if he could make out the difference between his wife of four years and a stranger, and a part of me didn't want to play this game any more, feeling it was going into dangerous territory. Yet, I dialled and gave the phone to Annie.

'Hey,' she said and smiled at the video call. Abhay was out with his friends at a loud place.

'Say hello to the gang!' he said and Annie waved to them. He was talking about how they had won the tournament and had come out to celebrate.

'That's great!' Annie replied. As he went on about the tournament and the others joined in with the details, Annie nodded and looked interested. I hoped he would stop suddenly and notice something was off. I let the conversation continue just so he could finally say, 'You're not Nandita!' But he didn't. And after five minutes or so he hung up. Again, my expectations about him had disappointed me.

Annie shrugged. 'That wasn't so bad.'

I was furious. How could Abhay not make out Annie wasn't his wife? Had I just wasted four years of my life on a marriage where my own husband was so shallow? Was he really in love with me? Didn't he know the difference?

I was feeling exhausted with the thoughts swirling and was getting a headache from the long day and conversations with several people who kept mistaking us. 'I'm going to head to bed now.' I indicated for Annie to leave. This game had gone on for too long.

But then Annie said something that would keep me thinking all night.

'You know what would be even more daring? If we took this further. We actually switched lives for a month.'

'What?'

'You could take my place. I'll teach you a few things about my job and workplace. It will give you a chance to have a job for the first time. And it would be a wonderful change for you. Allow you to try something new in life.'

I thought about it for half a minute before responding. 'I don't think it's a good idea. I'm not comfortable giving up my life.'

'Okay. Just a silly thought.' She hugged me and left.

The truth was that I didn't want to switch lives because I was scared. I'd never done anything so adventurous or dangerous in my life before. And I was barely convinced that Abhay loved me after that video chat. This vacation was supposed to give him perspective. It was supposed to make him miss me and long for me. Instead, he had been out drinking and he didn't even notice it wasn't me on the phone. I felt confused and angry with him. Angry with my parents for having forced me to get married when I wasn't ready. Angry with myself for not doing anything with my life. I thought that despite an arranged marriage, we had something in common, a love for family and each other. *But did we have anything in common?*

I messaged Diya. She immediately called me.

'Hey, babe. What's up? How is the vacay going?' She sounded chirpy on the video chat. I saw she was in her pyjamas watching TV.

'Do you think Abhay and I have anything in common?' I asked.

'Why do you ask?'

'Just tell me, na . . .'

She paused what she was watching and replied, 'You know . . . after a while . . . no couple has anything in common. Look at Mihir and me. We have nothing in common any more and we had a love marriage almost five years ago. I don't even think there's love any more even though we post photos together on Valentine's Day and our anniversary. We care about each other. That's love, I guess. Caring. Giving space. Being there for each other. But we all lead individual lives, really . . . Why do you ask?'

'No reason. I just wondered . . . if this marriage . . . of mine . . . was a mistake.'

'All marriages are a mistake, honey. But being single is lonely and boring. No one's happy with what they have any more. Everyone wants some change. But what? No one knows.'

'You are a bowl of sunshine today, aren't you? What are you watching?' I asked as she wasn't giving me the answers I needed.

'*After Life*.'

'What's it about?'

'It's about loss,' she said. 'We all go through the same motions and emotions, just at different points in time. And it's about finding happiness again.'

I didn't want to tell her that a lot had happened in my life in the last forty-eight hours. A loss of something I couldn't describe. But what she said triggered something in me. Maybe I finally had an opportunity to do something different with my life that no one had. A chance to be someone else. A chance to find out who I could be. A chance to be happy again. I could go on an adventure that could change my entire perspective on marriage and then maybe I would be the one giving advice to Diya about love and relationships. I had a chance to prove myself and make Abhay fall in love with me, finally.

Seven

Annie

How to Boost Your Ideas

Annie went for a run the next morning as thoughts swirled in her head. She knew this vacation wasn't just to take a break. Everything happened for a reason. She believed it. She had a vision board back home that had that quote written on it. She needed a strategy. She had to prove to Ranjana that she could get into a housewife's mind and thus get into the minds of the consumer base they were targeting, and hence, she was better than Sahil. But she knew Ranjana wouldn't allow any more days off. She had given these few days off in the middle of a campaign just because Annie had had a panic attack. But she would need to be back at work.

But if Nandita made the switch, Annie could be a part of Nandita's life for just a week or two. They would have to be discreet. They couldn't tell their respective sides about this. Because if she went in as Annie, everyone would be well-behaved around her and treat Annie as a guest. She wouldn't understand the nuances that went into the dynamics between a mother-in-law and a daughter-in-law. Or a husband and wife. She would be sleeping on a couch or in a spare room instead of understanding what it felt like to sleep next to a man who thought he was her husband. Those specifics were important to Annie. She could then use them as dialogues for her campaigns.

But would Nandita agree? And would she be able to pull this switch off? She seemed unsure about everything and a little naive. She could ruin the job for Annie. She would have to be trained to keep quiet and pretend to be working on a campaign, giving Annie daily updates so she could guide her better.

Annie's thoughts and breathing were interrupted by her mobile ringing. It was her mother, Leena.

'Hi, Ma,' Annie said and immediately wondered how Nandita would chat with her parents if they switched lives.

'How's my favourite child?'

'I'm your only child,' Annie slowed down her run to talk to her mother.

'Yes, but still my favourite. You know how proud of you we are.'

'What do you need, Ma?'

Leena was quiet for a while before answering, 'This month wasn't good for the shop. After the lockdown, we hardly made any profit. Everything went into the rent. And now your father needs to have an angioplasty.'

'What? Why?'

'The doctor has found some blockage in his artery.'

'Oh my god, should I come home?'

'No, no. It's not a major surgery. Chacha will be there. But . . . we'll fall short because well . . . Papa forgot to pay the last medical insurance.'

Annie groaned. Her parents had always been careless with finances even though they had been running a business for so many years. She had to manage everything for them. And sometimes when she was overloaded with work, she couldn't keep up.

'Fine, I'll send you the money.' Annie massaged her temples, feeling a headache coming on. After sending money to them, she knew she would not have anything left to move out of her flat. And Rohit, her ex, had messaged that he was planning to sell the flat and she needed to shift out. He had been kind enough to let her live there after they broke up a year ago. But she couldn't push her luck any longer by living rent-free.

'Bless you, *beta*. Eat healthy. Love you.' Leena hung up. As Annie walked back, she thought about her idea even more and how they would be able to pull it off. It would only be for a week or two and then she would work on the campaign and get that promotion.

She messaged Nandita to meet her for breakfast. She had to make this plan happen. It was the only way she could have a winning campaign and become the next managing director. Then she would be able to move out with the added raise in her salary and support her parents.

'I need a win,' she murmured as she headed to the coffee shop.

Eight

Nandita

How to Stop Doubting Yourself

I took a large gulp of my coffee, trying to process what Annie had just suggested.

'And what if people recognize us?'

'And what if they don't?'

'You'll have to get your nose pierced,' I said, pointing to my nose ring. 'And get your hair cut.'

'Haircut is fine. But nose ring? Ouch. Do I have to? Can't I just say I lost it?'

I shook my head. 'Abhay gave it to me as a wedding present to replace the small diamond one I had. So he'll get suspicious.'

'Okay,' Annie said, touching her nose and already feeling the pain.

I thought of one more thing. 'I have one very important condition if we are going to switch lives,' I said finally. I had been thinking about it the entire night. Annie raised an eyebrow. 'You can't sleep with my husband.'

Annie laughed so loud she had to hold her stomach. 'Yeah . . . definitely. Like I'm dying to do that!'

'I'm serious.'

Annie took my hand and looked me in the eye. 'I don't want to sleep with your husband. I just want to know what married life looks like. What your mother-in-law says to you when you wake up late. Nonsense things, really. Just relax as a housewife for some time. I've been so overworked. I had a panic attack before I came here.'

'Oh my god, really?'

'Yes. I want to watch Netflix and have someone pamper me. Someone like that fellow . . .'

'Hari.'

'Hari. Yes. Someone who can get me coffee in bed.'

'Chai. I have chai.'

'Can I just do a coffee?' Annie asked, looking away. 'I don't know how to have milky tea.'

I smiled.

'Please. Do this for me, Nandita. Please.'

Annie was an attractive woman in more ways than looking like me. She was more self-assured, confident, experienced. I wondered if I was making a mistake in switching lives. *Wasn't she whom I wanted to be for Abhay to fall in love with me? What if he saw it in her and fell in love with her?*

Annie continued, 'Do you guys do it . . . um . . . daily?'

'No!' I was brought back to the moment with her question. Abhay and I barely had any sex. But I didn't want to tell her that.

'Well then, I'll just say I'm on my period and it's extended. Men don't know anything anyway.'

'Promise, you won't sleep with him?' I asked again.

'I promise. I will not break this vow. Look . . . ' Annie said, after thinking for a second, 'If you get fired, my parents will lose the restaurant business.'

'What?'

'I pay the EMI for the space on my family business. My father will have to give it up to the bank or investors. My mother . . . well, she's not . . . um . . . how do I put this . . . she prefers I have this job. So, just please be careful.'

'Yes, of course. I won't screw this up . . . this is an opportunity for me as well . . . But isn't there like a man . . . boyfriend I need to watch out for?' I asked sheepishly.

Annie shook her head. 'You have no one to worry about . . .' Her voice tapered away as she looked to her left thinking about something. I didn't interrupt her thoughts.

It sounded like a solid plan. Well, sort of.

Annie thought out loud as she looked at me intently. 'I'll have to get glasses like yours if we are serious about this.'

'They're reading glasses. I don't need them all the time. But let's get your nose pierced.'

'And let's figure out hair. Is there a parlour close by?' Annie asked as she googled her question.

'And I need to give you some books to carry around that you should be reading. People will know you're not me if you're not reading a book.'

'Can't I carry an iPad and read a book from there?'

I rolled my eyes as she smiled. It felt nice to have a new friend. It had been so long since I had spoken with anyone who was just my friend. Besides Diya, all the women friends I had were part of a couple group that Abhay and I hung out with. His friends' wives. One had to be careful around them as they would gossip to their husbands which would eventually come back to Abhay.

We began to plot about the exchange, telling each other details about our lives such as our food preferences and people we knew, leaving out the finer details like our insecurities, our exes and the minutiae of what made us who we were. Because it might be easy to switch a life if we look alike, but it isn't easy to become someone else completely.

But we were going to do just that. I didn't know I would become someone else completely by the end of this project. And I didn't know how dangerous it was to switch lives with a stranger.

A few days later, I took the afternoon flight from Kerala to Mumbai to head to Annie's life, filled with apprehension and excitement. And Annie, bursting with ideas of what a housewife should do, took the evening flight to head to my home.

I knew this was the beginning of an adventure I could tell my children about and something Abhay and I would be laughing about for years to come.

Nine

Nandita

How to Have More than One Boring Life

It was around sunset when I entered Annie's apartment with her suitcase, her purse and her keys. I immediately wanted to message Abhay but when I checked the mobile, I was reminded that it was Annie's phone with a photo of herself in Paris on the home screen whereas I had one with Abhay and me.

Annie lived sparsely in an organized but small two-bedroom apartment. The walls were painted off-white and had blown-up photographs of herself on one wall. There was a chest of drawers on one wall with a few books and a cactus on top. There were soft blue couches with bright yellow cushions in the living area and an L-shaped sofa facing a large TV against one wall and a window against one side of the sofa. It had an open kitchen with bar stools in front of a large slab of black marble, which doubled up as a dining table. It was clean and tastefully done, unlike my mother-in-law's house.

I went into one room and saw that she had a large board with post-its and cuttings from magazines on a wall. There was a large stack of magazines on a desk that faced this wall. It seemed like a home office. There were a few plants on the windowsill. I went closer to see the board. It seemed like a vision board I had heard of. One photo had a strange man who said, 'I'm finding it hard to connect with people right now.' She had cut out words or written them in bold on large pieces of paper and pinned them on the board. *Be a Leader, not a follower. Become a Managing Director. Stay Motivated.* There were no photos of her family anywhere.

Wow. She really was a control freak. I guess she would fit into my control-freak family really well then. Everyone would be at loggerheads. Then when I told them it wasn't me, it had been Annie, they would appreciate me more!

I walked into Annie's bedroom which was all black and white with furniture and white bedspreads from IKEA. White bed and side tables with obscure-looking black lamps. There was a large plant in one corner against a window that was covered with dark curtains. There was nothing on her walls except a black IKEA full-length mirror and a sketch portrait of her done by a painter. *She really seemed to be obsessed with herself!*

The whole house was tastefully done. I wondered what Annie would think of my mother-in-law's expensive but hideous leather sofas and garish bedspreads.

I opened her cupboard and saw clothes neatly arranged. I suddenly felt embarrassed about how I had left my own cupboard, spilling with clothes. But I was in a hurry to pack and, after those drinks with Diya, I wasn't feeling too well to neatly stack anything up again, not that I ever did. I always had Hari to help with cleaning my stuff.

I went to the kitchen and opened the fridge to see all the things neatly organized in vertical order. But there was nothing but bread, butter and various types of cheese there. The cupboards had a range of masalas, bright red dishes and cookbooks that had stains on them, which showed they had been used. I was starving. I scrolled through Annie's phone to see if I could order some food from a restaurant. Thankfully, we had the same phone model. At least that was one thing we had in common. Software that we both understood.

I ordered a paneer dish for myself with some naan. I went to explore Annie's bedroom a little more. I lay down on her bed and must have fallen asleep because I didn't hear the bell ring. Then I heard the door open, and someone shut it behind them. I woke up with a start not knowing where I was or who I was supposed to be.

I called out, 'Abhay?' Then I corrected myself as I looked around to get my bearings. It had become dark. It was a different room. I was in Annie's house. I was supposed to be Annie. A woman I realized, I barely knew and with whom I had switched my life. It began to sink in.

'Annie! I've put sanitizer. Come out now, you OCD freak.' I heard a woman sing out and go towards the kitchen and rummage through the fridge. 'Have you cooked something? I watered your plants while you were away. Jyoti came and cleaned up yesterday. I didn't get any groceries except bread and butter. You forgot to send me a list.'

I walked out to see a woman looking into Annie's fridge. 'How did you come in?' I asked as I recognized Rhea, Annie's close friend she had spoken about. I didn't know she had a set of keys to the house, though. This could be a problem. I enjoyed my privacy. Even in my in-laws' house, no one entered my room unless they knocked or they would call me out to the drawing room to talk to me.

'Um . . . with your keys! Heeeellooo,' Rhea came up to give me a hug. 'I missed you. Look at you! You look great. This vacation has been so good for you. See, I told you!' She looked around. 'Are you going to whip us up some dinner? Or should we order?'

'I just ordered something . . .' I said, wondering why someone would expect food from a friend who had just returned from a vacation. Who was this self-obsessed woman? Diya would have brought food and wine for me rather than ask me to cook.

'You ordered?'

I nodded.

'You never order.'

I felt I was caught in the first moment of me being someone else. I tried to cover up, 'There were no groceries, right?'

'Oh, yes. Give me a list and I'll have it delivered when you're at work,' Rhea said nonchalantly, making herself comfortable on the couch. Annie hadn't told me she cooked so much. I barely knew how to boil water.

'So . . .' Rhea went on. 'I need to tell you something . . . Rohit has really been pestering me about you. You need to unblock him, bro. Just see what he needs.'

Annie hadn't mentioned anyone named Rohit.

'Um . . . who?' I asked as I got a glass of water for myself. 'Do you want some water?'

'Uh . . . no . . . I know you kicked him out of your life but you're still living in his apartment. Don't you have any whisky?'

'What are you talking about?' I asked, trying to make sense of what she was saying. Maybe Annie should have given me more details about the men in her life and not just her office colleagues before we switched lives.

Rhea came towards the cabinet and immediately opened one that had a few bottles of alcohol. 'Rohit Bhatija. Your ex. He's been messaging me. He wants to talk to you but you've blocked him! Whisky or gin? Though it looks like you've been drinking already!' she said as she took out two half bottles from the cabinet.

'Gin,' I answered. I needed a drink to begin my new life. She poured out two large drinks for us and went to the fridge as if it were her apartment. She found some Sprite, poured it into the two glasses and brought it to me.

'Cheers,' she said.

'Cheers to a new friendship,' I said automatically.

'New friendship? I've known you for a few years now!'

'Yes, yes. I meant a renewal . . . ha . . . ha,' I tried to feebly make up. 'What does Rohit want?'

'Arré . . . you're being very nonchalant about someone you almost married! He wants you in his life, obvio! I think you should give the guy a chance.' Rhea scrolled through her phone and found the messages.

'Why do you . . .' I wanted to know more about whom she was talking about and I've learnt that it's best to keep sentences incomplete because people invariably end up finishing your thought for you.

'Want you to get back with him? He's getting that divorce. He loves you. You love him. Read this.'

Aah. Got it. Annie's ex! I would have to message her later and get more details. I read the messages Rohit had sent to Rhea's phone. 'Tell Annie to unblock me, please. Need to discuss something urgent with her.'

I gave Rhea her phone back. 'See? Your face is flushed. You love him. Still,' she said.

I was feeling hot, actually, and was searching for the air-conditioning remote without trying to look as if I didn't own the apartment. 'This doesn't say anything about a divorce,' I replied. This was an important thing in Annie's life and I didn't want to commit to anything that she would regret later.

Rhea thought about it. 'After your abortion, how many people have you gone out with?'

I stayed quiet. I hadn't known about this. She continued, 'You've not gone out with anyone or fallen in love. Maybe because your heart was waiting for Rohit to return. And he has.'

I nodded. So Annie has not been on any dates. This was worrisome. What if she got attracted to Abhay?

Rhea said, 'Call Rohit or get on to the new app, Busybee. Remember the man I told you I met before you left?'

'No.'

'Well, things have got serious. I think he may be the one.'

I realized she was Annie's best friend. Like Diya was to me. I needed to behave as enthusiastically as Annie would have. 'Rhea! That's great news. Like marriage . . . the one?'

She nodded, working her happiness back. 'Do you want to see a photo?'

I nodded. Rhea showed me his photo.

'He's hot!' I said, genuinely meaning it. 'What's his name?'

'Karthik.' She smiled. 'He's forty-four. I know what you're going to say. That's old, but remember I'm turning thirty-seven in December so it's not that old.'

'No, no. Love has no age.' I tried to sound wise. 'If you're happy then I'm happy for you.'

Rhea went on for a while until I yawned.

'You look tired. I'll go. We'll catch up tomorrow.' She got up.

'Wait, what happened to my food . . .' I said as I checked my phone to track where the delivery man was.

'I'm not hungry. I must reply to Karthik. We've gone from Busybee to being busy . . . if you know what I mean . . . It will be a long night,' she winked. 'Oh wait. Are you going back to work tomorrow or still resting at home?'

I nodded. That was the plan. To get to a job as soon as possible so I could see what it was like. 'I'm going.'

'Don't have any more panic attacks. The managing director position is going to be yours anyway. Don't let Sahil stress you out.'

I nodded. I hadn't known the position was so important to Annie. I only thought she needed this job to help her parents with the restaurant. She had mentioned the managing director position in passing but I could sense there was something deeper at play here. I felt a shiver pass through me, which surprised me. Rhea was sweet and nice. A little nosy but a caring neighbour. And a little daft. She had not figured out that I wasn't Annie. And if I could fool her, I felt a little more confident about making the effort to pull this off at the office as well!

Ten

Annie

How to Be a Good Housewife

Annie was all set to live the life of a housewife. Nandita hadn't mentioned much about her life except:

a) Hari, her old, trusted servant from her parents' house, now lived in her in-laws' house and knew everything about Nandita. He was important to her. He also liked Bollywood films and wanted to become an actor.

b) Abhay liked watching shows at night and eating whatever his mother cooked. He had no libido. So not to worry. Just watch the shows and go to sleep. He played tennis four times a week so Annie could do whatever she chose on those nights as he met his friends afterwards.

c) Diya, her friend, regularly checked up on Nandita and wanted to meet often. So Nandita sorted it by chatting with Diya and saying she was going to be a recluse for some time as she had decided to focus on her book. So Annie didn't need to meet her.

All Annie needed to do was observe the dynamics between Abhay and his parents, shadow them wherever they went to get an idea of what interests an upper-middle-class family had and apply it to her strategy when she had to come up with campaigns.

Annie believed she had watched enough TV serials with her mother to understand what a housewife needed to do. This was research for Annie. And RESEARCH was everything! Annie had been working madly for the last six years in Mumbai trying to rise in her career while managing a revolving door of boyfriends until she met Rohit. And after dating for two years, Rohit had broken her heart a year ago to go back to his wife. But he had bought this flat when they were together and allowed her to stay in it as a gesture of kindness. The madness, broken heartache and hectic activity had given her stress and panic attacks recently. She was glad she had taken this break, in a way.

It was late at night by the time her flight landed back in Mumbai. She took an Uber to Nandita's home. She found the keys in Nandita's old tan leather purse, which Annie found hideous, and entered the dark apartment. She touched her nose. It felt odd to wear a nose ring but Nandita had insisted and they'd gone to a local jeweller who pierced Annie's nose just a day ago. It felt raw and uncomfortable. She shut the door as she put the keys on the console next to it. There were family photos there. Of vacations taken together. 'Eegghh,' Annie muttered.

Abhay heard her from his room and called out, 'Nandu, is that you?'

She followed the light towards the end of a corridor to see Abhay, Nandita's husband, sitting up in bed watching Netflix.

'Hey,' she said, not knowing how to react. He was an incredibly handsome man. She had felt an instant connection to him on the video chat from the resort. But she had never told Nandita how she felt, wanting to see if there was anything there in person. But seeing him in person she could feel a spark within her.

'Hey,' he said as he paused the show. 'How was the vacation?'

'Good. How are you?' Annie felt awkward standing in another woman's room, pretending to be someone she wasn't. *What conversations did married couples make?* She tried to remember if her parents had any normal conversations that weren't regarding the shop.

'I'm sick. I think I have a cold. My nose is stuffy,' he said, frowning. 'Ma and Papa had to go meet Chachu yesterday morning because he broke his hip in the bathroom. They'll be back tomorrow.'

'I need to, uh . . . take a shower,' she said.

'Ya, okay . . .' he said as he went back to watching the show. She entered their bathroom and saw there were more of his products than Nandita's on one side of the counter. There were towels in a drawer under the sink and a host of medicines in a box. Who were these people?

After a shower, she came out wearing Nandita's pyjamas. Annie ran her fingers through her new short hair and tried to figure out what to do with her towel. This was something one should know if one lived in a house. But these were things that she had forgotten to ask Nandita.

'Hey, Abhay . . . I'm going to hang this up . . . uh . . . in the . . .' She pointed, pretending to think of the word.

'Balcony?'

'Yes. Balcony.' She still didn't know which balcony. But she tried a new tactic. 'Do you want tea, or a soup or a drink maybe?' She could definitely use a drink, but she had to figure out where that would be as well.

'A drink sounds like a good idea,' Abhay said.

'Great,' she answered, 'Maybe I can help you . . . I'll have a large whisky with water and two cubes of ice . . .'

Abhay looked at her sharply, 'Since when did you start drinking whisky? Aren't you more into wine?'

Annie felt a little concerned that she might have given away a crucial piece of information for this experiment to stay on track. But she composed herself and said, 'I read that whisky has fewer calories. I've decided to switch.'

He nodded at the plausible explanation and went to get them their drinks. She followed so she could see where the bar was. He nodded towards the kitchen, 'Aren't you going to hang the towel?'

She realized the balcony outside the kitchen was the dry area and hung her towel there while he returned to the bedroom in a few minutes. He handed her the drink and said, 'Cheers.'

'Cheers,' she responded and clinked her glass before taking a large gulp. It was exactly what she needed.

They sat and watched a Netflix show that he had been watching earlier. Abhay was quiet, engrossed in the murder mystery. It was one that Annie had seen before. 'I liked Season 2 better in this series.'

Abhay paused the show to turn towards Annie. '*You* have watched this?'

Annie paused to think of the correct answer, 'There was nothing else to watch after a while at the resort. So you know . . . evenings got boring. I scrolled and watched this.'

Abhay seemed to buy into that logic. 'I told you not to go. I knew you would be bored without me. Fine, let's watch something else. What do you want to see?'

'Whatever you want, really. I don't care.' Annie took her phone to scroll through Nandita's social media and ignored Abhay, which made him even more curious to know what she wanted to watch.

'You know what I want to watch next?' He showed her his watchlist on his phone as he moved closer to her. She felt his ruggedness as his body touched hers nonchalantly. It sent sudden ripples through her spine.

She felt her face flush unexpectedly and avoided his gaze, 'Oh, this has my favourite actress. She's so good.'

'Yeah, I love her too,' he said as he turned to look at her.

'We should see that after we finish this one.' She stared into his deep brown eyes. *What was happening to her?* She got up to break the energy that had suddenly got intense. She found a pair of clean shorts in her suitcase. She couldn't bear wearing Nandita's clothes the first night that she was there. She would have to clean the cupboard to figure out where everything was.

'Can you rub some Vicks on my chest?' Abhay asked suddenly as he took off his shirt. Annie felt conscious of his bare body near her.

'Um . . . yes . . . okay . . . I think steaming might be good too?' she asked as he handed her the Vicks bottle that was on his nightstand.

'That takes too much time. This is quicker,' he said as he closed his eyes waiting for her to rub the Vicks.

She saw his flat abs and broad chest and gulped. She hadn't seen a man naked for so long. He's sick. This is housewife duty. Focus, she thought.

She started rubbing his chest with her left hand as he closed his eyes and moaned. 'Yeah.'

She could feel her face flush.

'Can you sit on me and use both hands, please?' he asked.

'What?' Her voice pitch went high. 'That's not such a good idea.' She knew she would be aroused and didn't want to put herself in a position that would make her do something she would regret.

He adjusted himself so his back was completely flat and ignored her comment. 'Sit.'

Annie slowly moved her body on top of Abhay. She started rubbing his chest in a circular motion as he let out a deep breath. As she was getting up, he put his hands on her hips and squeezed. 'Keep going.'

She softly rubbed his shoulders and then ran the tips of her fingers down his chest.

'Harder,' he moaned.

She rubbed his chest with long strokes moving down his torso and rocked her body up and down as she massaged him. She closed her eyes and tilted her head back. She could feel him getting hard against the thin cotton track pants he was wearing. He let out a soft moan. She ran her fingers across the length of his bare shoulders to feel his taut muscles. He had tan lines across his neck and arms from playing tennis. She let out a soft sigh.

This was the illicit affair she never wanted to have. 'I didn't think . . . I think we should . . .'

'You know how horny I get when I'm sick . . .'

'And you've not been sick for a long time, I guess . . .' Annie muttered.

'So long . . .' he moaned. Suddenly in one fluid motion, Abhay sat up and held Annie close to him with her up-tilted breasts and curved hips touching his body. He held her close to him and gave her a long, hard, deep kiss.

'You smell different.'

Annie figured it must be the perfume from her own clothes. She stiffened in fright. Annie could see he was hard for her as he tried to untie the knot of his pyjamas. He looked at her intently. 'It's been so long.'

Annie desperately wanted to give in. It had been a long time. He kissed her with a passion she had never felt before. She arched her back, ready to give in to this stranger. No one would know. This was research. She kissed him back with a fury that was pent up inside her. She felt powerful. Something inside her clicked. She knew what she needed to do. This wasn't going to be just an ordinary life switch. This chance meeting she had with her lookalike was for a reason. It was for her to switch her whole life around. This wasn't just for research. It was an opportunity.

But just as he was about to remove his clothes, Abhay stopped suddenly. He went to the bathroom while Annie lay there wondering what had just happened. *Had he guessed she was not Nandita? Had this experiment failed even before it began?*

'Abhay,' she called out to him. 'What's wrong?'

Abhay came out after a few minutes. 'Sorry, babe. I needed to blow my nose. Maybe this isn't a great time . . . '

'Of course.'

'I'm going to crash now.'

'So early?' she asked, confused about what had just happened. He hadn't confronted her. He hadn't accused her of not being Nandita. *What was going on?*

'It's been a long day,' Abhay muttered. She was perplexed but he turned over and went to sleep, putting off the light in their room. She slowly walked out into the drawing room to figure out how this household worked and what more she needed to do to be a part of it. She had never planned to sleep with Abhay, but she was very confused with what her body was telling her. After all, she wasn't in love with him. She'd just got carried away with playing housewife. And she hadn't been touched for so long . . . and the whisky . . .

Annie was not used to sleeping with anyone in her bed. It took her several hours before she could rest. But maybe it wasn't because of the snoring. Maybe it was because she had almost broken the vow to Nandita on the first night itself. Maybe it was because the plan was slowly forming in her head on how to make Abhay her husband.

Annie had taken a good look at the house once Abhay had gone to sleep. A large four-bedroom apartment in a fancy building with a huge kitchen and a gym downstairs. Abhay was wealthy and he had a family that loved him. He had friends that Nandita spoke about who were always there for him. Nandita didn't want any of that. But Annie did. This was her backup plan. If she didn't get the managing director position, at least she would have Abhay as a husband who could help with her parents' EMI and support her lifestyle. But she needed to do this slowly. If Abhay slept with her, he would know instantly she wasn't Nandita and maybe even get her arrested. But if she made him fall in love with her, then she could have it all.

Eleven

Nandita

How to Get a Corner Office

Annie had given me a few instructions on how to become a working woman.

a) Set an alarm to wake up on time.
b) Call an Uber well in advance to be on time for the office.
c) Don't make eye contact with Sahil, the fucker.

So basically, nothing useful.

I entered Annie's office half an hour before anyone else could arrive. I was so groggy from trying to wake up on time. Then I had to make my own masala chai and skipped breakfast. I missed Hari more than Abhay. One of the perks of being a housewife was that I could sleep till nine a.m., get an afternoon nap post lunch and have Hari wake me up both times with my masala chai in bed. All that would soon be eliminated from my life.

The office was on a high floor that overlooked several buildings in the Lower Parel area. It was a vast floor with different coloured, semi-circular cabins that faced several desks where the junior members of each cabin person's team sat. Each cabin was translucent so you could see each other but not pry into the boss's work. Several desks were individualized to the person's tastes with photos, plants and knick-knacks.

I went to Annie's cabin as she had instructed (take a left at the entrance and go straight down to the end) and saw her name on the door. What a wonderful feeling that must be. To have your own name on a door. Most parents are proud of their children for doing something great. But most of them never visit their children's offices to see their name on a door. I made a mental note to myself that if I had my name on the door, I would make my parents come to see it because it would mean it took a lot to get there. But then my parents would be happier if I gave them a grandkid instead of a paycheck.

Annie's office had a large desk perpendicular to a wall with a red chair behind it. She had an oval table on one side with a few chairs around it, which faced a large whiteboard. There were no photographs of anyone on her desk except a photo of herself after a marathon with the time written at the bottom. Her desk was clean except for a MacBook that was kept in the middle. A poster of Claire Underwood from *House of Cards* covered the wall behind her. It said, 'Am I really the sort of enemy you want to make?' It described Annie perfectly. Ruthless. Aggressive. Ambitious.

Now all I had to do was fill her mighty shoes. But I was exactly the opposite. Unsure. Reluctant. Flexible. *How did she even think this was going to work?*

I sat at her desk and opened her MacBook. I took a deep breath and straightened myself up. I was up to the challenge.

After all, this is what I had wanted for so long. To experience what it was like working and being part of a team. To know what a boardroom felt like, where important decisions were made. To feel like my opinion mattered to someone. I had heard Abhay say he was in a meeting and he had to get back to the boardroom so many times when I had called to chat in the first year of our marriage. I never imagined I would sit in one or have a cabin to myself.

I had a slight hope that he would recognize Annie from the previous night and call me. And we would have to switch back because he couldn't live without me, his wife. But there was no call and Annie hadn't replied to my message yet. I presume she was getting used to being in my shoes. I had told her I don't run so she shouldn't wake up at the crack of dawn as she had done at the resort. But habits are difficult to change.

We had agreed that we would change back if it got too much or someone found out and it would become a crisis. But until then, we would let this week go with living this life switch.

Sahil entered the cabin. 'Welcome back, Annie. How was your holiday? Whoa, nice glasses!' He sat on a chair, making himself comfortable for a long chat. Sahil was trim, muscled and sinewy, with straight, gelled black hair, a thick salt-and-pepper beard and dark eyes. I felt as though I had seen him somewhere before but couldn't recollect where.

'It was . . . it was great actually,' I tried to sound cool. 'How have you been?'

He looked at me for a long time. 'First time I've been in your cabin, and you haven't said, "What do you want, Sahil?" in that gruff tone of yours.'

I laughed. That sounded like Annie when she was upset, which I had seen briefly when we were dining and her order was delayed.

He got up. 'You might not have got it on your calendar yet. Meeting has been pushed to ten. Team shuffle and stuff.' He looked at me probingly to see if I would react.

I didn't. 'Great. Thanks for informing me. The meeting is in here?' I tried to see where the calendar was on the Mac. I had never used this before and was unfamiliar with the buttons. I made a mental note to look up some videos to see how this thing functioned.

He laughed. 'No, silly. In the boardroom as usual. It's Monday. Our regular nine-thirty meeting is now at ten.'

'Oh, yes,' I pushed my glasses up on my nose. 'I'm still in vacay mode, I guess.'

He winked as he left. *Where had I seen him?*

Annie had failed to mention that Sahil the 'fucker' was still handsome. Dynamic. Stunning.

I sat for the next hour in her cabin trying to figure out the laptop and opened several presentations that Annie had worked on. I was impressed. Annie was methodical and had great statistics in her slides. I would never be able to do all this. All I could do was type in a Word document.

I felt I needed to use the restroom, so I walked out of my cabin and went towards the corridor. But I kept going round and round, got lost, found the pantry where coffee was served and ended up back at my cabin.

A young girl came up to me looking eager and also terrified. She clutched a stack of papers close to her chest as if she was using them to protect herself against being hit.

'Welcome back, Annie ma'am. Meeting has been shifted to Queen.'

'What? The restroom?' I asked perplexed.

The girl pointed towards a boardroom that had the name 'Queen' on the door. Each corner of the floor had a boardroom that I hadn't noticed before.

I nodded. 'Sure. Sure. Yes. Um . . . you know I needed to use the restroom first. Why don't you come with me?'

The girl looked terrified as if I was going to murder her in there. 'Me?'

'Lead the way.' I waved my hands in front so as not to reveal that I had no idea about the layout of the office. 'And keep talking. Tell me about this week.'

As I passed a few conference rooms, I saw they were all named after court cards—king, queen, knight, page—depending on the size of the room.

The girl kept chatting about how she was forced to go to Sahil's team even though she wanted to stay with me. But it was peer pressure.

'Sure. Don't worry about it. We'll figure it out.' I finally arrived at the restroom. 'See you later.'

The girl seemed shocked that I was nice to her and left.

I looked at my watch and realized it was close to ten o'clock and I had better be on time for the meeting. I took a deep breath. This was it. This was my chance to prove I could be a working woman. If I could fool everyone into believing I was Annie, I would have the experience of my life this week!

I entered the Queen boardroom and took a seat at the large table closer to the screen than the head of the table. Several people whom I didn't know entered and told me they liked my new look. 'Glasses suit you, Annie,' they hollered.

Then Ranjana entered, walking confidently in a soft pink pantsuit and white shirt that was tailored for her pregnant belly. Her hair was swept back near the nape of her neck and her eyes were dark with kohl and determination. Sahil sat next to her. She looked at me and said, 'Annie, welcome back. Why aren't you sitting at your usual seat?' She pointed to the chair next to her. I hadn't known there were specific chairs for all. My heart was thumping hard and I hoped Ranjana wouldn't hear it.

'Oh, right.' I took my seat next to her.

'Okay. Let's get started. First, let's welcome back Annie. Hope you've got your rest and research done. We're looking forward to many more brilliant ideas from you from now on,' Ranjana said in a no-nonsense voice. Everyone clapped. She continued. 'We're presenting Sahil's idea about the Diamond washer and dryer next Monday. Annie, since you weren't here, Sahil has taken over your campaign.' She rattled on nonstop. Annie would not like this. And for the first time, I felt a pinch of anxiety that I was not helping Annie enough by being her. But I kept quiet. I had no ideas. I didn't know what to say or if I should even interrupt my boss.

Ranjana continued, 'So the presentation for the mental health app, MyTherapist, has shifted to tomorrow and the washing powder one has been moved to the twenty-first. So we don't have a lot of time. Did you get all of that? I hope you'll be able to present something, Annie. Also, Sahil is presenting the Busybee app on Thursday. Are you ready? Have you done your research on Busybee like Sahil has?'

And it clicked in my head. Busybee. Sahil was Karthik. Rhea's new love interest. The one she thought she would marry. The man Annie hated.

'Oh my god!' I exclaimed out loud. I should have warned Rhea that Karthik was Sahil. But now how would I tell Rhea? She would ask why I hadn't said anything earlier when I saw his photo. I sat there perplexed at what to do. On the one hand, I had to warn Annie's best friend that she was dating a fraud. On the other, if I did, I would give the game away that I wasn't Annie because I hadn't 'noticed' earlier. She was right. He was slimy.

'What is it, Annie?' Ranjana asked, looking at me.

'Um . . . nothing.' I tried to make up something as they continued to stare at me looking for a better answer. 'Am I supposed to present something?' I didn't recollect Annie mentioning that she had a presentation immediately on her return.

'No. I knew you'd be back today and I didn't want to trouble you during your vacation. So I've not sent the brief to you yet. And one day is really short notice for you.'

If I was going to gain the full corporate experience, I would have to work under pressure and see how I could handle it. I volunteered, 'Let me try, please.'

Ranjana looked impressed. 'Okay. I'll send it to you after this meeting.'

Sahil spoke sarcastically, 'If she can't come up with a decent idea in three weeks for the Diamond washing machine, how is she going to be able to do this overnight?' Annie had shared that story with me over drinks when we had spent ample time with each other. But it was more to the effect of how women aren't appreciated for their hard work while men can say anything and other women rarely question them. Come to think of it, Annie had only complained about how her ideas weren't accepted, instead of sharing what ideas had worked.

I wanted to speak up but my voice got caught in my throat. I looked down.

Ranjana ignored him. 'Moving on! Annie, I know you've not been here, but there has been some team reshuffling that's happened. Shivani will be reporting to you as a creative director. And the rest of your team will be reporting to Sahil.'

He gave me a sly grin.

I cleared my throat and everyone looked at me again. Again, I was rooted to the seat. Dear god. I thought quickly. 'I can manage a team,' I whispered hesitantly.

'She really—' Sahil started speaking.

'What are you suggesting?' Ranjana cut him off to look straight at me while she stood up to stretch her back.

I wanted to get the full range of experiences. I had heard Abhay talk about his team and I wanted to be able to do the same. 'I would like to get another chance at working with the team. Please.'

'But we've already—' Sahil spoke up again and I could see why he was so annoying.

'Fine,' Ranjana interrupted him again. 'Last chance.' She smiled at me and I could see why Annie said she would be firm but helpful.

I smiled. I sat there trying not to look down at my phone. There was still no message from Annie about her time with Abhay. I was dying to hear his voice and tell him I was in a board meeting. He would freak out.

I smiled and Sahil caught it. 'What's so funny, Annie?'

I panicked a little and shook my head. He looked at Ranjana. She probably figured that since she'd cut him off twice, she'd be on his side for this one.

'Nothing,' I squeaked.

'No, please share it with us.' She sat down on her chair holding her large pregnant belly and popping a button in her pantsuit.

I was in a spot. I had to think of something. I had vaguely heard her saying the marketing for the washing machine was not up to the mark. So I thought of what they were talking about and added to it. 'I was thinking about the Diamond washing machine idea.'

'The one you tanked?' Sahil reminded everyone.

'Go on,' Ranjana leaned in to listen to me.

'Yeah . . . um . . . I was . . . when I got marr . . . I mean, when my best friend just got married, she went to her in-laws' house and they played a prank on her. They gave her a whole bucket of clothes and said she had to wash them. She was so worried and she wanted to please them so she took them to the bathroom and came out to ask for washing powder. And that's when the whole family started giggling and told her it was a joke.' I laughed remembering how Abhay had told me it was his idea and his parents played along with it. I continued my story. 'They showed me, um . . . my friend where the washer-dryer was. And said she never had to do any housework. She asked them, "Not even cooking?" And they shook their heads. So then she blurted out, "What do you want me to do then?" And they answered, "*Jo tumhari marzi*", whatever you want. And that's how she felt accepted by the family and never did a single chore.'

Ranjana and the entire team were silent after my story. She just stared at me. I went quiet. I had goofed up. They knew I wasn't Annie. Crap. On my first day at a job, I would be fired!

'Annie,' Ranjana said slowly, 'that was . . . AMAZING!' She started clapping and everyone in the room joined in. 'This is it. This is our campaign.'

'What?' Sahil seethed. 'What about my idea?'

Ranjana ignored him to say, 'That's our tagline. Don't do laundry. *Karo jo tumhari marzi*. Prateek, you sort the hashtag. Annie, write this up and send it to me by end of day. I'll send it to the client. I think we've got it this time. Okay. Good work. I have another meeting.'

She clapped her hands twice and headed towards the door. I got up as well. I didn't know what I was supposed to write up but felt that I had somehow made her happy.

Sahil seemed irritated as he followed Ranjana to the door to plead his case.

I took a moment in the boardroom as people exited and breathed a sigh of relief. My first day was not so bad. I could do this. No one realized I wasn't Annie. She would be proud of me.

But just as I got back to my cabin, a petite woman in her forties with mid-length silver hair, purple glasses and an air of insouciance came into my office, 'Annie, so glad you're back.' She handed me a box of Bengali sweets as I sat down on the red chair behind the desk. 'I've brought this back from Kolkata. Had a wonderful week with my parents.'

'Really?' I asked, trying to rack my brain on who she could be as Annie had not shown me any picture of her on her phone. She had an air of authority about her, so I presumed she must be important.

'You're right. No one has a wonderful time with parents. But I think they've finally understood I'm not getting married, so they left me alone without setting me up on dates. How was your trip? Have you thought about what we discussed?'

I panicked on the inside but replied calmly, 'It's been some time . . . Remind me . . . what did we discuss?'

The woman cocked her head to one side. 'How you were going to work through your anger issues.'

'My anger issues,' I said alarmed. 'I don't have any . . .'

'Oh, darling.' She then called out to Shivani who was passing by the cabin. Shivani was tall and slim with the perfect oval face, dark eyes, bushy eyebrows and a pout.

'Yes, Koko.' Shivani barely entered the room, only poking her head in. I finally knew the woman's name. Koko was the HR head whom Annie had mentioned. A no-nonsense woman who was seemingly helpful but in reality didn't do much.

Koko replied, looking at Shivani, 'I'm looking forward to this new equation.' She turned to me and said, 'They will be assessing you, Annie, so try to make this relationship work.'

I looked at Shivani and asked, 'Who is they?'

Shivani pointed to herself saying, 'Me.'

'You and?' I asked, confused.

Koko clarified. 'Annie, we went through this last time. Shivani is non-binary. She addresses herself as they/them.'

'Oh,' I had heard about the term but had never met a person who was non-binary before. This would be interesting.

'And Shivani, you need to make Annie rock. We need this partnership to work, right?' Koko said enthusiastically and pumped her fists in the air.

I smiled. 'Ranjana said you'll help me with this Busybee presentation. I love that shirt, by the way.' I added an extra polite touch knowing that when you compliment someone, they warm up to you better.

But Shivani wasn't buying it. She looked at me and narrowed her eyes. I felt as if she could see through me. Again, my heart started beating wildly. I didn't know how much longer I could take of this life switch. Instead, she turned and left.

When my heart slowed down again, I wondered if I could just proclaim to be Annie's twin working here while she took some time off. I wouldn't need to fool anyone. And, clearly, I could come up with ideas as proven earlier. It was far easier to begin afresh than erase the memories of the past and work with Annie's baggage. I asked Koko before she left my office, 'What would happen if someone else came to work in Annie's . . . my place and I took an extended break?'

Koko's eyes grew wide as she put her hand to her head looking vexed. 'That can't happen. It's against organization policies that someone who has not been vetted by the system should come in. They could lose their job in a minute if they did that! That's fraud.'

'I didn't mean I would do anything like that,' I laughed nervously. 'It was an idea for a campaign,' I covered up. 'Switching places in life. Life switch! Ha ha.'

Koko said confidently, 'People would know in an instant. They're not stupid. And you could get fired or arrested for impersonating someone.'

'What?'

Koko nodded, 'Yeah, because you would be accessing confidential documents within a company.'

I gulped. Koko put her hand lightly on my hand that was on the desk and kept it there a second longer than usual as she looked at me. I wondered if she had guessed I wasn't Annie.

She smiled, 'Don't stress, Annie. You just need to come to me if you have any problem, okay?' She squeezed my hand and said evocatively, 'I'm here for you.'

As she exited, I realized that the HR head Koko was gay. And she had a massive crush on Annie/me. But the worst part was if anyone figured out I wasn't Annie, I would lose her job, and worse, we could go to jail.

Suddenly this life switch had become dangerous, and I didn't want any part of it.

Twelve

Annie

How to Train a Husband

'We need to switch back!' Nandita screamed over the phone as soon as she could get out of the office building.

Annie said calmly, 'Why? Did you lose my . . . your job?'

'No,' Nandita took a sharp intake of breath and added, 'I actually gave a great idea for the Diamond washer thing and Ranjana loved it.'

'That's brilliant. What's the problem?'

'If the HR woman finds out, we . . . you could get fired.'

'Well then, make sure Koko doesn't find out! And tell me about the idea, *na*.'

Annie had woken up early to go for a run. By the time she came back, Hari had returned and had made some disgusting milky cardamom tea for her. She promptly threw it in the toilet and made herself some black coffee when he wasn't in the kitchen.

Abhay had woken up to a sweaty wife showering and listening to a podcast about leadership in the bathroom. He went to sit at the breakfast table while Hari served him some aloo paratha.

When Annie went to sit at the table, Hari served a paratha which she looked at with horror. It was dripping with oil and it would bust her diet completely. She wondered if she could make eggs, but it might look suspicious as Nandita didn't know how to cook.

She saw Abhay was on his mobile phone and looked fresh. She exclaimed, 'You look better!'

'The allergy is gone. I'm fit and fine now.' He was distracted as he scrolled through his messages.

They avoided discussing what happened the previous night. She cleared her throat and said, 'You know, I'm going to make my own breakfast.' He looked up at her, surprised. She replied, 'Do you want eggs?' He shook his head.

She went to the kitchen and showed Hari how to make scrambled eggs the way she preferred it, soaking a red chilli in some oil and using that instead of butter. And then adding a dash of milk and sprinkling some oregano on top.

'I thought you hated eggs,' Abhay said suspiciously when she brought out her food.

'I'm transforming.' Annie relished her breakfast, not caring about Hari looking at her from the side of the door. Maybe she was being reckless but if she was going to be a housewife, it would have to be on her terms as well. She could not eat Hari's or anyone else's oily food for too long. She was used to cooking for herself.

'Okay, babe. I'm off to work. I have tennis tonight. You remember that, don't you? I'm going to have dinner with the guys. So I'll see you after dinner.' Abhay gulped down his coffee.

'Excuse me, I haven't finished my food,' she said firmly, looking up at him.

'What?' he asked as Hari handed him his lunch tiffin.

'I'm still eating.'

Abhay shook his head, implying he had not understood what she was saying.

She continued, 'Please sit with me. I'm not done eating. Five minutes. Food is not just functional. It's communal. It brings people together for a reason.' She didn't add that that was why she learnt to cook. So she could get her parents to sit with her to eat even though they were always too busy. And now she cooked for herself and ate alone.

Abhay sat down looking like a reprimanded child. 'I'm sorry. I didn't realize . . . You never said anything before . . .'

'And . . . I'd like to join you this evening.'

'Huh?'

'Playing tennis. I want to play tennis.' Annie knew that if she got into more activities with Abhay, she would know more about his life and what couples did together.

'But you hate tennis. And my friends,' Abhay said a little loudly.

'Really? Well . . . I would like to try. Again. With your friends. And tennis.'

Abhay was quiet for some time. She continued eating slowly to let him get used to the idea that his wife would join him. After several minutes, he replied, 'Cool. I'll see you at the courts at six-thirty. Are you finished?'

She nodded and then realized she didn't know where the courts were. She asked, 'How would I get there? To the courts.'

'I'll send the driver back for you after I reach. Be ready. Do you even have tennis gear? I thought you were more into swimming.'

Annie avoided answering and instead asked mischievously, 'Aren't you going to kiss me?' Abhay looked pleasantly shocked. He pecked her on her forehead as she called out, 'See you later, hubby.' She guessed that Abhay was back to being normal because he didn't kiss her on the lips. This is what Nandita had meant when she said Abhay wasn't into romance or sex any more. It didn't seem like that last night. But maybe that was an aberration because he was sick. She wondered if she should tell Nandita about it but thought against it. What she didn't know wouldn't hurt her.

Hari looked at her suspiciously but went back to the kitchen to clean up and then retreated to the servants' quarters on the other side of the flat. He had his own room with a TV and an attached bathroom.

Annie spent the day cleaning Nandita's cupboard and sorting out the room. Nandita was a slob and it took several hours for Annie to arrange everything according to her taste. If she was going to stay in the room, she needed it to be tidy.

Hari came to ask her about lunch but she said she would make her own salad, to which he retreated into his room for the rest of the afternoon in shock. She presumed Nandita never had salad and made it a point to eat more of Hari's food later to not raise suspicion or to at least teach him not to heap oil into everything. The first order of business she thought was to get rid of Hari. He was a pest who wasn't needed there. He looked at her suspiciously and smiled too sweetly when he brought her something. He was fishy. But she had to get into the family's heart for them to do without him. And she needed to know everything about this family.

She explored the house a little more. It had a large drawing room with a bar attached to one side and a dining area. There was a door to one side of the drawing room which led to an office. It had a large desk with some papers. She went around the desk and saw there was a diary, letterheads, some printed spreadsheets and jewellery designs. Behind the desk to one side was a steel file cabinet. She went through the file cabinet. Everything was neatly organized. She looked through one that had 'insurance' written on it. She took the file out and sat on the chair to go through it better. It was the entire family's medical insurance and life insurance papers neatly printed out and categorized. She checked out the nominee for Abhay's life insurance. Nandita Patel.

Annie smiled. She knew she would need to change that to Annie Singh. All she needed was two weeks to change his mind. After all, it was the same time in which she made Rohit forget his wife and fall in love with her. And when she had felt the relationship was on the verge of getting over, she guilted him into giving his apartment to her while he went back to the bungalow he shared with his wife. It had hurt for a long time that she couldn't make him leave his wife, but in retrospect, living rent-free was probably far more valuable than the love of a man who was not great in bed. But she had learnt those lessons and she would not repeat them here. She didn't want to be another mistress again.

She got a call on her phone. Diya. She picked it up.

'Hey! How's it going?' The voice chirped annoyingly from the other side.

'Good . . . great . . . you say?' Annie made her voice slightly higher like Nandita's.

'I know you're concentrating on your book, but I wanted to discuss my new idea. I'm planning to start journal therapy classes for teenagers. Should we meet for drinks? Same place?'

Annie hesitated before answering. 'Actually, I'm meeting Abhay later at the courts.'

There was silence before Diya asked, 'What? Why?'

'Oh, I dunno. Just thought I should spend more time around him. If he wants to play tennis at least I can watch, right?' Annie tried to sound casual.

'You hate tennis.'

Annie gulped. 'You know . . . someone at the retreat told me I should make more effort in my marriage. Gotta give it one last try, right?'

'Okay. Makes sense. Cool, I'll catch you later then. Tell me if your plan works and you get some action tonight.' Diya hung up and Annie realized that even Nandita's friend was lame. She didn't need to spend time with her. All Annie needed was to get Abhay to fall for her and his parents to like her more than they liked Nandita.

She walked into Nandita's in-laws' room. It had an ebony four-poster bed with side tables. A large chest of drawers faced the bed with photos of the family on it. On one side of the room was a dressing table with a mirror that had perfume and make-up and a small ornamental box. Annie opened the box to see an assortment of rings that Kamini kept in it. She put on one large sapphire ring to see how it would look against her skin. It felt good to be a daughter-in-law in a rich household. She could get used to this life, she thought.

She kept the ring on while opening the cupboards in the room. They were filled with clothes and shoes that were not organized as well as Annie would have liked, but she shut them so she wouldn't need to clean them. Her OCD was tingling to clean things up.

She sat on Kamini's side of the bed and put her feet up on the garish golden satin bedcover. What would it be like to have a married life for decades, she wondered. Sleeping next to the same man. Listening to his nonsense and agreeing with it. She'd seen her mother do it with her father and she had vowed not to have that. Until she fell in love with Rohit. But she would not think of that now. She would never have another heartbreak like that. She opened the drawer in the nightstand and found a thick red diary. She opened it and saw there were poems and thoughts inscribed in it. Annie read a few and acknowledged they were very good. She took a photo of one on her phone.

She went into her room and noticed the wedding photo on Abhay's side table. Nandita was beaming in a red-and-gold lehenga and hideous gold jewellery, carrying a large garland of flowers that hid most of her. Did she know what she was getting into when she got married? Annie wondered what it really meant to blend in and be a housewife.

When the in-laws came back from their trip, she would be ready to make them fall in love with her and forget about Nandita. Then she would slowly replace her in this large house with a man who was in love with her and a family who needed Annie, not Nandita.

She changed into Nandita's jeans and a nice blouse and smiled at herself in the mirror. They looked exactly alike. No one would be able to tell them apart. She splashed a little of the perfume that was lying on the dresser and felt ready and confident to execute the rest of her plan.

She heard a knock on the door. Hari came in with black coffee on a tray. He looked at her intently and said wryly, 'Your coffee, madam.'

Hari knew she wasn't Nandita.

Thirteen

Nandita

How to Avoid an Ex

After my mini meltdown this afternoon, I had gone back to the office and didn't step out of the cabin till it was time to go home. No one noticed me as I left the building. I picked up a bottle of wine on the way home in case I would ever need it. I returned home and just lay on the bed for a long time speculating if I had made a mistake with this life-switch idea. What was I thinking sending another woman to impersonate me as Abhay's wife? I was testing his love. And I was testing myself to see if I would survive in a corporate environment. Was I mad? Had Annie slipped something into my drink for me to even agree to this?

I fell asleep with exhaustion and anxiety and didn't realize how late it was when I woke up. My stomach was growling. I changed into a pair of shorts and a shirt when the doorbell rang. Dear god, that Rhea was such a pest. If I had to chat with her every day about her stupid love life, I might go crazy and tell her I'm Nandita and cancel this entire experiment.

I opened the door to find it wasn't Rhea. It was a man who stood there with a bouquet. He was of medium height with soft, wavy hair that fell just above his broad shoulders. His face was bronzed but I couldn't see beyond his mask. His eyes, though, were expressive and apologetic.

'Hi, babe. Can I come in?'

For a minute I stood there wondering who this could be until he said, 'I sent Rhea a message for you to unblock me, but I guess you didn't get it . . .'

Rohit. Annie's ex-boyfriend.

'Oh . . . No . . . I don't think that's such a . . .' I started to say as he entered, took off his mask and sanitized his hands. His after-shave left a scent as he trailed me inside. I finally saw who Rohit was. He was an actor in Bollywood who my sister Samaira had a massive crush on. She would be tickled pink to know that I had tried to throw him out of an apartment.

After I gathered myself, I asked, 'What . . . what are you doing here? I thought we had . . .'

'Broken up. Yes. But I think we need to talk,' Rohit sat down on the sofa without being invited. 'Can I have a drink, at least?'

I nodded. 'Help yourself.' I sat down and added, 'And make me one too, please.'

He went to the kitchen and poured out two whiskies into a glass. I hated whisky but I had to pretend that I was Annie. I could drink anything after this long day.

'Thank you.' I raised my glass and took a small sip.

'I know you've blocked me but I wanted to talk to you. Cheers.' He gulped his drink down in one shot, which alarmed me a little. He took a deep breath and spoke passionately, 'I still love you. Wait. Hear me out. I've been trying to live my life without you. I really tried. I worked hard. I finished that movie you said I should sign. It's going to be a blockbuster. You were so right. You always are my darling. I'm where I am because of you. Because you told me to do those last three films that have really made me famous now. And I earned twelve crore in the last one year.'

He sat down and looked at me as he held my hand. 'But babe, it's nothing without you. I need you back. I would give all of it up in a heartbeat if you agree to be with me.'

Why did men think that by saying how successful they were, a woman would fall in love with them or would go back to them? Women rarely care about a man's success. All I would care about is if the man paid attention to what I needed and asked me what I wanted and followed through with that. I couldn't figure out what he was proposing as he looked deep into my eyes. *Did he want to date or marry me?*

'Excuse me?' I asked, unable to remember if I had read anything about this Bollywood couple splitting.

He cleared his throat and took a moment to get another drink. I continued, 'Do you still love me?'

'No . . .'

At this point, I felt my head spinning a little. I hadn't eaten anything, and I missed Hari's cooking. I needed something oily in my stomach. I leaned forward to hold my head and Rohit took it as another gesture.

In one sharp, swift movement, he pulled me close and kissed me deeply. His soft mouth on my lips gave me a shock down my spine. It was sweet, dizzying and sexy. But wrong! I pushed him away and found clarity.

'No.' I said confidently as I stood up. 'You need to leave.'

'You're right. I'm sorry. Shouldn't have done that.' He stood up and then looked at me, his demeanour changed and his eyes steely. 'I'm sorry, but you need to move out in three months. I've found a buyer for this house.'

'What?'

I wondered what all that was about then. Him saying he loved Annie. What a sleazebag.

'I told him I'll give him the place in three months. If you find a place sooner, that's even better.'

I sat there feeling that it was something Annie should know about. I didn't speak. He looked at me strangely. He spoke with authority. '*You're not Annie.*' He spoke calmly and casually with a deep, menacing look in his eyes. 'Who are you?'

Suddenly I panicked. This was the first person who had figured this out. I didn't know whether to laugh it off, but the moment felt tense and awkward.

'Of course I am.'

'Okay then, what is our song?'

'Oh, dear god.' I tried to come up with an excuse for not knowing it. 'I can barely remember.'

He moved closer to me. I tried another tactic. Tenderness. I summoned up the courage to say, 'Rohit . . . I've had a really hard day.' I didn't want a stranger in this house any more.

'I could spend the night . . .'

What a creep!

I decided the only way I could make him less horny about me was to give him some shocking news. 'I had an abortion.'

It worked. It threw him off. He took a step back. 'What? When?'

'It doesn't matter. It was yours.' I said, not having all the details about it. 'It was traumatic. I don't want to relive the past, Rohit.'

'Oh, fuck!'

'You should go,' I said with finality.

'I understand.' He stood up. As he went towards the door, he turned to me and added as an afterthought, 'Um . . . but . . . uh . . . I still need to sell the flat.'

'Yes. Heard you,' I said as he nodded and left. I shut the door behind him. 'Jerk!'

I couldn't believe that Annie would go out with such a loser. Maybe this life switch was making me realize what a nice guy Abhay was. Even if he didn't understand me too well, he wasn't a creep. Suddenly I missed Abhay and felt like talking to him. But I knew I couldn't call him from Annie's phone. I opened Facebook to see his photo. His cover photo was of our wedding day. I looked so happy to be with him. But somehow, he wasn't looking into my eyes. And I had just noticed it. He was looking above at someone else.

I took the bottle of wine that I had kept in the fridge and sat motionless on the sofa. I didn't think I would need it so soon. I gulped it down as my mind whirled with confusing thoughts. I didn't know what had just happened. A strange man had kissed me. And I wondered who Abhay was looking at in the photo. I remembered that at that moment he had noticed his ex-girlfriend walking in with her husband. It was a surprised smile at her, not an amorous one at me.

The silence of the house felt overwhelming. It slowly became dark and I didn't switch on any lights as I sat on the sofa. There was no Hari to bring me a cup of tea or switch on the lights. There was no chatter of my father-in-law calling for his towel from the shower after his evening walk or the blaring TV in the drawing room with my mother-in-law in front of it. No sounds of a married life. Maybe this was what a single life was about. The life switch was slowly sinking in.

Fourteen

Nandita

How to Survive Marriage and Other Disasters

After I calmed down over the next few days, I felt this powerful surge of control. As if I could accomplish anything. If I could come up with an idea that floored my boss and stand up to a man, I could do anything. Abhay would be so proud of me if he knew all that I was capable of. I figured I needed more time to get the experience that would make me a different person for him. And then he would always look amorously at only me!

I wondered if I should ask Annie to help me with the presentation. But then after some thought, I realized this was my opportunity to do something different, to get over my fear of public speaking or having an opinion and I could do something for myself.

I woke up to the alarm ringing. After ordering some dosa and clearing my head, I checked the phone and realized it was our anniversary. Suddenly I felt very depressed. I had completely forgotten about it! I had planned a dinner for Abhay and me. Now Annie would be having it with him. I felt a sense of panic. I called Annie's number.

'Hey,' I waved at her in the video call.

'Happy anniversary,' she smiled back on the phone. 'I was wished this morning and it came as a big surprise. I looked so blank at breakfast.'

'Should we switch back? For just a day?' I felt sad that I was the one who had managed to stay married another year and I wouldn't be celebrating it.

'Well, he's playing tennis today so . . .' Annie shrugged and shook her head as if to say he was not really bothered.

'What? But it's our anniversary.'

'Yeah. But apparently, there's a coach who has come in from Serbia and he's coached Djokovic and all. He's friends with a guy named Ishaan.'

'Yeah, that's Abhay's best friend.'

'Well, he has come for just a day and will be giving the guys some tips. So Abhay has decided to do that tonight.'

'Oh,' I said, feeling happy that Annie wouldn't be spending it with Abhay but at the same time a little peeved that he hadn't cared it was our anniversary. *Would he have just let me celebrate alone?*

'So what are you going to do? Ma and Papa had planned a dinner, I think,' I said.

'I don't really care. Might go for a massage. Don't want to have dinner with them. They're really boring.'

'They haven't guessed you're not me?'

'They think you've changed and have started eating salad and jogging in the morning.' She laughed, throwing her head back.

I felt worried that I would have to keep up the pretences when we switched back. 'Oh no. I told you not to do that. I don't want to run when we switch back.'

'Don't worry. I'll fake a back injury and make sure when you come back here you'll be in bed the whole day!' Annie said with a smile. 'Or you could just tell them the truth.'

She was turning out to be a good friend. When this adventure was over and we hung out together, it would be great to see everyone's reaction. They would all laugh at our life switch.

I cleared my throat and said, 'How's your research going?'

'It hit a dent. Hari knows I'm not you.'

'Oh. Well, I told you he would guess. He's known me since I was fifteen years old.'

I could hear her sigh before she responded, 'What do you think I should do? I was thinking of giving him some vacation time.'

'I can just call him and ask him to keep quiet,' I replied.

'That won't work. Because he almost blurted out something yesterday.'

'He always wanted to be in Bollywood.'

'I'll ask a director friend if he'll take him on a shoot. Do you think your in-laws can give him some time off then?'

'That might work. He'll love it. My mother-in-law will be pissed that they have to find another cook, though.'

'Oh, don't worry, I can cook too.'

'Don't do too much. I wouldn't know how to explain it.'

'Yeah, but you're planning to reveal our plan once you come back, right?'

I hadn't given much thought to what would happen once I got back. I shrugged. I wanted to tell her not to get close to Abhay later. It was, after all, our anniversary. I didn't want anything to happen between them. But I didn't want to sound desperate.

'Let me know if you need any help with the office work,' she rested her palm on her face.

'I'm working on the MyTherapist app. I have a few ideas.' I discussed them with her and she seemed to approve of them. I knew I was on the right path. I didn't tell her that her best friend Rhea was dating Sahil. She would immediately want to return to give Rhea a good scolding.

For the next few days, I did everything possible to make a good presentation with my two solid ideas for the app. It was already downloaded on Annie's mobile and I browsed through it extensively. I had made hundreds of presentations in college for my psychology classes and this was going to be easy for me.

On Sunday evening, Shivani called. 'Annie, the MyTherapist presentation has been moved to Thursday. Tomorrow will be the Busybee app presentation.'

'What? Busybee?' I asked, hearing about it for the first time.

'Yeah. You know the app about dating . . . but it targeted friendships . . . rather than finding sex. Didn't Ranjana send you the brief?'

'Um . . . I don't think so . . . Maybe . . . I don't know where I kept it . . .' I fumbled.

'I'll send it right now. She asked if you can present something tomorrow.'

'Tomorrow? But I've been working on the MyTherapist app.'

'Yeah, anyway. That's been moved. Clients keep changing meetings. You know that.'

I felt panic rising in my throat. I didn't know I had to present anything.

'Annie?' Shivani asked, 'Are you there?'

'Yeah. Yeah. Sure . . . I was just . . . thinking . . .'

'Ya, whatever.' She hung up and immediately I got a mail on my phone from her with the brief.

I stood there stunned. How would I even figure out what to say in one night when it had taken me so long to come up with an idea for the therapist app? I barely knew anything about apps anyway. I only knew about games on my phone . . . which I didn't have any more.

I threw a pillow across the room 'Ugh.'

I stayed up all night with several cups of tea to come up with two slides and an idea for the Busybee app.

Finally, Monday arrived, and the clients entered the boardroom.

Ranjana whispered to me, 'Annie, if you don't have any idea, just stay quiet. I don't want you to screw this up!'

I felt my heart beating so hard that I thought it would come out of my chest. 'I can do this.'

Ranjana announced, 'Annie will go first with her idea.'

I groaned inwardly. I thought I would get some time to think if Sahil presented first, but luck just wasn't on my side.

'We've all gone through a lot during this pandemic,' I began. 'Each of us has struggled. Some of us tried to see the bright side and stayed positive. Some had massive mental-health issues. I have a friend who's just a housewife. Her name is Nandita. She was stuck in a house with her in-laws and her husband for many months. She did a lot of housework because they didn't want any help coming from outside and, well, her husband was working from home so he was in another room the whole day. She made tea and breakfast, cleaned and cooked for days, that went on for weeks.

'All her friends were working from home so they rarely wanted to chat when she was free and when she needed them. She had to listen to her in-laws repeating the news about how many lives were affected and creating more fear. I think we know those kinds of people, right?' I looked around and a few nodded.

I continued, gaining a little more confidence. 'And her relationship with her husband wasn't great. He kind of forgot that she was a person who had her own needs.'

Sahil interrupted me, 'What has this got to do with—'

I blinked at him and spoke, 'Let me finish, please!' I looked around and spoke with my voice a bit unsteady. 'All Nandita wanted was to connect with people, to share some laughs, have something in common with maybe a few who watched the same shows and wouldn't judge her. Maybe just a platform to vent out her frustrations. But she didn't know how to do it. Or where to go. She was lonely. And now, when the lockdown has been lifted and life is back to almost normal, the housewife is still lonely. The husband has gone back to the office, her friends have even more of a hectic life. That's where the Busybee app comes in. Busybee gives a housewife access to friends when she feels as if she has no one. It's an app to reach out to someone. So our campaign is about the lonely housewife instead of the single woman who wants to reach out and make connections.'

I showed a slide, 'Busybee. *No more loneliness.*'

I looked at Ranjana and smiled. I thought I had cracked the idea. I had worked and made it personal and thought it was fabulous. She would love me.

Ranjana was glaring at me, shocked and speechless.

Sahil snickered.

Mr Salgaonkar, the client head, cleared his throat, 'What has this got to do with our app?'

Sahil folded his hands and asked me, 'Yeah, Annie. What has this to do with the *MyTherapist* app?' He reiterated the word.

I had made the wrong presentation.

Shivani had given me incorrect information and thrown me off. I had worked through the night to present to the wrong client. It was now all jumbled and my head felt like it was spinning. I was rooted to the spot in terror. I could not believe I had made this blunder. I was going to get fired. Annie would kill me. And I had just lost her the managing director position.

Ranjana cleared her throat, 'Our Annie has made a mistake. Ha ha. She's actually just recovering from COVID . . . Brain fog! Please excuse her. In the meantime, Sahil has a presentation for you as well. Hopefully, it's on MyTherapist, Sahil?' She looked at Sahil to help her who nodded back with cool confidence. She scowled at me as I slunk into my chair hoping that no one would notice the tears forming in my eyes.

After he finished presenting, I excused myself and went to the bathroom. I needed to be alone. I forced back my tears. I had learnt a valuable lesson. Trust no one. I heard Shivani's voice and I came out to stand next to her. She smiled at me, 'How did the presentation go, Annie?'

She smiled and I knew she had done it deliberately. She had given me misinformation to sabotage me. I didn't look at her as I left to go back to the conference room.

My heart was still beating wildly as I sat down and gulped down some water. Sahil finished his presentation and Ranjana backed his idea, developing it further in her own words. Then they waited for Mr Salgaonkar to respond.

He looked at me and suggested something I never thought I would hear after an embarrassing humiliation, 'Would you like to modify your idea for us?'

I stared at him, unable to comprehend what he was saying. 'Excuse me?'

'I know you were mixed up.'

'She's really sorry. It was a stupid idea,' Ranjana interrupted, to which Mr Salgaonkar nodded and said, 'Hold on, Ranjana. I really liked Annie's idea of a housewife needing mental help. That's what MyTherapist is all about. Reaching people who don't think they need it. And we've seen an alarming rate of suicide among housewives. They're a huge market for us. If Annie could just rework the idea for us, I think it would be something we'd like to take further.'

I stood up in sheer joy, 'Yes. Yes, I will.' I ignored Sahil whom I could see glowering at me from the corner of my eye.

Ranjana tried to convince the client. 'And Sahil's idea?'

Mr Salgaonkar was polite but firm. 'It was a general idea of everyone needing a therapist. But it didn't connect. I liked Nandita, this housewife. I feel as if I know her. And that's what the app is about—people. And if Annie can add a therapist whom the housewife speaks to in the end, I think we could do this campaign. Send us the final look in two weeks, Ranjana. Probably once the brain fog wears out?' He smiled, got up and his team stood up as well. He came to shake my hand and then thought better of it and just nodded and left.

I stood there stunned as Ranjana walked the clients to the elevator.

Sahil seethed in anger, 'I had worked so hard for that presentation. You just snatched it from me.' I didn't say anything.

I realized that sometimes the best response to someone's wrath is pure silence. 'Dumb luck,' he said, as he walked away towards his cabin.

But I had worked hard as well. And I was beginning to realize that luck favours the brave.

Once again, I had proved myself in the corporate world. I was thrilled. In just a short time, I had accomplished more than I had in the last four years of my life. I could go back to Abhay and tell him that I was more than just a housewife. I could be a working woman too. And he would be so proud of me and love me.

But I didn't know Sahil would be up to something evil and ruin everything for me soon enough.

Fifteen

Annie

How to Fake It Before You Make It

Nandita was so gullible, thought Annie, as she gave Hari two thousand rupees and told him to go to Bhopal to meet her 'director friend'. He was so eager to star in a Bollywood film that he didn't ask any further questions.

'It's a small film about a village boy who finds a bag of money and becomes a rich man in the city. They're looking for a hero,' she had told him. He had believed her. He had convinced Kamini and Hitesh that this was his shot at a better life and he was leaving them for good. Annie had pretended to be sad and sent him off. She knew by the time he reached the small village it would take him a few days and then he would realize there was no shoot. He wouldn't have enough money to return and she would have Nandita's phone to not respond to him or send him any more money. She could delay him coming back for weeks. By then, Abhay would surely recognize her value in his life and let Nandita go.

She had been going for tennis lessons with him and he had started being more attentive to her needs. They went to watch a film together and she had kissed him in the hall. He had been pleasantly surprised and aroused. She had cooked for him and watched thriller shows on Netflix, all the while wearing the new boxer shorts she had bought for herself that showed off her long, lean legs. She knew he would come around soon enough. She had felt his arousal when they slept cuddled up together. She wondered what was stopping him from sleeping with her.

But Annie missed her old life as well. She knew if she was going to be Abhay's new wife, she needed to have a balance. She missed her job and making and spending her own money. They had hung out as a family for the last week and Annie needed some alone time for herself to plot how to make the family need her.

She decided to take herself out for lunch and read Kamini's diary, which she had taken from her side table drawer when Kamini was out with friends. Maybe there would be some insight that could help Annie bond with Kamini as well.

Annie went to her favourite place, Olive, to have lunch. She saw a group of teenagers sitting at a table clicking photos and giggling. 'Kids nowadays,' she muttered. As she was passing them, one of the teenagers wearing torn denim jeans that showed off too much of her thighs and a black AC/DC T-shirt, a nose ring and black nail polish, with straight black shoulder-length hair waved to her. She smiled but then the woman who was probably about eighteen or nineteen said, 'Nandita! It's me.'

Annie took off her glasses to figure out who the person was. A friend of the girl said, 'She's purposely ignoring her sister.'

Sister!

Annie didn't know Nandita had a sister. But she was so young. There must have been at least a decade's age gap.

The girl got up and hugged Annie. 'Hey, sis! Wass new?'

Another girl with curly red hair grinned, 'Yeah Nandita, join us. And then you can use Abhay's credit card.' They chuckled as Annie shook her head.

'No . . . I have some work to do.'

'What work?' Nandita's sister Samaira asked Annie. 'Tell us about your new work.' She drew up a chair and Annie was forced to sit with a bunch of teenagers who seemed to know her but she didn't know anyone's name. But eventually, someone mentioned Nandita's sister's name and Annie remembered that Nandita had vaguely mentioned Samaira one evening at the resort.

'Sam, you're such a bully. And she's your elder sister,' the redhead said. Annie looked at them and wondered why she was stuck in the middle of talking to teenagers.

Sam ignored her friend and looked directly at Annie. 'How come you've not spoken to Mom in three weeks? I'm curious to know what work you're doing.'

While Annie tried to think of an answer, the waiter brought their food order. But instead of eating it, they all whipped out their phones and started taking photos of it. Raina the redhead seemed to be in awe. 'Samaira, you take the photo. You're best at it.'

Annie saw this as an opportunity to leave.

But Sam spoke, 'Nandu, don't go. You didn't even come over when Ma called you. Mamu had come over after ages and really wanted to meet you.'

Annie had seen the texts but had simply replied that she was busy. She didn't want to attend family functions that wouldn't help her cause. 'I'm sorry I missed it.'

'Ma had made your favourite sambhar rice. Nothing I liked, as usual,' Sam complained but before Annie could respond, Raina let out a deep sigh and looked up. A tall, well-built man with an air of arrogance walked towards them.

'Oh my god,' Raina's eyes bulged as she squealed. 'It's Rohit Bhatija, the actor!' She caught Samaira's hand as their jaws dropped.

Annie froze as she saw him walk towards her. She was pretending to be Nandita. He could not come up to her. No, no, no. She slowly turned to walk away. Please god, don't let him come towards me, she thought. Sam was already pissed. She would blow her cover and god knows what hell would break loose.

But he did.

'Hey,' he gave Annie a big hug. 'How are you?'

The girls gawked. Annie smiled as she took in Rohit's cologne. She had forgotten how warm and comfortable his hugs used to me. She closed her eyes for a split second to take in a familiar person's aura. 'I'm fine. How are you?' They both looked at each other letting everything around them fade away.

Then Sam cleared her throat. 'Sis! I didn't know you knew . . . where did you meet . . . I mean . . . Aren't you going to introduce us?' Annie's heart raced faster. Rohit knew she was an only child from Delhi. How was she going to say she had a sister now?

Annie introduced everyone reluctantly, 'Rohit meet Samaira, Raina and . . .' The other two girls introduced themselves. Then they took a few selfies with him which gave Annie enough time to compose herself.

'Okay, enough. Bye, girls.' Annie led Rohit to another table. Sam looked in amazement at her supposed sister. She suddenly had far more respect for her than fifteen minutes ago. Annie knew she would have to tell Nandita about it later that day.

Rohit sat down and took her hand. She withdrew. 'What?'

'Listen, I've been thinking about you.'

'Why?' She had blocked him, if she recollected. Mumbai was such a small city after all. And everyone bumped into each other all the time.

He wasn't paying attention to her words as he seemed to be in his own head about what was troubling him. 'I've been really rattled about what happened to you.'

'Excuse me?'

'I feel like it was my fault.'

'Still not getting you,' Annie put her elbows on the table and tried to look interested.

'The pregnancy. The abortion.'

Annie took her elbows off the table and sat back. Her face dropped. 'What? Who the fuck told you?'

'You did?'

'When?'

'At your apartment. My apartment . . .'

Annie could feel her anger rising. Rhea must have told Nandita thinking she was her and stupid, naive Nandita would have blurted it out to Rohit.

'It was your fault. But it's over. Let's fucking move on.'

Rohit nodded, looking sheepish, 'Can you please unblock me? I can't reach out to you at all.'

'That was the point.'

'Annie . . . I'm selling the place. I mentioned that . . . the night . . . um . . . anyway . . . have you found a place?'

'You want me to move out of the apartment?'

'I'm sorry, babe.'

'Fuck!'

'I told you two weeks ago. I thought you would have started looking!' He apologized. Annie was furious. Nandita could have mentioned this to her at some point in the conversations they had had! Annie had always believed she was a strong, independent woman who made her own choices and decisions. But it all felt too much. Annie put her head in her hands as her hair flopped down on the table.

'I can help you with some brokers,' he suggested.

Sam came over in that instant. 'Bye, sis! Bye, Rohit. Nice meeting you. Would love to have you over at our house, right Nandita?'

Annie knew she had blown it. The life-switch experiment was over. Annie looked shocked at both of them. Sam left as Rohit looked at her suspiciously.

'What did she just say?'

'Nothing,' Annie tried to cover up.

'She called you Nandita. Who's that?'

'She's my cousin. She's mental . . . just forget it . . .'

Annie stood up and spoke, 'Fine. I'll move out. And then I never want to see you again.'

'Annie!' he shouted out but she had already walked out of the place and refused to hear him.

Now she knew she had to work harder to make her plan work. She needed Abhay to fall in love with her quickly so she could move into his house. And the only way she could do that was to remove Nandita from his life completely.

Sixteen

Nandita

How to be Resilient

A few days later, Shivani sent me a text message. 'Sahil has got COVID. And so have I. Please get yourself tested.'

I freaked out. 'No, no, no, no!' I shouted in my cabin as soon as I read it. I called Ranjana who answered immediately. 'Yes, I know. I'm making an announcement.'

She spoke on the intercom for the entire floor to hear. 'We have arranged for an RT-PCR test for everyone. Please take the test and return home for the day. Masks are being sent around; please take one if you don't have one. The result will be sent to your mobile and to HR at the earliest. I request you to return to work by tomorrow morning if you are negative.'

'There go my plans for Goa,' said Faiza, a young and brilliant copy editor, as they all burst out laughing.

I grabbed the Mac, put on my mask, got the test on the way out and left for the day. I did not want to fall sick. The whole purpose of being in office would be ruined.

Rhea messaged me while I was on my way home in a cab, 'I've got COVID.'

'Oh no. How?' I responded, which seemed to be the appropriate first reaction to the news. Obviously, if Sahil had it, then so would Rhea, if they were still dating.

'I have no idea,' Rhea texted. 'Anyway, I'll be isolating in my apartment for the next week, so please send me some home-cooked food,' she wrote, thinking I was Chef Annie.

'I will,' I promised with a little bit of panic. I didn't know how to cook. I had barely managed to help Hari during the lockdown. What home food could I send her? But I didn't want to think about that right now.

I finally had a day off from work. It felt exhilarating. To be able to do nothing for a whole day? I knew exactly what I felt like doing.

I took a home COVID test that came out negative and I decided to head to the club for a swim.

As soon as I hit the water, I felt relaxed and finally at ease. I swam several laps for over an hour when I suddenly heard a familiar voice.

'I'll meet you at the courts, okay?' Abhay called out as he left the gents' locker room.

'Five minutes,' Annie called out.

They were at the club together. *Was she playing tennis with him? When did this start?*

I decided to spy on them to see what equation they might have, what Abhay might be feeling about Annie. And if things became too cosy, I might step in and stop it from going further.

I changed into Annie's clothes in the pool changing room. Putting on my sunglasses, I walked to the courts outside. I sat at a distance so they wouldn't notice someone watching them play.

'Jump and serve. Then you'll get power and motion to move forward,' Abhay said as Annie did as he instructed.

'It's tiring, Abhay. How do you do this?' Annie called out after serving several times.

'It's only been ten minutes. Keep going.'

I smiled. I could see she was getting as exhausted as I used to when I tried to take an interest in tennis. He was exacting and competitive.

'I need a break. The sun is so hot on my side. Look how tanned I've become.'

'Okay, let's take a break,' he said suddenly and they sat down on the players' chairs. I couldn't see them properly from where I was, so I tried to get a better view, going to sit several seats above and behind them in the stands.

'You didn't tan easily before,' Abhay laughed.

'I never played in the sun.'

'I like your tanned skin, though,' he smiled seductively at Annie.

'This is the first time I'm hearing about it, Mr Patel.' Annie flirted back.

He brushed her hair out of her face. 'Well, there's always a first time . . .'

What was happening? When had he become so flirty?

My mind went into overdrive. Was he flirting with Annie or did he still think it was me?

'I like this new you, Nandu. That spa did you good,' he said. A part of me sighed with relief. He still believed Annie was me. But was she playing the part too well?

'Ready to play a game now?' he asked. 'Or a whole set? Maybe you'll beat me.'

'Oh, you'll definitely beat me, Mr Patel,' Annie said as she drank some water, which spilt on to her shirt. Taking up a towel, she rubbed her neck and cleavage very slowly. *What was she trying? Making him lust after his wife or her?*

But Abhay didn't take the bait. I knew he would not fall for any seduction. I know my husband well.

'Fine. One set. Let's go,' Annie said. Then she stood up, turned around, put one foot on the chair and bent down to tie her shoelace, giving him a good look at her perfect, round behind in her short white tennis skirt.

I was raging mad. I stood up and that's when Annie saw me. She took a step back as if she suddenly had been confronted by a ghost.

Abhay had moved off to practise serving, so he hadn't seen her reaction. I didn't have to be worried about him. I gestured to her as if to say, 'What the hell are you doing?'

She shook her head rapidly, 'Nothing,' she mouthed. 'Nothing has happened.' But I was hopping mad. Another woman was trying to seduce my husband. I walked slowly down the steps to get closer to them and stopped a few rows behind Annie's chair on the court.

'You serve first,' Abhay called out to Annie. If he noticed me, maybe this whole game would be over. I stood still. I took off my sunglasses but didn't call out to him. Shouldn't a husband know when his wife is around? I could see him clearly. Couldn't he see me?

He didn't. As usual. He went back to collecting the balls at the other end of the court and preparing for his game with her.

Annie picked up her racket and gave me a thumbs-up sign. 'It's fine. Relax!'

I decided I had seen enough. Either I had to exchange now or leave and let this life switch continue.

But by the look of it, no matter what Annie's shenanigans were, Abhay would only give as much as he always gave me.

Maybe she needed to learn that not getting sex was also one of the miseries of being a housewife. A life of having the perfect man who makes you laugh, supports you, gives you space and lets you be but doesn't have the libido to satisfy your primal needs. Yes, let her understand how frustrating that can be too.

I would go back to the office tomorrow and learn as much as I could from this job. I was in a much better situation than Annie, who would be rejected by Abhay and who would have to listen to my in-laws' taunts every morning about not being pregnant.

My phone beeped as the COVID test result arrived. Negative.

I saw Annie groan as she lost another point to Abhay who laughed and berated her for being so bad. 'Come on, babe, buck up!' he screamed.

I'd heard it all before. I was looking forward to going back to her apartment and having a glass of wine by myself in peace. I needed to count my blessings about this life switch instead of being suspicious and anxious. I put on my sunglasses and left them to their tennis.

But I didn't know what this tennis match would mean for me later and how they bonded because Annie lost. I didn't know that I could have stepped in then and saved myself a lot of heartbreak.

Seventeen

Nandita

How to Be a Boss

Annie told me that no one named Mark had messaged me. I sent him a Facebook message asking him to contact me on social media and not on my phone when he arrived. He understood because he believed that all Indian wives hid their exes from their husbands and the phone was a place where anyone could see if a message popped up. He said he was arriving in a week. Enough time for me to get the corporate experience and go back to Abhay and tell him about my adventure for him to fall in love with me. Then when I met Mark I would tell him what a great life I lived and he would be jealous. I don't know why I needed my ex to be jealous when I was in a happy marriage. But then, if you met your ex, wouldn't you want them to be a little upset for letting you go? My plan was solid!

I tested negative and so did most of Annie's old team. Everyone came back to the office except Shivani and Sahil and then the rumours started. They were having an affair. I didn't question it. I wasn't into rumours. I just wanted to get the experience of corporate life. But I learnt that rumours were a large part of it as well. And the more I questioned, the more I got to know about what a working woman's life was like.

Soon I started jotting down my experience in a journal.

Question 1: Why were there always late-evening meetings?

There was mostly no work done during the day, but Ranjana always found something for the team to do when it was time to leave. On Wednesday evening she told us that our teams had to come up with a new campaign by Friday. On Thursday evening she kept a board meeting at six in the evening to discuss the progress of the campaign. On Friday she asked for the presentations at seven in the evening.

I wondered what Ranjana was doing throughout the day that she couldn't finish the meeting during normal working hours. But her secretary kept saying she was busy with other meetings. Meetings is the keyword for corporate life. If you have several meetings during the day and walk and talk, ate and took notes, read and sent emails, you seemed to be busy, and the company was happy with you. But it didn't mean you were actually being productive.

I had not got the hang of just looking busy. So several times I was caught reading a book, staring at my Facebook page or just looking out of the window of Annie's office when someone entered. But I was creative. Ranjana slowly started chatting with me about campaign ideas. We spent several afternoons going over presentations and she began to rely on me more.

Once I came up with an idea for eggs that the government wanted to promote for healthy living.

'Have a mother-in-law make eggs for the daughter-in-law. Role reversal. Maybe she's a newlywed and doesn't know her way around the kitchen. The bride can't cook. But the mother-in-law can and feeds her a different form of egg every day. And the daughter-in-law makes her coffee. They sit and chat. Bonds built over yolks.' I had commented. Maybe I was thinking of what could have been with Kamini and myself but never was. After all, advertisements are an exaggerated, idealistic reality.

Ranjana had liked the idea, and this gave me the courage to say I wanted every team member to leave by six every evening. She was appalled.

'They need to have a balanced life, Ranjana,' I argued.

'But you've always kept them back till nine or ten to do work,' she said. I shook my head, 'Not any more. I want them to remain fresh with ideas and sitting in an office for twelve hours isn't going to do that.'

When I made the announcement the next day that everyone was supposed to leave by six every evening, there was a collective gasp. A few stayed back to check if I was playing a prank. I picked up my purse to leave as well announcing, 'Go home, guys. Watch Netflix!'

The atmosphere in the office changed from the next day itself.

Question 2: Why was everyone so artificially nice?

The biggest problem about a corporate job was getting people to like you. Everyone was artificial and smiled when you passed by but rarely spoke to you when you asked them questions. I needed people to like me. But everyone hated Annie. And feared her. So they avoided me.

At first, I thought I would casually ask them about their lives. But they all seemed as if they were in a military marching band, standing erect and answering in monosyllables every time I went near their desks.

'How was your evening?'

'Fine.'

'Did you do anything fun?' I would probe.

'Not really. Just watched some shows.'

And when I asked them what they were watching, they were all those crime shows that I could never get into. I felt as though I was being judged for my choices. Abhay would have seen all the shows that the team was mentioning. He would know exactly what to say to them.

No one wanted to open up to me. Even when I took my lunch to a table where the team sat, they would clam up and talk about the weather or someone's disease of the day—cold, cough, knee pain, lower back injury. Everyone finished eating quickly and went back to their desks, leaving me to eat alone.

So I started watching the crime shows too and could start talking to them about it. 'I cannot believe that he was the murderer,' I said to a few who had recommended one show to me. 'I sat up all night bingeing it.'

'It's so good, right?' they asked. I nodded and they recommended a few more to me. I understood that I wasn't there to correct them or teach them or tell them what to do. I needed to learn from them. They had more experience than me. So, often I would go to them and ask, 'Guys, please can you tell me what this means? Google is no help.' And they would explain something to me.

Once at lunch, they were all talking about their love lives and I blurted out, 'Yeah, but how do you get a guy to fall in love with you?' They presumed I was the single Annie asking and they felt sympathetic towards me. I also got a few great tips.

• Stop making yourself available.
• Do something else with your own life so you don't need to rely on him.
• Be interested in what he does.

Valid points that I knew I was trying already with this life switch and I made a mental note to attempt to enjoy tennis again after I switched my life back.

Since then, the team started coming into my office and asking me for advice on several things and I was happy to be a mentor if they needed me.

Question 3: Why did corporate structures have a lack of clarity and create fear?

'What's going on?' I asked as I entered the office one morning to see Sahil and a few people huddled up whispering.

'There's going to be a corporate merger and some of us may be laid off.'

'What?' I asked, alarmed and hoping that I would not lose Annie's job because of a merger.

'But by then Ranjana would have taken her golden ticket and exited, leaving someone to pick up the pieces.'

'Really?' I asked.

'This company has no clarity. Ranjana just wants us to work and go round and round before this merger happens.'

Another team member felt afraid and asked, 'Yes, but where will it all lead to? What will happen to us? Also, no more funds are coming in for marketing or anything so how will we progress with anything? What are we supposed to do?'

I realized that keeping people in fear was one of the greatest ways to keep people in check. It meant you could spread rumours, talk incessantly about a future that you didn't have control over and rarely do any work as it allowed you to keep your people in anxiety and uncertainty. Which could result in some sort of illness that everyone had at some given point in time and spoke about at lunchtime!

The lack of clarity permeated into most parts of every employee's life in some way or another eventually.

I realized that I would not make a massive difference to the larger organization but I would reassure my team members to start working again.

'How many companies have merged over the last one year?'

They didn't have an answer.

'How long was the merger conversation in place?'

Again silence.

'How many people got fired?'

'Millions,' someone spoke enthusiastically. I looked at him wearily. 'Really? If a person is valuable to a company, do you think his boss or an HR person is going to fire him? And do you even know how much money they got to be fired?' They stayed quiet.

'So why are we worried about something that may or may not happen? Let's chat more about this over lunch and get back to work for now, huh?' I went back to my cabin and saw that the team had gone back to work as well. I had done my research and it had come in handy. I realized that going to work wasn't always about making presentations and sitting in meetings. It was also interaction with the people and chatting with your team. It was learning something new every day and appreciating the process.

I had started getting the hang of the game and began to enjoy myself.

But before I knew it, Sahil and Shivani were back in the office and I needed to keep my guard up again.

But when Sahil came to visit me in my cabin, he didn't look so smug.

'How are you feeling?' I asked.

'A little weak but my brain has been functioning perfectly well.'

'Good to know. It's been boring without competition here,' I said.

He smiled and I tilted my head and winked.

He got up and commented, 'Well, I need to start kicking your ass again, right?'

I laughed nervously, not knowing what to say.

'Hey,' he said in a softer tone, 'Thanks for helping Rhea and me. I really love her.'

'None of my business,' I assured him. But he felt as though he owed me an explanation.

'Karthik is my middle name. I like it more than Sahil. But when I joined here, Ranjana introduced me as Sahil and I didn't want to correct my boss on my first day so it kinda stuck.'

'Cool.'

'You've changed, Annie. It's kinda nice.' He looked at me more intently.

I raised my cup of coffee and said, 'Cheers to a new era.'

I felt my time here was done. I had got the experience and now I could convince my family that I could take on any job. The only person who was still not on my side and who had a lot of power in the office was Shivani. I had just two days before the switch back to convince Shivani to like me.

Eighteen

Nandita

How to Be Invisible without Being Isolated

I had won over everyone in the office except for one person, Shivani. I decided that I would incorporate all that I'd learnt in psychology and NLP to win her over. I don't know why I needed her approval. But it was something that I had been thinking about for the last few weeks.

Instead of talking to Shivani in the office, I decided to take her out for a nice meal. And using Annie's corporate card made it easier to go to a fancy place rather than a regular café. I made a reservation at a restaurant I'd heard a lot about from Diya.

Shivani reached there at the same time I did and appraised the room.

'This seems very fancy.' Shivani noticed the Chinese restaurant had couples sitting at tables with candles all around. 'And romantic.'

'Yes. My bad. Maybe we should go somewhere else,' I suggested as the waiter came to tell us our table was ready.

'Every place in this city will be full. We might as well eat,' Shivani said, following the waiter. She seemed more easy-going than she was in the office. I took a deep breath and prayed the night would go well.

After we ordered, I asked her what she liked to do in her spare time.

'Look, you can cut the crap. I know you're here to butter me up.'

'I'm not,' I spoke unconvincingly.

'You are so full of . . . thank you,' she said to the waiter as he brought her a tall iced tea.

I got defensive. I'd never had a person in my life who didn't like me. And for a moment I forgot I had to be Annie. 'Okay, tell me why you don't like me. What have I done to you?'

'Forget it.'

'No, please,' I said in a kinder voice. 'I want to know. I'm trying to change.'

'When I joined, you kept me on your team. And with just one mistake, you pushed me out. You got me transferred to Gauri's team. And when she quit, you didn't even want me back, even though I had proved I could do good things. You don't give people second chances. You push people too hard. You change directions to get what you want without telling people about your plan. You leave people behind. You aren't a team player. You're only thinking about what's good for you and becoming managing director.'

'Okay,' I said, slowly understanding why everyone hated Annie. 'I was too busy focusing on myself.'

I took a deep breath and drank my glass of wine in one gulp. 'I guess I was trying to establish myself too.'

Shivani pursed her lips. 'See, there you go again. Defending yourself. Forget it. You'll never change!'

I needed to take a break from being Annie. I excused myself to go to the bathroom. When I got back, I saw that Diya and her husband, Mihir, were entering the restaurant. I didn't know where to hide so I stood behind a wall. Diya was on the phone doing an Insta reel as she said, 'Reviewing this Chinese restaurant today, guys. I'm just loving the décor. Major romantic vibes happening. And I'm here with my hubby. Hashtag couple goals.'

I could hear her but she couldn't see me. 'Crap,' I said to myself. How would I get out of this one? I was probably in there an awfully long time because Shivani sent me a message. 'Are you okay?'

I came out gingerly to see that Diya had been seated far away from us. So I could quickly finish my meal with Shivani and leave before they noticed.

'I have a bad stomach,' I groaned. 'Probably the dimsums didn't suit me.' I gulped down some water.

Shivani didn't care as she chewed her rice and Thai chicken curry.

'I think I'm going to pay the bill and go. You finish slowly. I need to head home,' I felt uncomfortable as I saw Diya get up to visit the restroom. And my table was right in the direction of the restroom.

'But I want dessert.'

'I'll, um . . . leave some cash . . . I'll go figure the bill . . .' I quickly got up to go to the waiter and avoided Diya completely.

I let out a sigh of relief as I hid behind a large wall in another section of the restaurant. I had to think fast. What would I say to her if she spotted me? She would ask me to join them and I didn't know what to say about who Shivani was. I didn't know what to do. But I found our waiter and asked him to give me the cheque quickly. I didn't need any of the food packed, thank you.

I saw that Diya had got back to her table and the coast was clear. I went back to my table. By that time Shivani had finished eating and was scrolling through her phone. 'Dude, this is the worst dinner ever. Where were you?'

'We need to go. I'll make it up to you.' My body was shutting down in panic.

'What the . . .'

'I'm so sorry,' I took out Annie's corporate card. The waiter took forever to bring the machine. He stood there for a long time and then finally said, 'This card is not working.'

'Fuck,' I muttered as I looked through her wallet to find another one. But then realized I knew the PIN only for that card. And all the cash was finished.

I looked up at Shivani apologetically. 'You don't happen to have any money, do you? My cards are blocked.'

'Annie!' she said as she gave her corporate card to pay for the meal. 'I can't believe this.'

I apologized once more but got up to leave. I had almost got to the door when the waiter shouted out 'Madam, you forgot your mobile.'

I looked back as he brought my mobile to me. But Diya and Mihir had seen me too. Diya waved to me. I pretended not to notice them. I could see her getting up and coming towards me. The waiter gave me the mobile. I turned to Shivani to say, 'Why don't I meet you outside? I'm just going to say hi to a few friends.'

But she stood still and folded her hands.

'What are you doing here?' Diya asked and hugged me. 'Why haven't you met up? I've messaged you like a thousand times. What's been going on with you?'

I hugged her back and for a moment I thought I could get away with it. Shivani stood next to me and smiled. Diya looked at her waiting for me to introduce her.

'You know I've not been feeling well ever since I got back. I just needed some space.' I tried to cover up while Shivani the nosy human being stood listening to the conversation. Ugh, she was so annoying! No wonder Annie didn't want her in her team.

'How's Abhay? Have both of you . . .' Diya asked as she kept looking at Shivani.

'No, not really . . . I'll tell you about it soon. I have to run.'

Diya finally asked, 'And who's this?'

'Hi, I'm Shivani, Annie's colleague.'

Diya looked at me, 'Who's Annie?'

Shivani pointed at me, 'She is.' Diya looked at me perplexed while my head began to spin. I took a step back trying to brace myself and hold on to something only to bump into a man who was entering the restaurant.

I turned around and gasped. I put my hands to my face. 'Mark.'

Mark looked pleased to have bumped into me. 'I sent you a message two days ago. Where have you been?'

Diya looked at him in amazement. 'This is Mark? Your ex-boyfriend?'

Mark looked at me with a twinkle in his eye, 'So you've told everyone about me, huh, Nandy?'

'He calls you Nandy, Nandita?' Diya asked. 'That's hilarious! But why is she calling you Annie?'

I suddenly realized Shivani had heard the whole conversation and called out to me.

Shivani looked straight into my eyes and asked, 'Who's Nandita?'

Mark asked, 'Who's Annie?'

I looked from one to the other as my voice caught in my throat. I muttered, 'Me . . .'

Diya's jaw fell. 'O.M.G. Can you do this again for my Insta reel?'

Nineteen

Nandita

How to Get People to Do Stuff for Free

For the first ten years of my life, I had only seen my parents fight. I wondered if they had a happy marriage. They led individual lives where they rarely interacted if they could help it. They even attended my school events separately.

Then my sister was born when I was ten and they changed overnight. Suddenly they were more loving towards each other and her. They started doing things together. They started going for morning walks together, my father started making tea for my mother every morning; they attended plays, movies and parties together. It was all a shock for me who was so used to seeing them bicker. Then they took up a course in marital therapy. I laughed my teenage head off. My mother and father becoming counsellors was ludicrous to me. But soon they started doling out marital advice to their friends that seemed to work.

When they got certified as marriage counsellors, they started telling me the secret to a happy marriage. This consisted of ideas like adjustment, finding your own hobbies to keep you busy, small ways of giving attention to your husband, participating in group activities. I was left baffled.

My sister, Sam, saw her parents have a loving relationship. I always told her we had two different sets of parents. She had a normal childhood while I had a dysfunctional one. And yet she chose to rebel while I was the one trying to please them. I wanted to be happy and positive so they would fight less. Later, when they discussed marriage with me, I agreed so they wouldn't have to argue again. Sam could just get away with murder because they pampered her as if she was the princess of Windsor.

So, all my life when they were fighting and even later, I immersed myself in books. Romance novels and Mills and Boons and classic love stories. I wanted to believe that there could be passion in a person's life and not just adjustment. That there were sparks and not just simply asking for what you want, as my mother told me. I believed that the person who loved me would know me without me having to say anything.

At eighteen I left for Yale to study psychology because my essay gave me a scholarship that was unheard of in the Gujarati community. And that's when I met Mark. He was the embodiment of the romantic notion in my head. He spoke Shakespeare and Milton to me. He helped me with my classwork by becoming a subject I could analyse and later, he showed me what it meant to have a passionate relationship and analysed me.

But I was an Indian who believed that the person you have sex with should be the person you marry. Yes, I was traditional and old-fashioned. But Mark thought that passion wasn't enough for marriage. We belonged to different communities, cultures, upbringing, had different ambitions—he wanted to be a screenplay writer in Hollywood, and I wanted to be a psychologist in India. I never wanted to stay in America forever. I missed the comforts of my home too much. Hari's cooking, chai in bed, weddings every November and December, a large family that was nosy and loving. I wanted all that in my life. Finally, I wanted Mark to 'adjust' to me.

And he couldn't.

So, when I came back it took me a while to get over Mark. Obviously, I told everyone I had not fallen in love with anyone and my virginity was intact. What would my parents think? My parents had met Abhay's parents at a party for common friends. That's when they got to know Abhay was single and ready to settle down. They invited us to their house just to see if Abhay and I would get along. When I saw Abhay, I was instantly attracted to him and he to me. And we both said yes. A few months after marriage I truly fell in love with him when one night, he took me to see a play that he didn't understand but knew I would love.

Since then, I have been in love with him. It just takes simple things to make a wife devoted to her husband. Understanding what she likes and going out of his way to do them for her, even if it's not in his comfort zone. And with the notions that my parents had put in me, to adjust in any way one can to make the marriage work, that's what I had been doing.

But Abhay had not fallen in love with me. He didn't have the passion that Mark did. He didn't understand my smile or jump on me like Mark, who couldn't keep his hands off me. He didn't quote poetry or write songs for me. And then slowly my marriage became a comparison between what I had given up and what I had to adjust to.

But how could a daughter of marital counsellors actually choose to get divorced? I never thought of divorce. I knew marriage was for life. And I would get Abhay to fall in love with me one way or another. I had tried everything from trying to enjoy tennis to inviting his alcoholic friends for dinner, who would go through entire bottles in the liquor cabinet and start slurring by midnight. Then he started going for drinks with them after his tennis and stopped inviting them home because he saw how annoyed I would get.

So, I thought this life switch would be my last attempt to get him to fall in love with me. He would realize that I wasn't a housewife who just sat at home waiting for him to return from his parties or a plants blogger who could earn no money. I wanted to prove something. And this would spark the passion for me as a woman, to be something more, to put my education to use, to make everyone proud.

And I had ruined everything.

Obviously, I hadn't seen Mark's texts because I didn't have my phone. Annie did. I needed to see her ASAP so I could explain the whole situation to her. I would go to Ranjana and apologize and sort everything out for Annie. It was a simple, funny story. I'm sure she would understand.

It was Saturday and Annie and I were supposed to switch back. But Ranjana called me into her office. I saw through the glass doors that Shivani was sitting there with Koko, the HR lady.

My bravado left me. I had never been so scared in my life. My heart was in my mouth. I took a deep breath to enter her cabin.

'Hi, Ranjana,' I started. 'I can explain.'

'Who are you?' Ranjana asked with folded hands. 'First, tell us that.'

'I'm Nandita,' I began. And I told the whole story which left the three of them gaping by the end of it.

'You've been fooling us the entire time?' Ranjana asked, shocked. 'Where is Annie? Get her here.'

'I honestly don't think . . .' I stuttered.

'Now!'

I took a moment to think. I knew Annie would be packing her things and heading to the restaurant in a bit to exchange our lives back, with her job intact. I called her but she kept cutting the phone. And then she put it on silent.

'She's not picking up,' I said nervously.

Ranjana was livid. Koko, however, was amused. 'I really thought you were Annie. Shivani, how did you guess this?'

I glared at Shivani, who could have kept quiet and let it be. Instead, she spilt out, 'Apparently, a man named Mark kept calling her Nandy, Nandita and going on about how he wanted to catch up with her, while she was being super creepy. And then there were her friends who were asking who's Annie. I put two and two together.' She crossed her hands smugly.

'I can explain,' I tried to calm everyone down.

But Ranjana was agitated. She threw up her hands. 'What should we do, Koko?'

'I think we should fire—'

'Wait,' I interrupted. 'Let me explain, please. I'm sorry I fooled everyone into believing I was Annie. It is my fault. I just wanted to be part of a work culture. I'm a housewife who's not been allowed to work my whole life. When I met Annie, I gave her the idea to switch roles so that for a moment I could be someone else. And maybe . . . just have my husband respect me again.'

I took a moment to pause before I continued, 'And Annie has worked here for so long. She's been a great worker and

I know she needs this job. And this was all my mistake. I forced her to do this absurd thing. Please just forgive me. Forgive her.'

Koko looked at Ranjana and me. 'Your life seems to be a tragedy, whoever you are. But really, company policy is very strict.'

Shivani laughed. 'How absurd. Are you stupid? You can't just take over someone's life!'

Ranjana sat down on her chair. She tried to lean forward with her pregnant belly to give me a hard stare. 'Annie should not have agreed to do this. We can all get into trouble if it leaks to clients. I'm sorry . . . but you're . . . she's fired.'

I put my hands to my face and let out a little sob. 'No. Please. No.'

Ranjana turned around. 'Koko, Shivani, I want this to be kept quiet. No one shall know that she . . . was not Annie. Not even Sahil. Understood, Shivani? We will look like fools here. And if clients get to know that an amateur was giving advice and presentations, then there could be lawsuits.'

Koko nodded. Shivani smiled at me. Ranjana looked at her specifically. 'I will break the news that Annie decided to quit effective immediately to join another agency. So, everyone just shut up about it. Koko, Shivani, you can go now. You . . . Nandita. Stay.'

Koko and Shivani left me alone in the room with Ranjana. I couldn't control my tears. I felt awful. The one condition that Annie gave me I had broken, and I couldn't face her.

'I thought I was good here,' I sobbed. 'I thought you liked me.'

'I did,' Ranjana said with a tinge of melancholy. 'You had really good ideas. But I can't keep someone who's a fraud. That's illegal, I think . . . but unethical for sure . . .'

I nodded. 'Annie will kill me.' I wiped away my tears. 'I tried so hard. I thought I made a difference. And now I'll go back and tell my family that I lost a friend's job as well. Abhay will hate me. I hate myself.'

I sat quietly feeling the enormity of the situation. Ranjana just passed a tissue box to me. Finally, I got up to leave. I needed to tell Annie immediately and I would just go home and confess it all to the whole family. Maybe Annie would know what to do. After all, she had worked here for six years. They would forgive her, right? My mind played tricks with me as it jumped from the most desolate scenario to a more hopeful one.

'Nandita,' Ranjana spoke softly. I turned around to see her holding her belly and looking at me. 'You were good. Your ideas were very different. You should try to pursue this line.'

'I don't think that's possible. Thank you, though, for all your help.' I wiped my nose with a tissue that I took from her desk. But just as I gathered my purse and opened the door, Ranjana let out a yelp. 'Ow.'

I turned around. She was clutching her belly and sitting on her chair leaning back dangerously.

'What happened?' I asked concerned.

She didn't answer me. She was just breathing rapidly. 'These are Braxton Hicks,' she breathed deeper. 'They'll go away.'

I looked around to see that the office was empty. Koko and Shivani must have left already. I didn't know what to do. I stood there watching her breathe. Then it stopped but she still looked anxious.

'Should I call someone?' I asked, paralysed whether I should leave or help her.

She pointed to her mobile and gesticulated for me to pass it to her. She dialled her husband's number. It was unreachable. She looked at me alarmed. 'He's on a flight to Delhi.'

'What about your parents? Shall I call them?' I asked, wondering if they were still alive as Ranjana was already forty-eight years old.

She shook her head. 'They live in Delhi. They're too old anyway.'

I helped her up, but she bent over in pain again. 'This is not supposed to happen for another six weeks. It'll be fine. I'll just go home and lie down.'

'We need to get to the hospital,' I said, taking charge. 'Should I call an Uber or an ambulance?'

Ranjana shook her head and spoke through her pain, 'I have a driver downstairs.'

I nodded as I helped her get to her car. But I didn't get in, hesitant, wondering what the protocol was. She'd just fired me. She didn't know me at all because I was suddenly no longer Annie. I was a stranger to her.

She rolled her eyes. 'Nandita . . . Get in.'

'Yes, yes, of course,' I was frantic as I got into the car from the other side, relieved that she was being nice to me but worried that I wouldn't be able to make the meeting with Annie. And instead of switching our life back, I was now fully immersed in hers and headed to the hospital with her former boss.

Twenty

Annie

How to Fall in Love with a Married Man

Annie had spent almost four weeks trying to fit into Abhay's life. She went to tennis games with him, hung out with his friends and even went to his jewellery shop to see what she could learn about the business. Hitesh, Abhay's father, had never seen his daughter-in-law so involved with their business. He was impressed.

Annie even gave a few suggestions on how to improve their social-media marketing. 'I'll make some reels for you, Papa, with different pieces, and we'll post them on Instagram. I'll share it and if you're okay to spend some money, we'll get just one celeb to repost it as well. Let's do it next week when there's a holiday and it's a festive occasion.' She gave a few ideas and told Abhay to make the reels. She had so much fun that she forgot it was part of her plan. She began to fall in love with Abhay.

'You're a genius, *beti*,' Hitesh said when his shop was flooded with customers.

'Just wait, I'll make a website for you to sell stuff online as well,' she said.

But the only one who was suspicious was Abhay's mother, Kamini.

'How does this girl know so much? I thought she said she had done only English in college. Marketing *kahan se aaya?*' she told her husband, who stayed oblivious to the minutiae of a couple's life.

'*Kya farak padta hai?* I can finally see Abhay is happy. It's been four years, Kamini. I honestly thought we made a mistake with this match. Our only son. Also, I think she did psychology.'

Kamini reached out to hold his hand as they chatted in their bedroom at night. 'This is not Nandita. It's someone else, Hitesh. I know Nandita. She is dull, passive. We thought we were getting a sweet, homely girl. But we didn't realize it wasn't what Abhay wanted.'

'Then why did he agree?' Hitesh asked. '*Woh bhi toh rishte ke liye na bol sakta tha.*'

Kamini sighed. What could she say about men and lust? She'd seen it as a model. She knew it drove men to do anything a woman asked. Abhay had been in lust with Nandita. Not love. And, as Kamini knew, the lust dies if it's not ignited often with intelligence and mutual interests. But still, if this was someone else, she'd never admit it. And there were a few times when she tried to get Annie to reveal her true identity by asking probing questions that Annie could not answer and dodged gently.

'I'm forgetting where you went for your second anniversary, Nandita. Was it Bali?' Kamini would ask over dinner as they sat down to eat together.

Abhay would pipe in, 'Singapore, Mom.'

Kamini would give her child a dirty look as if to say, *Don't be such a foolish man. I'm trying to show you she's not Nandita.*

The next time she would ask, 'Nandita, you borrowed the yellow *paithani* from me last Diwali. I can't remember if you gave it back.'

Annie would answer, 'I think it's in your cupboard, Ma. I don't wear yellow. You must be mistaken.'

The one thing Annie knew she had was a good memory. And she remembered all the details Nandita had given during their life-switch boot camp where they asked each other's favourite colours, people, friends, hobbies and dislikes.

She knew that she might never win over Kamini's affection, but all she needed was Abhay's love.

The day before she was supposed to switch back, Annie hatched a plan to see if Abhay really loved her and if her plan had succeeded. She knew Hitesh and Kamini would be busy that evening and Abhay was playing tennis and would come home by nine o'clock.

Annie finished packing and waited.

As Abhay entered he saw Annie sitting with her suitcase in the drawing room, waiting for him.

'Nandu? What's this? Where are you going?' he asked, confused.

'I need a drink,' Annie headed to the bar and got a drink for herself. 'You want one?' He shrugged as she poured him a drink.

'Where are you going?' Abhay asked again.

'I'm leaving you, Abhay.'

'What?'

'I don't know if you love me. I don't know why I'm in this marriage. We never have sex. It's like you don't need me. So then, what am I doing here?'

'That's ridiculous!' Abhay's eyes flashed with anger and disappointment.

'How does it matter, Abhay? I've done everything to make you fall in love with me. I guess it's not enough.' Annie turned to the bar and smiled to herself. She could see her plan was working.

'Why aren't we more physical? Clearly you don't want me!' Annie said as she gulped down her whisky.

He took two strides towards her and kissed her with a passion that shook her.

'Abhay . . .' she whispered, meekly protesting. 'You don't need . . .'

'Don't . . .' he murmured as he pulled her shirt over her head and kissed her neck. His lips continued to explore her soft ivory flesh as he roamed down her body towards her breasts. He swiftly removed her bra and licked her hard nipples. She threw her head back to moan as he moved slowly down and unbuttoned her jeans.

'Abhay . . .' she said softly. 'Anyone can walk in . . .'

'No one is going to come . . .' He bunched up her jeans at her ankles and brushed his lips over her panties. She could feel herself get wet as the top of his fingers slowly moved down her thighs and then up again. He moved his fingers under her panties and rubbed two fingers across her vagina. Slowly. He rubbed her clit with small circles. Gently tugging her panties aside, he thrust his tongue deep inside her, spreading her legs as she balanced herself on the bar. She grabbed his hair and moaned deeply as his tongue went deep into her crevice, his beard making her nerves tingle.

'Fuck,' she said as she felt her body clench. He stood up suddenly and took his shirt off. She bent down to kiss his nipples. She kicked off her jeans and kissed him on the mouth. He picked her up in one swift swoop as her legs wrapped around his torso. He carried her to the sofa and she collapsed into it with a giggle. He unbuckled his jeans and she helped him pull them down, slowly running her fingers over his thick, hard penis.

She sat up to take him in her mouth, licking him slowly from the tip to the sides and then moving her mouth over him in slow, long advances. He pushed her back gently as she settled into the sofa. He moved his body slowly over hers as she lay on her back welcoming him into her folds. Her breasts tingled with a sense of urgency. She could feel the sexual magnetism between them that she just couldn't deny any longer.

'Abhay . . . I love you . . .' she moaned, allowing herself the liberty to let go.

She buried her face against his throat and reciprocated when his lips brushed against her mouth. He sucked at her breast whole, as it sent shivers of ecstasy coursing down her spine. She closed her eyes. It had been so long since she had been kissed. Since anyone had made love to her.

'You're mine . . .' he whispered as he devoured her body, entering her again and again. He took his time to explore, to move, to look deep into her eyes. Then, she closed her eyes, enjoying every minute of his lovemaking. He shifted inside her slowly, knowing his enormity and her depth.

Annie groaned in pleasure. 'Why did we wait so long?' she whispered.

He only smiled. As he rocked her slowly and then harder and faster, she succumbed to his domination. Then suddenly he stopped, sat up, moved her right leg across his shoulder and to the other side, turned her over and penetrated her deeper. Flesh against flesh. His body lying on top of hers. He went deeper inside her, rubbing against her clit as he took longer movements. Panting harder. He held her breasts as he moved quicker, firmer, deeper. She closed her eyes as she could feel his breath on her ear.

And then a moment of explosion as Annie's entire body tingled with a thousand shards of ecstasy.

They lay there exhausted, exhilarated, elevated.

Breathing in deep, soul-drenching drafts of air. He moved to the floor and lay panting, sprawled naked against the cool marble floor of his parents' drawing room.

'I need to . . .' Annie got up to head to the restroom, grabbing her clothes on the way.

She looked into the mirror and realized she'd finally slept with Abhay. And it wasn't only because she wanted to usurp Nandita's life. It was because she had fallen for Abhay.

She had to reveal this switch. She needed to tell him she was Annie. She needed to know whether he loved her too. Clearly, he had shown that he desired her. There was still lust in this relationship. But was it for Nandita or for her, Annie?

She came out with a big smile. She had to tell him how incredible he was. And that she'd made his libido come back. That they were meant to be together.

But when she walked up to him, Abhay was standing in their room with her purse and his mother's ring in his hand.

'What's this?' he asked. Annie saw the ring and realized that she had forgotten to put it back after her first day there. She had not used the purse until now and had completely forgotten about it. 'Isn't this my mother's? What were you doing with it?'

'Uh . . . I can explain,' she said. 'It's not what it looks like.'

'Okay,' he was calm and very unlike anything she had seen earlier. 'Tell me then.'

Annie gulped. 'I was . . .'

Abhay interrupted her, 'And no more lies. Just tell me who you are finally. Because you're definitely not my wife.' He shut the room door behind him as he sat on the chair with his arms folded, waiting for an explanation from Annie.

Twenty-one

Nandita

How Not to Be a Loser

Later, I wouldn't remember that time as the night I helped a woman give birth. Or as the night I didn't switch my life back and how everything changed. I would remember the one and half hours I was stuck in traffic while Ranjana screamed and shouted, making her driver try to cut red lights to get to the hospital.

But Mumbai traffic would not budge if you weren't in an ambulance. I cursed myself again for not calling one. 'It would have taken an hour to get to us anyway,' Ranjana reminded me.

'You know we can go to any hospital, why go so far?' I asked.

Ranjana stared at me as if she would chew my head off, 'Have you ever given birth? No, na? Then shut up. You only go to the doctor you're comfortable with. Do you want a stranger to see your girl parts? No, na? Then shut up.'

'Okay, then,' I said, as I looked out of the window at the car next to us.

At first, Ranjana played some songs from her playlist. But her battery soon died, so she took out her power bank to charge it. Ranjana's pain intensified sporadically, she started chatting with me.

'So tell me about you, Nandita.' Ranjana asked. 'Distract me.'

I went blank. The only thing that came into my head was the opening song of a Dharma movie. My life felt as dramatic and vapid.

'Come on. You've got to have something. Who is this guy who Shivani met?' Ranjana asked me with a wink. 'Lover, husband, what?'

'No one.' I answered. Seeing Mark that night had brought back all those feelings I'd had when I was at university with him.

'No one?'

'He's Mark. My ex.'

'Aha.'

'There's no aha. There's nothing really.'

'Of course there is.'

I started to protest and recalled the night when I had fumbled and had looked at Mark, and he reached out to embrace me. I said, 'Maybe there still is. I don't know. Why do exes come back into our lives? Is it some unsolved stuff? Unresolved energy perhaps?'

'Listen to me, girl . . .' Ranjana started as she clutched her belly. 'Fucking an ex might be a good way to get revenge on your spouse, but it will only leave you disgusted with yourself.' Ranjana breathed deeply.

'But—' I started to speak but Ranjana cut me off.

'Don't make excuses to have an affair. Tell your husband what you like. What you want. What you need. And if he refuses to give it, have the courage to walk out. And then be with the man you want to be with. See if your boyfriend wants you then. Most men just want to have sex with a married women because it needs no accountability or responsibility.'

I took a moment to grasp this. Had I told Abhay everything I wanted? Did I just keep quiet and sulk every time he didn't want to go to a play? Didn't I just go along with his plans with friends but resent him afterwards? Before I could respond, another contraction hit her. 'How far are we?' Ranjana screamed.

The driver turned around, 'We are still at JVLR flyover.'

'Fuck, we've been here for the last thirty minutes. I fucking hate Mumbai traffic.'

I tried to change the topic. 'You are a firm believer in marriage?'

Ranjana cut me off. 'Marriage is great for some time. But like everything else, it sucks. But we blame the marriage more than anything else in our lives. Life is supposed to be awful at times. It's not supposed to be rosy and happy. Marriage, jobs, children, even vacations are supposed to be boring and awful after a point. Nothing remains static. We are supposed to evolve to figure out what else, what more. Do you think I'll enjoy sitting at home and looking after this baby? Hell, no. After some time, I'll want to come back to a job.'

'So why are you leaving and giving up this managing director position?'

'Because I want to try something new.'

'New?'

'Start my own company. I have plans. Let's see.' Ranjana said as the traffic began to move. 'Oh, thank god.'

'Ranjana,' I asked, 'do you think I have a chance to get a job at the agency?'

'As you? Or Annie?'

'As me,' I asked and realized she was joking and laughed again.

'Yes, you have potential. But you need to know why you want it.'

'What do you mean?'

'If you want a job just for a pay cheque then you'll be average at your workplace, any workplace. If you want it to prove something to someone then you'll never be happy. So you need to know *why*. Why is this job the best for you?'

'Now it feels like something my college professor would say,' I murmured.

'Most things in life need a why. Why this marriage? Why this man? Why this choice? If you have even a rough answer, you'll be sorted. Otherwise, you can flounder through life trying to find happiness and it never finds you.'

They had almost reached and Ranjana thought she shouldn't say any more as she was just focusing on her breathing.

'I really liked working with you, though . . . You had some great ideas. Better than Annie's.'

'Really?' I asked, pleased that I could be smarter than Annie who had worked there for several years.

Ranjana's phone rang as her husband finally got the messages. She spoke to her husband as soon as he landed in Delhi and he just took the next flight out from the airport itself.

But it was several hours later and after many more contractions and pain that Ranjana delivered a baby boy. I stayed with her throughout, holding her hand and not caring that Annie might have been waiting at the restaurant. For the first time in a long time, I hadn't thought about going home to Abhay. I was just focused on a woman delivering her child as I helped her breathe through it all.

Ranjana's husband arrived to watch his son being born and I finally took leave of the couple in the early hours of the morning.

As I was leaving, I wondered about what Ranjana had mentioned. Figuring out my why. Why do I want Abhay's love? Why do I need to stay in this marriage? Why did I want Annie's job so badly now?

But before I could answer all that, I needed to get back, charge my phone and tell Annie to just come back to her home instead of meeting at a restaurant near the office, which we had planned earlier because Annie wanted to go straight to her cabin to work. The office was shut on Sunday. And the office was shut permanently for Annie.

I had no idea how to break it to her that I had broken my vow to her and lost the job. Not once did Ranjana say I could have the job back. I guess it wasn't in her hands any more.

But I didn't know that not having a job was going to be the least of my concerns. Because I wasn't the only one who had broken a vow.

Twenty-two

Annie

How to Face Reality Gracefully

Annie took a deep breath and rang the bell. It felt strange not to have the keys to her own house. Nandita opened the door for her.

'Welcome home.' They hugged each other. Nandita was all packed. She didn't want Annie to feel she had taken over her home. She'd made an extra effort that morning to clean up the way Annie liked it.

'You got some real plants?' Annie asked as she looked around her place.

'Yeah, I needed to water something. You can give them to Rhea later, I guess.'

'No, no, I'll try to look after them.'

Nandita wondered if she should ask Annie if she wanted a cup of coffee and then felt awkward as it was her own place. 'Should we do a coffee?'

'You drink coffee now? The number of people who gave me the disgusting milky tea while I was you and now you drink coffee?'

Nandita laughed. 'I had to be you so I started drinking coffee but with milk and sugar!'

Annie made a face and mouthed 'Milk?' She went to her kitchen and made coffee for both of them.

They sat down to tell each other about the significant thing that had happened to them.

'How's the job? Ranjana? Slimy Sahil? Tell me everything.' Annie said. 'How was your experience? You ready to get a job now or you've had enough?'

Nandita began with the easier aspects of office politics, the campaigns and Koko hitting on her. Annie laughed and listened. Then Nandita asked, 'How was your research as a housewife? Do you think you have enough to become the next managing director?'

'I think so. It was lovely, really. I never thought it would be this nice to be accepted by a family.'

'They accepted you?' Nandita asked, a tad surprised. As far as she remembered, it felt restricted.

'Yeah. I did things that I wanted to do and convinced them that I had changed.'

'Oh god. Like what?'

'Well, you need to run in the morning!'

'I told you not to start that!' Nandita groaned as Annie laughed.

'I cooked. Made some light soup and salads for myself that the family started enjoying,' Annie said with a mischievous smile.

'Oh my god!' Nandita smiled as she leaned back on the sofa. 'I think I'm just going to stay here a little longer.'

Annie laughed and poked her. 'Aren't you missing your husband?'

Nandita didn't know how to respond. Instead, she asked, 'Do you want to switch phones?'

Annie nodded as they gave each other's phones back. They spent the next ten minutes going through messages and emails.

Nandita saw the messages from Mark. She wondered if she should respond. Annie had ignored them. She sent a message, finally saying, 'Let's meet tomorrow if you're still here.' And immediately he responded that he had come for a project to Mumbai so he would be here for some time.

Annie saw Nandita think and send a message. She knew it wasn't for Abhay. But she didn't know how to tell her about what had happened between Abhay and her. They had decided it would be best if they didn't say anything at all.

'So, anyone guess you weren't me?' Annie asked finally.

Nandita took a long time to respond and sighed, 'Yes.'

'Who?'

'Shivani.'

'Oh, don't worry about her. I can twist her into keeping quiet.'

'It's not that.' Nandita felt anxious. 'Shivani told Koko. Koko told Ranjana.'

'Fuck!' Annie blasted and got up to pace as Nandita shrunk away from her, 'Why didn't you call me?'

'I tried but you didn't pick up. And then later my phone died when I took Ranjana to the hospital to deliver her baby.'

'She had the baby?' Annie asked in a shrill tone.

'Yes.'

'Fuck. That means she is going to announce the meeting in a week or so when she can get to the office. I don't have time.'

Nandita was confused, 'What meeting?'

'The managing director presentation. Sahil and I had to make a deck and present to the board as to why we're likely candidates. We have to get the votes of the team and the board. It's a massive presentation. I have only one week to prepare.' Annie closed her eyes and thought. She would present from the viewpoint of knowing the housewife, the single woman, a family and working individuals. Already she had the deck in her head, the slides just jumping out. 'Tell me about the team. You had said you could get through them, right? I want to know everything so I can be you for a bit and get their votes.'

Nandita cleared her throat. 'Yeah, the team really likes me . . . you I mean. But there's something I need to tell you.'

'What?'

'Um . . . truly I . . . it wasn't my . . . well it was . . . but . . .'

Annie came and sat next to Nandita. 'What are you saying?'

Nandita looked up and held Annie's hands. 'I got fired.'

Annie stood up. 'No, no, no, no, no! How?'

'Well, Shivani said . . . um . . . that I wasn't you . . . and since I had told Koko I wasn't interested in her . . . I don't know . . . it's just got messy . . .' Nandita scrambled for words and an apology.

'Ranjana would not fire me. She loves me. She is strict but she's on my side. She'll give me another chance.' Annie's voice rose in panic.

'Maybe you should call her,' Nandita suggested. Annie nodded and started dialling the number. But Ranjana didn't pick up. She looked at Nandita. 'What should I do? I told you not to lose my job. That's the one thing I need. You broke our agreement! How could you, Nandita?' Her voice grew loud as she started to hyperventilate.

'I'm sorry . . .'

'You're sorry? You've ruined . . .' Annie sat down and started howling. Nandita felt helpless. She had never meant to break the pact. She felt terrible. But then she had an idea.

'I can take you to her. I know where she is,' Nandita offered. 'You can convince her to give you your job back.'

'Okay. That's a good idea. I need this job.' Annie grabbed her purse. 'Let's go.'

Nandita left her packed suitcase behind and picked up her purse.

They went downstairs and hailed a cab.

'Everything will be fine, 'Nandita tried to assure Annie. 'It's just a mistake. She said it in anger. You'll be okay, Annie. '

Annie tried not to hyperventilate. She kept looking at her phone for some clue on how to reverse this horrible thing that had happened. She was apprehensive to tell Nandita that she had broken her pact too. She had slept with her husband and she had been exposed in more ways than one.

There were so many things on her mind about the last three weeks—her meeting with Rohit, the pressure of getting her job back and making a presentation that should have happened a whole month away. But the thing that was on her mind was her last conversation with Abhay.

'Where were you going with my mother's ring?' he had asked, confused, angry, a flash of betrayal showing on his face.

'Abhay, it's not what you think.' Annie had pleaded. 'Nandita and I switched our lives at the Kerala resort four weeks ago.'

'You fucking what?' he said as he sat on the bed. 'Mom said . . .' he started recollecting the last few weeks.

Annie bent down in front of him. 'I was not running away with the ring. I forgot about it. I had tried it on . . . I've never seen . . . and then it was still on my finger when

Ma . . . Kamini walked in and I panicked. I dropped it in the purse. I don't even use this purse. I was just giving it back to Nandita who I was supposed to meet tonight. We are supposed to switch back.'

'Switch back?' he asked incredulously. 'What is this? Am I just a puppet in this whole scenario? Why would she . . . why did you . . . I'm just . . .' He was at a loss for words.

Annie sat on the bed next to him not holding his hands but clasping her own tightly. 'Firstly, I would like to introduce myself. Hi, I'm Annie. I work at an advertising agency. I'm a senior manager there . . . hopefully I will become a managing director. I did this switch with Nandita . . . because I . . . I needed to understand a family life better . . . to get better at my job which a man is going to take away from me because . . . well, he's a man . . . and I don't really have a great family like you do, Abhay . . .' she said as she could see him look at her with kinder eyes.

'And Nandu?'

'Uh . . . I think you'll have to ask her . . . she mentioned that she wanted to get the experience of a job . . .'

'She did this because she wanted to get a job?' Abhay turned to ask Annie incredulously. 'I didn't want her to have a job because I saw how stressed out she became when she had one.'

'When?' Annie asked trying to recollect any conversation with Nandita about her previous employment.

'A long time ago. Nandu tried a job, but she was anxious all the time and her boss hated her. I thought I was being helpful by telling her to quit. I told her to take it easy . . . figure out what she really wanted to do. But switching a life . . .'

Annie stayed quiet to let Abhay figure out his thoughts. Ultimately she said, 'Abhay, this life switch has taught me one thing. To never take a husband for granted. Abhay . . . I've fallen in love with you. And I want to be with you. Tell me, do you want me too?'

But Abhay looked away, unable to decide what to say. This was too much for him to handle. He had cheated on his wife who had cheated on him. He was attracted to another woman but still married to her lookalike.

Annie knew when she had been rejected. She nodded, still hopeful. 'I'm going to leave my number on your phone. Um . . . when you decide what you want, call me.'

She left the ring on the table as she picked up the purse. 'I love your parents too. Even though Kamini hates me. But I think maybe . . . never mind.' She left the words unsaid as she left Abhay's home and went to switch her life back.

But when she met Nandita, there were too many things on her mind. Her anxiety began shooting up as she saw her mother calling on her phone. How could she tell Leena that she didn't have a job and couldn't pay any more for their restaurant? She was letting her parents down. Abhay hadn't called her yet. She didn't have any more words left in her. What if her plan had failed?

She took a deep breath to cross the road but her blood pressure shot up. Her head spun out of control and she collapsed on the pavement. She let go of the phone that she had been clutching in her hand. The phone that pinged with Abhay's message.

Twenty-three

Nandita

How to Control Your Temper

I couldn't believe I was back in the same hospital a day later.

I paced in the emergency room. A nurse tried to calm me down as she brought some papers for me to sign. I was no one in Annie's life. *How could I take the responsibility if something happened to her?* I didn't know whether to call Rhea or Annie's mother. I couldn't think. I signed the papers because they needed to perform surgery on Annie.

I don't know how long I sat there staring into space. I could comprehend people coming and leaving. Staring at me. A nurse whispered to another nurse that my twin sister had gone in for surgery when the shift changed at dawn. They asked me to go to the canteen to eat something or have tea. I refused. I couldn't move. I wouldn't be able to keep anything down anyway.

I should never have done this life switch in the first place. What if something bad happened to her? What would I tell her parents? All Annie had wanted to do was give me a chance to be something else, do something great and I had screwed it all up.

I opened my purse to take a tissue out to wipe my tears. There were two phones inside. I remembered I had picked up her phone and her purse before the driver rushed us to the hospital. I saw the message from Abhay on my phone. 'Where are you?' I didn't know how to respond. Was he looking for me or Annie?

I saw the message on her phone from Rhea asking the same question.

I didn't just have one life. Now I owned two lives. And I didn't want either of them.

But with two lies, two phones and two numbers, I didn't have a single person to call. I had no idea who would understand me or what I had gone through. I wondered if I should call Abhay and tell him what happened. But he would ask too many questions and be shocked and hurt that he had been deceived. I didn't need that conversation right now.

Just then, a doctor came out of the OT. He saw my face and seemed paralysed. 'Are you related?'

I nodded, 'Yes.'

'Your sister is in recovery. We had to do an extensive surgery which was successful. She's doing okay. We have to wait for her to wake up though. Then we'll know more. You should get some rest.'

'I can wait,' I said, relieved to hear that the surgery went well and that Annie could call her parents herself after she woke up. 'How soon will she be back to normal?'

'That we can't say. We'll know more in the next few days . . . and we can only hope for the best.'

'Hope for the best? What are you saying, Doctor?'

'The next forty-eight hours are critical.'

I bit my lower lip, trying not to cry. If Annie died . . . No!

'What can I do?' I asked.

'Wait.' He left without giving me anything reassuring. I was left alone to figure out what to do. I didn't know how much Abhay knew about this life switch.

But I thought of one person who did know about it. And maybe she could give me some advice.

I knocked and entered the room. Ranjana was messaging on her phone. 'Nandita,' she said with a smile, 'How sweet of you to come.'

'You didn't think I was Annie?' I asked with a wry smile as I handed the present I had bought from the gift shop for her.

'Thank you. You know, I always knew you weren't Annie.' She waved her hand.

I wanted to believe her. 'Really?'

She winked at me.

'Where's your baby?' I asked.

'Since he was born a few weeks early they've kept him under observation.'

'Oh my god. Is everything okay?'

'Yeah, yeah, he's a fighter like me.'

'Have you thought of a name?'

She shook her head. 'My husband and I can't decide. You just missed him. I threw him out because he was fussing too much. Told him to go back to Delhi for his meeting.'

'You what?' I laughed and sat down on the sofa near her bed.

'Men are a big pain. And now I have two of them to look after forever!'

I laughed after a long night of exhaustion, anxiety and loneliness. Suddenly I felt as if the last two days had taken a toll on me. I put my face in my hands and wept softly and uncontrollably.

'Hey, it's okay, Nandita. It'll be okay.'

I shook my head. 'It's not okay. Annie is in a coma. And it's all because I told her I lost her job.'

Ranjana sat up, stunned. I felt ashamed about my life switch.

'How? What happened?' she asked.

I looked down. I had been awake for almost twenty hours and my brain wasn't functioning any more. She could see I was troubled. I needed to tell someone. I was going to burst if I didn't.

'I can't remember the exact time. We were supposed to switch back and she suddenly had a panic attack or her blood pressure shot up and she collapsed. She's out of surgery but the doctor is saying the next forty-eight hours are critical. I don't know what to do. Tell me what to do,' I rambled on.

'You need to call her parents first,' Ranjana said as I nodded agreeing with her. 'You can't do this on your own.'

I was quiet. *What would I even say to them*?

But Ranjana finally spoke firmly. 'What were you people thinking? What a stupid idea in the first place. How would you . . . oh my god . . . like you both were demented!'

I was shocked at her outburst.

'Go home. Pray that she wakes up. Or her parents can sue you. You'll have a long court case against you. And if it wasn't for me, the company would put both of you in jail for fraud.'

I was nauseous and ran to the restroom to throw up from anxiety and panic. When I washed my face and came out, I apologized for my behaviour.

Ranjana wasn't having any of it. 'Listen to me,' she said in a firm tone. 'I'll give her job back if she wakes up. But, with both of you switching lives, I don't know if the board will agree to making her managing director any more.'

I felt there was some relief in that. At least she would have a job.

'I understand. She'll be relieved to hear that when she wakes up. Thank you.'

'Call her parents. They need to know.' She spoke with authority. So I did what she suggested. Annie's mother, Leena, was distraught and decided to fly from Delhi to be with Annie. But she said it would take her a day to leave. She could only get in by tomorrow. I didn't tell her we had done this ludicrous experiment to switch lives or that I looked like her. I said I was a friend and Annie had high blood pressure and had collapsed.

I messaged Abhay saying I would be home by the evening.

I knew she was in the ICU, so I told the nurse I would go home for the night but would keep my phone on. She still hadn't woken up. But I was ready to meet my husband and share the truth. I needed some support. Annie hadn't mentioned if he knew about this exchange. But I missed Abhay. And I knew that, in his heart, he missed me too. And we were meant to be together to solve all problems. I felt a deep sense of happiness as the cab made a turn into the lane where my building was. I was finally home where I was supposed to be forever.

Twenty-four

Nandita

How to Learn to Speak Up

I took an Uber back to my own home after a month. I was ready to crash into bed. My head was throbbing from all the pain and trauma of the day.

I rang the doorbell and my mother-in-law opened the door. 'Where are your keys?'

I stuttered. 'Um . . . I forgot . . .'

She walked back to the drawing room where she was watching a film with some of her friends. I peeped in to see that they all had a glass of wine and were giggling about a romantic comedy. Kamini had always had a battalion of female friends, a tribe that she had collected growing up and with her varied interests. I had been a recluse and had only stuck to Diya all my life. But some collect a community as they pass through life, which increases with age. And then there are others who walk alone with maybe a compatriot or two who may leave as well until there's nothing but loneliness accompanying them.

And then one begins to embrace it so that loneliness becomes a best friend. And that's why some get married. Just to drive that feeling away, not knowing that it only becomes stronger as you go deeper into married life if you don't find the correct person or enough self-love. You just hide it better than you did before.

'Where's Abhay?' I asked as she took a sip of her wine.

'I thought he told you.'

'Tennis.' I said with certainty.

She looked puzzled. 'No. He's gone for a meeting with Papa.'

'Meeting?'

'Some wedding jewellery planning for a bride and her family. Didn't he tell you?'

I shook my head as I went to my room. I went in for a shower and threw my clothes in the dustbin. If I wore them again, I would be reminded of the worst day of my life. I just wanted to lie in my own bed and sleep. Sheets that smelled of home. A nightstand that I had known for four years. Small things we take for granted when we don't have them. I had never appreciated being home as much as I did then. Knowing where everything was and who everyone was in my life. I felt comforted and relaxed. I got into bed and sighed, happy with the familiarity of the surroundings and closed my eyes.

I dialled Abhay, but I hadn't realized I had used Annie's phone.

Without listening to me, he picked up and replied, 'I'll call you back, Annie.' And suddenly I was wide awake all over again.

Twenty-five

Nandita

How to Live Two Lives

Annie still hadn't woken up after four days and I was worried. Her mother and I had been taking turns at the hospital but there hadn't been any improvement. She was still in the ICU and was finally being shifted to a room since all her vitals were stable but she hadn't woken up.

'How will we be able to afford all this?' her mother asked me as we both looked at the patient in a fancy room.

I stayed quiet. I didn't know their financial situation and Annie had never brought it up. But the fact that neither of her parents had called her over the last three weeks had been telling. At least I had my iPad and had spoken to my parents for a brief bit through Facetime.

Annie needed the job. She needed to make a presentation to the board. She needed to try to get the managing director position. I kept telling her this as I sat next to her for hours every day. But I also had another reason to sit there: Abhay.

He hadn't said her name again. But when he came back that night, he realized it was me and not her. He said he had figured it out early.

'Nothing happened, baby. I am all yours,' he smiled at me as he kissed me deeply, making me forget why I had even done the life-switch exchange. It all felt normal again. He was attentive and excited to tell me about the new wedding jewellery he was designing. But something felt off. I looked at him with mixed curiosity. I wondered if I should ask him when he knew it wasn't me. Was there a moment that he didn't and had tried something with her? Had they broken my agreement? But I was scared to know the truth. What would I do then? Where would I go if I left Abhay?

When I told Diya, she said, 'You sent another woman who looked like you to pretend to be his wife? And you expected him NOT to sleep with her? How crazy is that? What were you thinking?'

I hadn't known what to say. How could I have been so stupid? So trusting of a stranger? But I knew Annie would tell me the truth of what happened and how. If I knew one thing about her it was that she was brutally honest to a fault. It was why her team didn't appreciate her and Ranjana did. She couldn't lie or fake sincerity. I wondered how she did as a housewife. What she must have said to Mama and if my in-laws had guessed. There were so many things I needed to ask her but she just wouldn't wake up.

By the fourth afternoon, I went out of the hospital to sit on the lawn outside and think. I saw Ranjana with her husband and their baby leaving for home. I ran to their car to say goodbye to her. She saw me and said, 'You're still here?'

'Yes.'

Ranjana turned to her husband and said, 'This is the one I was talking about . . .'

'Nice to meet you,' he said warmly.

'How's Annie?' Ranjana asked. I shook my head. 'She's still . . .'

I showed Ranjana Annie's mobile in one hand and mine in the other. 'I'm living two lives now. She hasn't woken up.'

'What?'

'I've been helping her mother as much as I can by being here during the day. But the doctors are wondering what's gone wrong. She's in a coma,' I said as tears stung my eyes.

Ranjana turned to her husband and said, 'Wait in the car. I need to go see Annie.'

We both went up again to see Annie in the room sleeping peacefully hooked up to monitors.

Ranjana held her hand and spoke words of encouragement to her, assuring her that she had her job and she wanted her to come back to make more presentations. After all, Sahil wasn't as great a leader as Annie was. But Annie didn't move. Her eyelids flickered and for a moment I was hopeful that she would open her eyes. But she didn't.

Ranjana stayed for a few minutes but then turned to me and said, 'I need to go. The baby will wake up.'

I nodded, silent, unable to comprehend what to do or say. I'd never been in such a precarious position in my life. But she said something that shook me from my stupor.

'Nandita, you'll have to make Annie's speech.'

'Excuse me?' I stuttered.

'I think I can convince the board that you need to make Annie's speech . . .'

'What? I'm not . . .'

'You could be her for so many weeks. Maybe you need to be her one last time. Or maybe you need to be you. Your choice. You have to try. Otherwise, the board will pick Sahil by default. And Annie would hate hearing that and will never wake up.'

'But Koko? And . . . Shivani and Sahil?'

'I'll convince the board. I'll tell you when you can make it. I'll give her a week to wake up.'

'Ranjana, I can't,' I started speaking, my voice trembling. 'I can't give a presentation of what she's done for the last six years. I barely knew what to do in these last four weeks,' I pleaded.

'You'll figure it out,' she said as she hugged me and left.

Ranjana's words spun in my head. I wondered what to do. What if she had let me down and slept with Abhay? Should I make the presentation as Annie for her to succeed or as myself for a job I could have there?

I saw a message pop up on her phone from Rhea. 'Babe, Karthik is acting shady. Need to talk.'

I remembered I hadn't told Rhea about Annie in the hospital or that Karthik was Sahil as Rhea had not been in town recently. She hadn't seen that Leena was in Annie's apartment. I figured out a perfect plan to know if Abhay had slept with Annie. All I needed was to get Rhea on my side.

Twenty-six

Nandita

How to Catch a Liar

Before I could implement that plan, I needed to do one thing. I had to figure out why Shivani had betrayed me. I had been so nice to her and thought we were getting along at the restaurant. Just because Mark had popped into my life unexpectedly didn't mean she would tell Koko and Ranjana that I wasn't Annie. There was something there that was bothering me.

I also needed to call Mark. I had waited for four years to see him again and when I did, I hadn't imagined I would be in such a precarious situation. But there were so many things happening in a matter of days that I needed to prioritize what to do first.

After Ranjana left, I decided to go to Shivani's apartment. I wanted to sort out what had gone wrong that she would be so cruel to me.

As soon as I reached Shivani's apartment complex, I saw Sahil get out of his chauffeur-driven BMW and enter her building. What was he doing here? He didn't live here. I knew for a fact that he lived in another part of town because Rhea had told me. I was sure he was here to work on his presentation to the board with Shivani.

I waited for ten minutes and then went into the building. But I didn't know her apartment number. I read the list of all the flat owners' names in the wing that Sahil had entered. It didn't have Shivani's name anywhere. She had clearly rented the flat. I tried to see if Sahil had made an entry in the guest register, but there was nothing. He had been here before. I tried another approach. I asked the watchman, 'Which floor has sahib just gone to?' The watchman looked at me blankly.

'The man who just went in about ten minutes ago? Tall, fair, black hair, blue shirt, dark jeans. He left his sunglasses in the taxi,' I said as I showed him my own sunglasses case.

The watchman was clueless. 'I had gone for tea,' he said.

I sighed. Thousands of security guards were employed in buildings across Mumbai but not one of them knew what the meaning of security actually meant. I asked him again, 'Which apartment number did you call last?'

He shook his head. I was stuck. My plan was falling apart. I didn't know which apartment they would be in. I looked at Annie's phone to see if she had put an address in the contact details against Shivani but there was nothing.

Just then a middle-aged, slightly dark-skinned, curly-haired, plump woman who was carrying groceries came and pressed the lift button. I took a chance and offered to help. 'Hi. Can I help you?'

'Thank you, dear,' she said as she waddled to the lift.

'I'm Annie,' I said. 'I work with Shivani. Um . . . we were supposed to work today at her place. She told me her flat number but you know how it is, once I got here, I just forgot.'

'Oh, that happens to me all the time,' she said.

'You don't happen to know her, I suppose?' I asked.

'What does she look like?'

'Short hair. Bushy eyebrows.'

'Oh, lovely eyes but has a scowl all the time?'

'Yes, Shivani does have nice eyes!' I said.

'Oh ya. Cranky thing. She's . . . they're in 502. Across my hall.'

I helped the lady with her grocery bags to her door and she asked if I wanted to come in. But I refused, saying I needed to work.

I reached 502 and put my ear to the door to figure out if I could hear anything. Nothing. They must be plotting their presentation against Annie. I would find out what he was going to say and why she had betrayed me.

I rang the doorbell. Shivani took a few seconds to open the door. She must have seen from the peephole who it was and realized it was her boss. I heard a door close in the distance.

'Annie?' Shivani said as she opened the door more alarmed than surprised. 'No, wait. It's you. What's your stupid name again?'

I ignored her and barged in as a door closed from the corridor in her flat. 'I wanted to talk to you.' I was expecting both of them to be working on a presentation but there didn't seem to be a laptop around or Sahil.

'Um . . . actually, I'm a little . . . busy,' Shivani fumbled as she became conscious of what she was saying.

I played it very coolly. 'It won't take long.' As I looked around, I could feel something was off. There was something unusual about the room. Why wasn't Sahil in the dining area working on his presentation? Why were her clothes crumpled and her hair untidy?

I stood there near her sofa and then suddenly rushed towards her bedroom. I don't know what possessed me to do so. She didn't see that happening and charged after me to stop me.

'Hey you . . . you can't . . .'

But it was too late. I opened her bedroom door to see Sahil quickly putting on his shirt. I stared at him in shock. He had told me he was in love with Rhea. She was planning to marry him. How could he betray her with . . . wait . . . wasn't Shivani queer?

I turned and saw Shivani looking a little more troubled than when she had opened the door.

'You can't just go in . . .'

I had the upper hand all of a sudden and knew it. I calmly went back to the drawing room and sat on the sofa. 'Can I have a glass of water, please?' I asked politely, making sure they knew I wasn't going anywhere. It gave me some time to formulate my thoughts.

She went to get a glass of water as Sahil exited the room and said cheerily, 'Nandita, how lovely to see you.'

'Oh, you know I'm Nandita. Guess the secret is out,' I said as I stared at Shivani who gave me a glass of water.

Sahil came and sat on the sofa, 'Would you like a cup of tea? Coffee?'

'No,' I said firmly. 'I would like an explanation. I came here to ask Shivani why she betrayed me when I had only been nice to her. But I guess you're the reason, isn't it, Sahil? You've played both Annie and Rhea. Good job.'

'Rhea?' Shivani asked suddenly. 'Who's Rhea?'

'Oho, naughty boy . . . Sahil hasn't told you?,' I said as I folded my legs and gave no more explanation. 'I would like a cup of coffee, thank you.'

But Shivani and Sahil did not move to make me a cup. They just stared at each other. If anyone had told me a month ago that I would be confronting strangers about their love lives in a month's time, I would have found the situation ludicrous.

Sahil went to Shivani and said softly, 'It's the girl I was seeing before you. That's over. I told you.'

Shivani nodded. They quickly made up. And I was put on the spot again.

'Well, I guess I still need to hear Shivani say it,' I declared while putting on the recorder on my phone.

'Say what?' they asked.

'That you wanted me . . . Annie to get fired. So Sahil could win the managing director position.'

'That's ridiculous,' Sahil said. 'I didn't even know you were you, and not Annie. How would I get you fired?'

Shivani folded her hands. 'Nandita, I didn't know you'd get fired. I thought it was funny because we all hadn't caught this exchange or whatever it was you did. I told Koko, who came over after you dropped me. We are . . . friends. We had a few more drinks and I told her. She called Ranjana in the morning.'

So it was Koko who had a grudge against me or Annie for not becoming friends with her. I heard Shivani and things began to settle in my head. I stared at the ashtray on the table. I felt exhausted. I had been running around for so long trying to live a life that wasn't mine. I felt I needed to do the best for Annie. And yet I didn't even know if Annie had betrayed me. I was silent for a long time.

'Nandita?' Sahil said, bringing me back to the present situation. 'I like competition. Annie is great competition. I want us to compete at the board meeting on Monday. I don't want to get it by default. I don't even think that's possible. They'll put up other candidates and delay the meeting, I presume. Ranjana just wants it to be over quickly because I've heard she's had her baby. If Annie is not there, Ranjana will need to come back to the office and she doesn't want to do that. If she hands over her position, she gets a large payout and can go on to motherhood. It's actually a complicated process which you probably didn't know about or wouldn't even understand!'

I heard him and realized Ranjana had been playing the game too. She wanted me or Annie to be there on Monday so she could retire quickly with a fat pay cheque. Maybe . . . she wanted me to fail so she could give the position to Sahil. If I didn't show up, she would have to remain in the office and wouldn't get her payout. It was all coming together.

I understood what I had set out to achieve. Corporate life was everyone looking out for themselves. And people might seem friendly, but they would never be your friends. A lesson Annie had learnt and had been trying to teach me. But then, I had to learn it on my own. Was it too much to understand, withstand and continue in this maze of office relationships and politics? Or was it something that fuelled one to do better, learn and become more aware like a lion in the jungle? I knew Annie was a lion but was I one too?

Just then my phone buzzed with a message. I looked down and it pulled me out of my reverie.

Sahil cleared his throat to say, 'Nandita . . . about Rhea . . .'

I looked at him. I had forgotten about her completely. But he continued. 'She's not the one for me. I told her I needed time and she freaked out. She's needy, clingy . . . calling me constantly. She rarely understands my work or even wants to.'

'That's not . . .' I shook my head.

'I told her it's over but she's creating drama, wanting to meet me and talk. I just don't have the time right now. I need to work on this presentation. Please . . . if you could . . . keep this thing between Shivani and me private. I would be really grateful,' he pleaded.

I felt anger rising in me. I wanted to scream about what I had to do for everyone. What was anyone doing for me? My life was in utter disarray and no one seemed to care. I knew I had to look out for myself.

I turned to them and said, 'I will be presenting as Annie on Monday. I would be grateful if you pretended I was Annie . . . and not tell anyone, even Koko, that I am Nandita.' I looked directly at Shivani as I said it and then at both.

'Where's Annie?' Sahil asked, confused. 'Why won't she be there?'

I didn't answer his question. 'You don't need to know that right now. All I need is your assurance. And I'll keep the fact that you're seeing Shivani so quickly after breaking up with Rhea to myself.'

Sahil nodded, followed by Shivani. She said softly, 'I'm sorry, Nandita. I didn't mean to get you fired.'

I nodded, grabbed my purse and left. I ran all the way out of the building until I stopped to take a breath and realized the voice recorder was still on. I shut it off and saw the message that had buzzed earlier. I had used Annie's phone.

No one knew that Annie was still in the hospital and I hadn't had the time to tell Abhay all the details until I knew what had happened. But it all seemed pretty clear now.

It was a singular message that took my breath away. It shattered everything in my life.

The message had come from Abhay. On Annie's phone.

And it read, 'You're right. Can we meet?'

Twenty-seven

Nandita

How to Plan a Revenge

Leena called me to ask if I could sit with Annie for some time, so I headed to the hospital again.

'I'm just going to buy some groceries so I can cook something for Annie. So she has good food when she wakes up. I just wish . . . I just wish . . . my Annie could wake up and see . . . that I love her . . . that I don't . . . It was my fault. All this that had happened. She took this pressure on herself because her father and I . . . if we hadn't . . .' Leena sobbed.

I tried to comfort her. 'Aunty, please don't worry. Annie loves what she does. She enjoys the pressure. She thrived on it. She would be bored otherwise. Your daughter is stronger than you think. She'll wake up soon and eat your food and you can tell her all that you want to. I just know it.'

'You're a good friend, dear,' she said as she hugged me and left. I felt miserable. I wasn't a good friend. In fact, I doubted if we would be friends when Annie woke up. And, hopefully, that would be soon so we could go back to our own lives.

A nurse came to check her vital statistics.

'When do you think she'll wake up? What did the doctor say?' I asked the sister.

The nurse looked solemnly at me and said, 'He'll take his rounds around twelve.'

'Okay,' I said, exhausted from the day already and it had just started.

'You don't worry. Your sister will be fine.'

And then I lost it completely. 'She's not my sister!' I screamed at the poor nurse. 'I want her to wake up so I can murder her.'

The nurse was visibly upset. She almost called the security guard before I calmed down. 'I mean . . . she is . . . she is my sister . . . I just want . . .'

The nurse understood. 'It's okay. Sisters fight. Even I fight with my sister. I miss her since she is married and staying in Kerala. But she's my best friend. I tell her everything. I know what you're going through, dear. You don't worry. Doctor said she will wake up. She's just taking time, no? Resting. You also go home and rest.'

I shook my head. 'I'm okay.'

'I'll send you lunch later. Eat something,' the nurse said as she smiled and left. I felt grateful for someone who had said a kind word to me, who was not deceiving me, who seemed to indulge me. After almost half an hour of waiting, I got impatient.

'Annie!' I screamed near her face 'Did you sleep with my husband?' But there was no movement and a dead silence filled the room.

I realized I needed my best friend too. I needed advice. I didn't know how to handle this situation alone. So I called the one person who I knew always spoke clearly and bluntly. I dialled the number and said, 'Hey, it's me. I'm at Powai Hospital. Can you come here? I need your help.'

My best friend had always been a straight shooter. She didn't mince words and was always on my side, even when we didn't agree on several things in life. But it was time for more than moral support. It was time for some sound counselling. She dropped all her work and came to see me immediately. And I realized I would never take this friendship for granted.

'What do I do with this message?' I asked Diya.

Diya came close to Annie and lifted her hand. It fell when she dropped it. She looked surprised and smiled wickedly. 'Can I take a selfie with a coma patient? My Insta would blow up.'

'Yes. You must,' I answered wryly. 'Coz everyone will think it's your best friend who's in a coma.' I pointed to my face to remind her of the resemblance.

Diya smiled. 'Can she hear us?'

'Yes,' I nodded. 'That's why I want her to hear this. And wake up.'

'What do you want her to hear?'

I moved closer to Annie and spoke loudly, 'I still love Abhay. And no matter what you say to him or what moments you shared, we are married. And we will have a life together.'

We stayed quiet for some time, waiting to see if there'd be a response.

'Why don't you ask him about the message?' Diya asked finally.

'He'll deny it.'

We sat in the room in silence for a while until she said, 'This is really creepy. Can we get coffee somewhere else?'

I picked up my purse and we headed to a café across the street.

We sat down and ordered our Americanos.

'Cheers,' she said.

I replied, 'Cheers.'

'To nothing? You must really be glum.'

I raised my cup and said with a tinge of anger, 'To me figuring out if my husband cheated on me.'

'Whoa. Back up. First of all, you're jumping the gun. You don't even know what happened.' Diya responded with sincerity, and I knew she was incapable of being fake with me. 'He loves you. And he hasn't slept with her. It was probably a great dinner. You're making this up in your head. Stop worrying. Go ask him about it. It'll be a simple answer.'

'If I ask him, he'll deny it. That's why I'm here . . . to ask her.'

'Well, clearly she isn't saying anything.' She turned and asked me with an afterthought, 'What happened to Mark? The one love that you told us about? Did you meet him after that night in the restaurant?'

I shook my head. 'I haven't had time.' I waved my hands around. 'Have you seen my life over the last one month?'

'You should. Maybe if you slept with him you'd feel better.'

It sounded so tempting. But getting even with your husband didn't mean sleeping with another man to spite him. It would only make me feel worse if I did it for the wrong reasons.

'I want to be in a better head space before I meet him.' I had told myself. And now I had nothing. Not a job, nor a faithful husband. I didn't want to just have an affair with Mark. That was never the intention. It was meeting an ex to prove that I had done something more with my life, without him.

We stayed quiet before Diya asked me a question that shook me. 'Are you the same person you were when you fell in love with Abhay?'

'I don't know . . . I don't think I've changed that much,' I said, thinking about it slowly.

'Haven't you? I knew a different you in school. And then even when we were apart in college, you used to tell me everything about Mark and your courses. You were so passionate and excited talking about him and all the stuff you were planning to do together. Like opening that clinic. Becoming full-time psychologists. Helping people. And then you came back and suddenly you became a housewife.'

'I was forced to get married!'

'Okay,' she said, looking away from me while sipping her coffee. 'And then, over the years, maybe you just lost yourself. You were working on a novel. You thought about starting a clinic and using your psychology lessons to earn money. What happened then?'

'I was trying to be a good housewife.' I wanted her to believe me. But she nodded, knowing me too well. I continued, 'You know, I did like the work. And the office. My team had been good to me. I hadn't thought of my clinic for so long. That was a dream with Mark. Maybe some dreams are only for a certain point in time. You're meant to evolve out of them.'

'You don't need Mark to open a clinic. Or maybe find work somewhere. And not think so much about Abhay.'

'So I should just forget that he cheated on me?'

'He *may* have cheated on you. But so what? So many husbands cheat on their wives. And vice versa. Don't make it your whole identity. He gives you so much more too. That should be enough.'

I shook my head, 'It doesn't work like that with me. It just doesn't. I can only get on with life if I know.' We had finished our coffees and she looked at her phone.

'I have to get to work, honey. I wish I could stay with you longer.' Diya smiled sympathetically at me.

'It's okay. I need to figure out if Abhay cheated on me.' I stood up and called for an auto.

'Where are you going?'

'To be Annie one last time,' I said with authority.

'What are you going to do?'

'Seduce him as Annie.'

'That is not a good idea at all,' she said as we exited the café. 'That's dangerous. You're playing with your life, Nandita. I don't support this.'

'I now know why I did this life switch. It wasn't just to work or get to know myself better. It was to understand what love meant. To truly accept someone for who they are. And till now, I wanted to figure out if Abhay truly loved me. But now I know it was for me to understand if I truly loved and needed Abhay. I have to do this. So I know for sure. I will finally know if Abhay loves me. And if I should be with him.'

'You're happily married. Don't upset everything you've built. Not for one night. Not for her. Don't let her win.'

'It's not about winning, Diya,' I said. 'It's about love. I can't stay with someone who doesn't love me. I did this experiment to win his love and respect. Now it's his turn to win mine. I need to know the truth.'

For so long I've been trying to fit into everyone's world. First my parents', then Mark's, then Abhay's, then Annie's. I've wanted to fit in to be loved. Because I didn't know who I was or what I wanted. But now I needed people to fit into my world. And maybe I didn't know myself completely yet, but I knew I was tired of being a side character in everyone else's world or being in someone else's shoes. It was time to make my own world.

Diya looked at me intently. 'Nandita, there are some truths you don't need to know.'

I nodded, knowing that my best friend had my best interests at heart but she would never be able to understand what I was going through. She had been in a great marriage where her husband was constantly romantic towards her. He was far more in love with her than she was with him. She wasn't the type of person who needed truths in her life. Her truth was set. She would be in her happy marriage forever. But I was still unsure. And it bothered me to the point I was unable to sleep properly at night next to Abhay.

'I'm here for you. Call me,' she said as her Uber came up to the curb and she got in.

Abhay messaged, 'On my way.' He really wanted to meet Annie. And I would play the role of my lifetime to figure out if he needed me or Annie. And, more importantly, if I needed him too.

Twenty-eight

Nandita

How to Seduce Your Man through a Life Switch

It isn't difficult to be someone else if one tries. But it's easy to take on another's identity and live like them for the rest of your life. All you need to do is leave everything you know and become another person. People do it all the time. They assume the personality of someone who isn't them. Sometimes they take on the identity of someone who's died. But, most times, we switch from playing a hero to a villain to a side character even in our own lives. It all depends on how much power we feel like owning and projecting at any given point in time.

I never had any power. I was a people pleaser from a young age because I wanted my parents to stop fighting. And when my sister was born, I wanted to be the good elder sister.

'Don't make so much noise, Nandu. The baby is sleeping.'

'Stop fighting, Nandu. You're the elder one. You should know better.'

'Give her your books, Nandita. We can get more for you later.'

I retreated more into my shell, got good grades and finally left after my twelfth boards. The freedom I had at Yale gave me wings to be who I wanted to be. But when I had mentioned I wanted to start a clinic after college, my parents refused to allow me to stay a minute after my graduation. They sent me a flight ticket and told me either I come home, or they would never speak to me again.

I couldn't take the emotional blackmail and I returned. But it wasn't just that. Mark had said he didn't believe in marriage. He would open the clinic with me and we could be together but we could not get married. My parents would never have accepted a live-in relationship. And I still needed their approval to live a happy life.

Now Sam is supposedly in a live-in relationship with her boyfriend and my parents don't know. I learnt of it when I saw her Instagram page and she was waking up to 'coffee in bed' in a place that didn't look like her room at our parents' house. Or maybe they do know but have turned a blind eye to her shenanigans as usual. Only I needed to toe the line. And I always have.

Here I was at Annie's apartment not knowing who I was any more. Maybe I had become more like Annie than I thought. I had kissed her ex-boyfriend just like she had kissed my husband. But no, I hadn't kissed back. I had stopped it. I wasn't Annie. I was still in love with Abhay.

And that hurt the most. That I still loved him.

But I needed to stand up for myself. I needed to know if this marriage was a mistake. And if that were the case, I would tell my parents *they* had made this mistake. They had chosen a man who cheated on me.

I opened the door to the apartment and walked in. It wasn't just Annie's place, it had been mine too. I had read several of the books on the bookshelf, reorganized the sofa to move towards the window to get more light and bought several plants to look at when I was reading on the sofa. I had got used to the coffee Annie had, worked out how to use the machine and enjoyed an espresso now and then.

Living a single woman's life for the last month, I had realized far more about myself than I'd done in the last twenty-eight years. That I could take care of myself. And maybe, just maybe, I didn't need approval for anything after all.

I shook myself out of my reverie. I noticed the clean dishes at the sink, and some khichadi made for one person. Leena had been staying here alone for a week while her daughter lay in a coma. I had not come back here ever since I went back home. I had felt something was missing there as well. There was no Hari and everyone seemed to have got busier with their lives. My in-laws had said nothing and Abhay hadn't mentioned anything to them. It all felt surreal. To go back and see nothing had changed. Or maybe everyone was playing a part I didn't know about?

As I walked around the small house, I began to feel I could have a life like this too. Why had I got married so young? Maybe I had been scared to be alone. Maybe it was love. Maybe it was an escape. The last month had helped me experience all that I could be. The life switch had been a real eye-opener for me.

Now I needed to know if I should go back to being a married woman or choose to be a single woman for the first time in my life. And if Abhay wanted to make a switch as well. Had he picked the wrong person? Had he fallen in love with Annie?

I wore Annie's clothes, denim shorts and a black top. I combed my hair and put on some lipstick. The doorbell rang. This was it. I was going to be Annie for Abhay.

'Hi,' he said, standing there with his hands in his pockets, smiling sheepishly.

I opened the door so he could enter, 'I got your message.'

He walked in and swept me up in one move, folding me in his arms and giving me a long kiss. I wondered whether it was because he thought I was Annie or did he recognize me?

When he let me go he smiled and said, 'So good to see you this way, Nandu.' He walked around the apartment. 'So this is where you've been staying . . . wearing her clothes? Being her?'

I was shocked that he knew in a second. My face betrayed my emotions. He continued, 'What? You didn't think I would know my own wife?'

I felt a wave of relief overcome me. I threw my arms around Abhay and kissed him with the passion that I had always felt. And, for the first time, he reciprocated with an intensity that left me breathless. He had changed. He had missed me. And everything was going to be all right.

He wrapped his arms around me and said, 'Shall we make use of Annie's sofa? Or . . .'

I guided him to the bedroom.

I still couldn't get the message out of my mind, though. I turned to him and asked, 'What did you mean by "You're right"? Why did you want to meet Annie?'

'Hmm?'

'You sent a message on Annie's phone. I read it.'

He sat up looking surprised and asked, 'How did you read it?'

I had thought about the various questions that may arise when I asked him, so I was prepared for this one. I replied, 'She sent it to me.'

Abhay thought that was plausible but there was a small moment when he frowned.

'Well?' I insisted on knowing the truth. He took a long time to reply. And that's when I knew . . . something wasn't right.

'Babe . . .' Abhay drew me into his arms again and said, 'It was nothing. Some stupid argument about something. She said she had facts and I said I had learnt it in school. Something like that . . . I don't even remember.'

'Abhay . . . Just tell me . . . Why did you want to see her?'

'Um . . . I think I got a forward proving I was right or something so just wanted to, um . . . complete the conversation . . . What's with all this interrogation, Nandu? I just feel . . .' He got up to head to the bathroom and shut the door behind him.

I felt I had insulted him by asking too many questions. After all, I had placed him in this scenario. He had given me an explanation. I needed to let it go and just believe him. *Didn't I?*

But there was still something bothering me. I just couldn't place my finger on it.

'Where is Annie, though?' Abhay asked as he exited the bathroom and went to the other bedroom to check out the apartment. He stood in front of her vision board while I went to the bathroom to think of a reasonable answer to his question. Where was she? What could I say?

How could I tell him that I was responsible for Annie's coma? Would he understand? I went to the other room to tell him the truth but I saw him touching Annie's running medals. He smiled and cocked his head as if he was remembering something. An intense wave of jealousy passed through me. *What had I missed? What had I done with this life exchange?*

My phone rang and he turned towards the door where I was standing watching him. I went to the sofa where I had thrown my phone when he had swept me up in his arms. At that moment, everything changed for me. With that one phone call and what ensued, my life switched more than any life switch I would ever have done.

Leena was calling. I picked it up.

'Nandita,' she said excitedly. 'Annie's awake and she's asking for you.'

I looked at Abhay and repeated her words, 'Annie's out of her coma. We need to go to the hospital.'

Abhay's face fell and he became ashen. 'Coma?' he asked, confused. I had never seen such a reaction from my husband in the four years I was married to him. And again, the butterflies in my stomach began to bother me.

Twenty-nine

Nandita

How to Win a Husband

I felt that someone had run over me with a steamroller. My insides knotted up as I felt ill at the thought of confronting Annie with Abhay. After I hung up the phone, I wondered for a flash of a second if I should lie to Abhay and say I had an errand to run and go to the hospital by myself. But then, Abhay had just confessed his love and my heart said there was nothing to be worried about. A little thought crept into my mind, though. It would be fun to see Annie's face as she realized that the switch had taken place and Abhay was now more in love with me because he missed me. I had won. I got what I wanted from this life switch.

I turned to Abhay and said, 'Annie's out of her coma. We need to go to the hospital.'

Abhay's reaction was natural but it made me flinch. 'What? Annie? What happened?' His genuine concern disconcerted me for a second. *Why should he care so much? She was nothing to him. Wasn't she?* She was just play-acting as his wife. Or had there been something more with the message that he wasn't saying?

'I'll tell you on the way,' I said as I grabbed my purse but suddenly stopped. I realized I couldn't wear these clothes to a hospital. I quickly went inside, changed into jeans and a long kurta and came out. Abhay looked at me in wonder.

'You just know what to wear . . . you know?' He smiled appreciatively.

'I went to a convent school till twelfth grade. Strict moral and dress codes were taught. Guess some things just remain in your life, right . . .' I reminded him.

I saw him gaze at me with a half-smile as I asked, 'What?'

He shook his head and turned off the lights as we left Annie's house. 'Will you drive?' he asked with a sarcastic smile. I gave him a look as if to say he knew I never did. He muttered to himself, 'Should have known then.'

Even though he asked about how Annie landed up in the hospital, I didn't give too many details about the accident, only saying that Annie had been unwell for a few days. I wanted to gauge what he was thinking with the questions he asked. But he was clever enough to keep the questions to a minimum as well. He seemed concerned as a friend but not anxious as a lover. Was he putting up a front or was his immediate reaction to the news his genuine feeling? I couldn't tell and I decided to confront both of them when we reached the hospital. I needed to figure out the truth otherwise it would haunt me forever.

There were some wives who guessed that their husband was having an affair. Some looked the other way. Some denied it. Some encouraged it as it kept the husbands out of their own busy lives, but they continued to stay together for the sake of society. But I knew that there were only two reasons for people to stay in a marriage—out of duty or out of deep love. And I loved Abhay. It scared me to think that I could lose him. My mind was exploding, thinking he might love someone else. My heart filled with dread as I choked back the thought.

When we got to the hospital room, Annie wasn't in her bed or in her room.

I asked the nurse at the nurse's station where Annie had disappeared.

'Your sister? She went with your mother to the lawns. She said she needed fresh air.'

Abhay gave me a strange look when the nurse said 'sister'. I didn't reply.

When we went towards the lawns, we realized that only a few people had come out. Large cumulus clouds had gathered, indicating there might be rain. There was a small pathway around the garden and I could see Annie in a wheelchair with her mother pushing her.

I walked rapidly towards her with purpose as Abhay tried to keep pace.

Before I could reach them, Annie saw me heading towards her and asked her mother to stop pushing.

I reached her and took large deep breaths to gather my thoughts. 'Thank god!'

Abhay caught up with me and remarked that Annie seemed different in a hospital gown wrapped in a shawl. She looked frail and scared. I could feel that he wanted to rush to her, do something for her.

'I'm so glad you're awake,' I said as I hugged Annie. 'How are you?'

'When did you . . .' Abhay began, but Annie cut him off.

'A little woozy but I needed to get out. How are you, Nandita?'

'I'm just . . . so happy to see you're . . . awake,' I said, relieved that she was coherent and there was no brain damage.

Annie looked over and said quietly, 'Hi, Abhay.'

He waved to her. 'Hey.'

Annie's mother Leena got a call from Annie's father and she picked it up as she moved slightly away from us to talk to him.

'Annie,' I started speaking. 'Ranjana gave you your job back.'

I thought the news would make Annie jump up for joy and begin running around the lawns. Instead, for the first time, Annie only nodded and replied, 'Hmmm . . .'

An orderly came to interrupt our conversation by saying, 'It's time to go in. The patient cannot be here for so long.'

Abhay moved towards us, 'Well, now that we've seen her, maybe we should come back later, Nandu? Um . . . she needs rest.'

'Just a minute,' I said as I stopped him from taking Annie inside. 'This won't take long.'

Annie looked up. I leaned down to her and whispered, 'Annie just tell me what happened between you and Abhay.'

'What? What do you mean?'

Abhay looked uncomfortable as I tried to watch both of their reactions to this confrontation.

'Nandita . . . what are you trying?' Abhay asked as he tried to intervene.

I ignored him and looked straight at Annie. 'I got you your job back. I didn't break our pact. Now please tell me. Did you break our vow? Just say it. So we can truly switch back. Otherwise . . . I won't be able to . . .'

'Why would you even ask that?' Annie looked surprised. Was that a quick glance at Abhay? I didn't see his reaction.

'That's enough chatter,' the orderly said, and Leena hung up to come towards us.

I took one last chance.

I pulled out Annie's phone and showed it to her. 'Abhay messaged you without knowing I had your phone. What does it mean, Annie?'

She paused and told the orderly to wait. She gulped before answering me softly. 'Why don't you ask him?'

'For god's sake, Nandita, I told you—' Abhay started.

I cut him before he could complete his sentence, 'I heard what you said. I need to hear it from Annie. I know she can't lie. She's been brutally honest all her life. That's why people in the office don't like her because she tells the truth to their faces. It's a rare gift. So be honest with me too, Annie.'

But before Annie could speak, Abhay stepped forward and said, 'Okay, I'll tell you.' I looked at him for a moment as he averted his eyes from Annie.

Annie held her breath. Would he speak his truth? This was the moment he had to choose between the two women. He could confess and plead for forgiveness from his wife or he could confess and let both of them know who he really loved. Instead, he said, 'I figured out that Annie wasn't my wife a few nights ago. I confronted her and she accepted it. That's all. We had a drink and got to talking about her life. Because I wanted to figure out if you two were twins or what. Because the resemblance is uncanny. I needed to know more about her. One thing led to another . . .'

He paused to find the correct words as I held my breath in anticipation.

'But it led to . . . a great conversation that evening. I thought we could remain friends but we felt we needed your permission first. That's all.'

Abhay's words tumbled out of him. He was looking directly at me to see if I was convinced. I was surprised that he could think of a lie so quickly on his feet when given the opportunity. But a part of me really wanted to believe him. It's just that moment for wives. When they know something is wrong. But for the sake of history, a shared past or even children, they decide to let it go. So I did. And sometimes that's all one can do. Believe the lie so one can have a more peaceful life. After all, I did all this to see if my husband still loved me and was willing to lie to me to save the marriage. Right? *Right?*

Annie heard his words and felt hollow inside. She had seen the passion in his eyes that night. She had felt his longing for her when they hugged before they parted again. He had smelt her hair, held her close and she had seen the tears in his eyes. She knew he wanted her. Yes, they did have that conversation about her life, her dreams and who she was. But they had also made love again. After the confession. Before the dawn broke. Before she had to leave. He had cheated on his wife. She had broken her vow to her friend. She had failed the rules of the game. She had destroyed their marriage. But she wasn't going to tell the truth if Abhay hadn't. This was his choice to make. No wonder he had sent the message. Because he wanted to hook up again. And he got caught. This was his mess to clean. Not hers.

'We need to go inside now,' the orderly said in an authoritative tone. They all filed back into the main lobby in icy silence as I collected my thoughts on how to confront Annie in a more rational manner. There was something that wasn't sitting well in my heart. Why couldn't I let it go? Because I knew that I wasn't at ease. And I would never be until Annie told me the truth. 'Only one guest at a time can go up,' the orderly said when both Abhay and I tried to enter the lift.

Leena said, 'I'm going to find the doctor. Papa wants me to ask him something. Darling, I'll see you in the room a little later.'

'How did you get my job back?' Annie called out to me, peeping from her wheelchair while the orderly raced ahead as fat droplets of rain started pouring down.

'I'll meet you at the car in ten minutes,' I told Abhay as I followed the orderly back into the hospital.

When Annie was back on her bed, sitting up, the orderly allowed me to enter her room. 'Tell me all about what Ranjana said. She's something huh?' Annie said smiling at me as if all was well.

'You have to make a presentation in a week,' I said finally. 'For the role you wanted. The MD position.'

Annie looked confused, 'But you said . . .'

'Ranjana gave me . . . you . . . your job back.'

'But I won't . . . what will I . . .' Annie struggled to find the words as she looked out of the window thinking of her role and maybe the presentation she would need to make.

I stayed quiet to give Annie a moment to gather her thoughts.

But all Annie said was, 'Thank you. I knew you wouldn't let me down. I'll be ready. I am the next managing director.'

'Is there anything else you want to . . . say . . . ask?' This was probably the last time we would speak. I knew she wouldn't be the friend in my life that I thought we would become. That was gone. I didn't feel it any more. So I hoped maybe she would just be honest with me.

But she just shook her head.

'All the best,' I said, turned and left.

I called to tell Abhay I was going to say bye to Leena, who had gone to meet the doctor, and then come down to the car. But suddenly, I remembered I still had Annie's phone in my purse and I wanted to leave it with her finally. This life switch was over. I didn't want it any more. I was happy to go back to being a housewife for some time and figuring what my next steps would be. Maybe another job. Maybe a new hobby. Whatever it was, I was ready to let go of all this ill feeling and welcome Abhay into my life. I couldn't wait to tell him about all the wonderful things I had done over the last few weeks. It would be far more interesting than any Netflix show he would have picked for the evening. I smiled as I headed to Annie's room.

As I walked into Annie's room again to leave the phone, I saw someone was already there. Abhay.

And there was no more denial. The truth was right in front of me.

Abhay was sitting on Annie's bed, holding her hand and kissing her on the lips.

Thirty

Nandita

How to Cancel Your Ex

What is it about love? We chase it from the moment we are born, wanting to be loved by parents, friends, partners and even colleagues. We seek love all the time, in every relationship. Its form changes because love, as we all know, is like water; it's important to all but how much we need varies from person to person. Some say love is the purpose of life. Seeking it, finding it, keeping it. And without it, we are just lost and lonely souls.

All my life I had been seeking love from people. My parents were so consumed with fighting and then loving my sister that they never really cared to see how much love I needed. I desperately sought love from Mark and even though he said he loved me, I shunned him because he didn't want to marry me. And then for four years, I tried everything I could to make my husband fall in love with me, but in a heartbeat, he fell in love with another woman, only proving that he didn't love me in the first place.

I couldn't make anyone love me the way I wanted. The only way to find love was to not seek it any more. I gave up on love.

When I walked in on Abhay kissing Annie, my world collapsed. I stood there shocked and paralysed. It wasn't only that they had lied to me and made me believe that nothing had happened, it was because they were blatantly going to carry on an affair behind my back!

But the shock intensified because I saw Annie open her eyes and notice me. And when Abhay turned to see I was standing there, there was a slight smile in the corner of her eye.

I had been played all along! From the moment she met me, she knew that she wanted my life. I had been chasing her life for an opportunity to make my husband love me.

But she had been eyeing my life and I realized my life had been perfect as well. I had an amazing husband, a loving family and supportive friends. I didn't need to exchange my life at all. She had planned to take over my life completely. Now she had her job back and she had my husband.

My mind was reeling. I didn't know what to say. I stood there, furious. I threw her phone at her. She ducked.

'Nandita!' Abhay screamed at me. 'What are you doing?'

'Fuck you!' I shouted back as I walked out of the room, running down the corridor to the lift to get as far away from him as possible. Abhay came chasing after me. I couldn't hear what he was trying to say then. The voices died down in the hospital. I got into a cab. I didn't look at him. It wasn't because I was feeling betrayed by this disloyalty of a kiss.

I knew this little act of infidelity was a result of the bigger act they must have performed. I left because I realized that I had been chasing him to love me for so long and all that I'd done, was for him—and it was all for nothing. The betrayal felt deep and cutting.

I didn't know where I was going. At first, I thought I would go home, but then I knew Abhay would land up there and his parents would try to convince me that it was a mistake and I should forgive him. I didn't want to meet Diya because she would tell me to leave him and I wasn't sure that was the correct plan yet. I had no job, no financial security of my own and parents who were living their own lives and didn't need me as a burden.

I needed a place where I felt safe and could think, and cry and maybe drink. I messaged the one person I knew who would welcome me without judgement. Mark.

The taxi dropped me off at his hotel. He opened the door and I entered, collapsed into a chair and sobbed.

Mark opened the fridge and gave me a mini bottle of wine without saying a word.

I looked at it and said, 'These are so expensive!'

He rolled his eyes saying, 'We can afford them. We're not in college any more.'

And suddenly I started giggling. The whole situation was absurd. I was in my ex-boyfriend's hotel room because my husband had cheated on me with my lookalike who had taken over my life. It couldn't get more ludicrous than that. How had I landed myself in this position? And, more importantly, how would I ever go back to my old life?

Mark with his dark eyes, pale skin and impish charm sat on the bed away from me to allow me space. He had always been thoughtful and generous. I took a swig of the wine and it got over in two gulps.

'Wow, these are small,' I commented. He casually went to the fridge and got me another one. He took out a beer for himself and we raised our drinks to each other with a nod.

'You know who you look like?' he asked smiling. I shook my head. He continued, 'Bottoms-up Bianca!'

I laughed out loud, almost spilling my drink. 'Yes, I remember our old professor. She was the best teacher I've ever had.'

We recollected our college days as we drank some more. He didn't ask me what I was doing in his hotel room and I didn't ask if he had been waiting for someone else. After all, it had been five years since we had seen each other. His life would have changed. He could have been married or had a girlfriend or many girlfriends. But it didn't feel like that. For the first time after so long, I felt as if I belonged somewhere. In the strange hotel room with an ex-lover who knew me really well and wanted me with him at that moment.

I stood up and went to sit next to him on the bed. I leaned in, held his cheek and pulled him in for a long kiss. He still smelt of Paco Rabanne aftershave; warm, familiar, more home than Abhay had ever been.

He pulled away for a bit and said softly, 'Nandita, you're a married woman. I don't want you to have any regrets. I don't want to take advantage—'

'Shhh . . .' I murmured as I kissed him again.

Why was I doing this? For revenge? What did I want to prove by cheating on Abhay? That just because he had, I could too?

But I wasn't that type of woman. I was angry and bitter with Abhay and resentful of Annie. But wasn't the whole situation my doing? Did I love Mark enough to sleep with him? Would I be making another mistake?

I got up quickly and my head swirled. Mark stood up to keep me from falling.

'I think you better lie down, Nandy,' he said as he gently lay me on the bed and took my shoes off.

'Why did you leave me, Mark?' I asked him finally. 'I tried to find our love in my marriage and I never got it. You damaged me.'

Mark didn't answer. Instead, he said, 'I think we need to order food. Do you still like aglio e olio pasta or do you want Indian?'

'I've had Indian for so long. I want something American,' I said with a wry smile.

'You haven't changed a bit,' he said as he pulled me close to him and kissed me.

'I think I'll have another drink,' I said. 'Can we order a bigger bottle of wine?'

He smiled and ordered an expensive bottle for us. We caught up about old times as we sat casually on the bed facing each other. I told him about my life switch.

Mark found the humour in Annie taking over my life and Abhay falling for Annie. He laughed when I told him that I had caught them kissing in the hospital room.

'It's not funny!' I said even though he made me feel it really was.

'Yes it is.'

'Are you laughing at me?'

'No, honey. Not laughing at you. But trying to make you see the humour in all this,' he said. He kissed me casually on the lips as if we were still lovers. And the casualness of it made me feel so comfortable. Abhay never gave me these casual hugs and kisses in our marriage. I had to beg him to touch me or hold me and he had kissed Annie so casually. Was that what we all wanted in a relationship? The need of another person for you? And not just to do things but to hold you, kiss you and be physically intimate, knowing that you belonged to each other as no one else did. Mark continued, 'I'm laughing because he's such a fool for losing such a brilliant human being. For choosing someone who looks like you but can never be you. What a loser. What did you call this again?.'

'Life switch.'

'Seems more like a lie switch. You caught him in a lie.'

'Which is?'

'This marriage.'

I stayed quiet, staring at him. In a heartbeat, he had made me feel important and worthy and shown me a new perspective.

'Remind me again why we broke up?' I asked, smiling.

He shrugged, 'You needed to live in India.'

'No, because you didn't want to marry me. I was heartbroken and decided to come back,' I said with finality, giving him something to regret.

'Do all relationships need to end in marriage?'

Doesn't love deserve that? A progression?

He stood up and lifted me with his hand. He looked into my eyes and spoke softly, 'The good ones deserve another chance.' And then he pulled me closer and kissed me deeply and I let him.

I pulled away for a bit and answered firmly, 'I can't do this Mark. I still love Abhay. Even though he has hurt me, I am still in love with him and sleeping with you will only make me feel worse.'

'I love being with you, Nandita.'

And then what Ranjana said dawned on me. Men didn't want accountability. There could be love, respect, desire and humour in the relationship but only a man who chose to be committed would take on responsibility.

Mark saw my mood change. 'I don't understand, Nandita. He cheated on you. You're not doing anything wrong.'

'Just because he did doesn't mean I should. I don't need to stoop . . . I mean . . . If I do . . . there will never be any reconciliation.'

'I didn't mean . . . I'll call you a cab. Go home, Nandita. Do what you need to do. But just know this . . . don't compromise on who you are to stay married to him. Not all marriages have love. And not all those who love need a marriage.'

My rant was over. I gave Mark a long hug. I knew he didn't love me either. But I didn't need him to. And I wouldn't make the mistake of cheating on my husband with another man who wasn't in love with me. I deserved better.

'Thank you, babe,' he said to me. 'For coming tonight. I didn't think I would ever see you again.'

I held his face with tenderness and left. As I walked out of his room, I felt a part of the old me die. The one that was unsure about being loved, the one that needed validation from a man. I felt I could be anything I needed to be because nothing was going to stop me any longer. I had to live my own life the way I chose it and not because of my circumstances.

Maybe I was foolish to believe in love. To believe that I could still make my marriage work. That despite everything,

Abhay would still fall back in love with me. It's not easy to fall out of love with someone. No matter how much he has broken your heart. You still believe that he will come to his senses eventually and love you again. And I was going to hold on to that hope.

But just as I was exiting the lift, I saw my sister Samaira entering with a man about twenty years older than her. Both of us were stunned to see each other.

'Nandita,' she said anxiously, 'What are you doing here?'

Thirty-one

Annie

How to Steal a Husband

There are two things you can't plan for in life. Love and death. You don't know when you'll fall in love and with whom. And you don't know when you'll die.

Annie knew this was her second chance at life. To come back from the dead, to wake up from a coma. She wasn't going to miss this opportunity that the universe had given her.

She knew she had made an impact when she saw Abhay with Nandita. There was something in his eyes. But he had played it cool. She had gone along with his denial to his wife. So that's how he wanted it to be. Just casual? Was she just an affair for him? She didn't have enough time to process her feelings. Nandita and Abhay left and she was alone with her thoughts.

Maybe this life switch hadn't benefited anyone except Abhay, who got to sleep with two women now. Lucky bastard.

But then he came back. Her feelings weren't wrong.

She could see it in Abhay's eyes that he wanted her. The last few weeks she had enjoyed hanging out with his friends, running with him in the morning, occasionally playing tennis with him which he had taught her. They had bonded over his business, and she had given him ideas on how to market the jewellery better. She had modelled with the jewellery for a campaign they had thought of together. She was meant to be with Abhay. Not Nandita.

And yet Nandita was legally wedded to Abhay and she would never leave him. And he didn't have enough courage to leave her. Which would leave Annie as the 'other woman' all over again.

Annie felt she had said enough before she left his house. If she came across as desperate he would definitely not choose her. But if she walked away, he would feel he'd lost her and might come after her. Which he did.

'You're going to run again, right?' Abhay asked, worried about what this coma would mean for Annie.

'I don't know. What do you care?' Annie spoke softly as she looked away.

He held back a sob. 'I hate to see you like this.'

She heard the change in his voice. She took his hand and said, 'I'm so glad you're here.'

He had sat down on the bed looking towards the door and taken her hand. 'I'm there for you if you need me, Annie.'

Annie had nodded. He could have just squeezed her hand and left. What he had said was enough for her. She hadn't expected any more. He had not been part of her goals, her destiny.

'I wish I hadn't left you that day,' she said. 'I know if you need to be with your wife . . . I know this was stu—'

He leaned in and kissed her. It was a deep, meaningful kiss that meant what he had offered. It meant something more.

She felt that she had finally lucked out. And things were going to change.

Just at that moment, Nandita had walked in.

Annie's face had frozen as she saw the look on her face. She hadn't meant Nandita to find out this way. Only when she was better and Abhay had made up his mind completely did she want her to know. To maybe tell her together that things would be changing. Nandita had looked shocked, hurt, angry and visibly upset with both of them.

A smile left Annie's lips. At the timing. And the absurdity of the situation. Of this whole life switch that was meant to be fun and had turned into an actual life switch. She was sure Nandita walking in on them was destiny's way of giving her Abhay quicker. Nandita had been so angry that she had flung her phone and left.

Abhay had stood in shock for a second and looked at Annie. 'Fuck!' he exclaimed.

Annie pleaded, 'Let her go, Abhay!'

'I need to . . . sorry, Annie . . . I need to speak to her . . .'

'Abhay . . . this is a sign . . . Abhay!' Annie called out as he ran after Nandita. Then she waited but he didn't come back. And he didn't respond for several days.

Leena had come in later and Annie had been upset to see her mother fuss over her. Leena made a big deal about Annie having soup and asked the nurse several questions when they were taking Annie in for an MRI.

'Stop it, mother!' Annie said finally, after several hours of tolerating Leena.

Leena was taken aback. 'I was just—'

Annie interrupted her loud enough for the entire floor to hear, 'You only want me to get better so I can start giving you guys money again.'

'That's not true.'

'For the last six years, you've only called when you needed money. Have you asked how I am? Who I am with? How *I* am managing?'

'Annie, why are you even saying that? We tried but—'

'You barely tried.'

The nurses wheeled Annie away even as Leena sat in the room waiting for her to come back.

The nurse helped Annie with the MRI. Annie was thankful she didn't say anything to her during the entire process. She lay quiet and still inside the machine, thinking of all that she had gone through in the last six years. All she had managed alone, from broken heartbreaks to wins and losses at work, horrendous colleagues, the lack of friends. The pressure, mental stress and lack of support. She had become who she was not because she had chosen it. But because there was no other option.

When she was wheeled back, Annie saw her mother was still there, waiting for her, looking concerned. It irritated her no end. She ignored her mother, pretending to sleep so she could just leave.

But Leena had something to say and waited patiently until Annie finally looked at her and asked, 'What?'

'I've never pushed you to give us money. It was just going to be a loan anyway.'

'A loan? When were you going to pay back the loan? You have so much debt already from taking loans from people for a place that is old and no one wants to live there.'

'Don't talk like that. It's a family-run business.'

'It runs on MY money! It makes no profit. Just sell the damn place and live comfortably. But wait, why will you take my advice? You only take advice from the men in your life.

Papa, Chacha or even Amitabh, who is the most useless cousin I have, who doesn't know how to invest at all. But you only took money from me. Advice? Never!'

Leena stayed quiet. 'Okay.' She got up as the nurse walked in.

The nurse said, 'The doctor will be here soon. The patient cannot get agitated.'

'I'll go home for now. I'll come back later,' Leena said.

'Ma,' Annie said finally, taking a deep breath and feeling sorry for her outburst. But Leena had already picked up her bag and wiped a tear from her eye as she was leaving.

Annie called out, 'Ma . . . I think you need to head back to Delhi. I'll call Rhea and she'll take me home tomorrow. Papa needs you more than I do. I'll be fine.'

Leena didn't say a word. She just turned and walked away from the room, down the staircase and out of the hospital.

Annie was left alone in the room, wondering who was left in her life any more. But as her anger rose, she realized she didn't need anyone. She would manage on her own as she always had. And she always would.

The doctor entered and looked at her. 'Well, how is the patient today? Where did your mother go?'

'I'm okay. She's tired. She's just gone home,' Annie said not wanting to give any more details. She felt lost and desolate. Abhay had not been picking up her calls and her mother was angry with her. She felt as though there was no one in her life who she could count on. She desperately needed to become managing director now. It was all that was left.

Dr Padmanabhan, elderly and a little portly, with dyed hair and spectacles, looked at her MRI results for a long time.

'Am I dying?' Annie finally asked.

'No, you've made a miraculous recovery. It's unprecedented. I wish your mother or husband were here for me to share this with you.'

'Share what?'

'The good news,' he said.

'What good news?'

He smiled at Annie, 'You're pregnant.'

Thirty-two

Nandita

How to Be a Good Sister

When I met my sister in the lobby with a much older-looking man, I seriously forgot all my problems for a second and just stared at her. She looked like a deer caught in headlights. She didn't take that lift going up. Instead, she gestured to the man to leave without her and he got the hint.

My face revealed my feelings. 'What are you doing?'

'What are *you* doing here?' she asked. She had always been so cocky, impudent and so self-assured that it made me sick. But meeting a man so much elder to her meant there was something wrong. I immediately left my own woes aside to be a concerned elder sister. After all, I still loved Sam no matter how bratty and immature she was. I needed to figure out what was going on in her life for her to choose this man.

'Sam, either you tell me or . . .' I couldn't finish that sentence because the lift doors opened and I realized Mark was exiting from there.

'Hey, you're still here?' he said with a smile as he came towards me. 'Wanna grab . . .'

He saw the look on my face. Sam noticed it too. She gave a wicked smile. 'Well, well, well,' she said as her body language changed. 'You were here to see him. In his room. And you're giving me a moral lecture? I'm not the one who is married.'

'Nothing happened!' I defended myself.

She nodded her head, 'Sure! First Rohit and now this guy . . . you know what they say about people in glass houses . . . should not be throwing rocks at others!'

I pulled her hand and dragged her to the corner of the lobby. Mark followed but I told him to sit on a couch, which he did.

'Samaira, that man you're with . . . who is he?' I asked furiously.

'What do you care?'

'I'm your sister!'

Sam shrugged and replied, 'Please . . . you left when I was eight. You returned when I was in my teenage years. You've hardly been there as my sister.'

I took deep breaths to calm down. I had tried to be there for her through my weekly phone calls and every year when I had visited my parents. But she was always out for some class or visiting her friends. *How was I supposed to connect with her?*

'Sam . . .' I tried a softer approach. 'I'm concerned. He's much older than you. And you're going to get hurt. I don't expect you to be a virgin but are you . . . are you in love with that man?'

She folded her hands and asked, 'First, you tell me who's that.' She turned and pointed to Mark who was sitting on a couch.

I knew that if I wanted to get anything out of my sister, I needed to be honest. 'That's Mark. My ex-boyfriend from Yale.' Sam's eyes grew wide. She waited patiently for me to reveal more. So I took her to another couch and sat down. 'He was in town and I wanted to meet him.'

'Why did you go up to his room to meet him?'

I bit my lower lip. 'I went up there to sleep with him . . . to hurt Abhay . . . but I couldn't do it . . . I didn't want to.'

Sam suddenly looked concerned. 'Why did you want to hurt Abhay?'

But I wouldn't answer any more questions until she told me what she was up to. 'Who was that man you were going up with?'

'Just a friend.'

It was my turn to raise my eyebrows to display curiosity and surprise. She continued, 'He's a pilot. I'm dating him.'

'Samaira!'

But she wasn't listening any more. 'Why did you want to hurt Abhay?'

'Is he married?'

'Aren't you married?' She again exaggeratedly pointed to Mark sitting on the couch who looked at me and raised his head as if to ask what was going on.

I knew I had to tell her the complete truth otherwise Sam would walk away and I would never be able to connect with her. 'Abhay cheated on me. With . . . Annie.'

'Who's Annie?'

'She is a woman whom I met at the resort I went to last month. She looks exactly like me.'

Samaira's jaw dropped as I nodded to confirm what I said. 'Yeah. She looks like me.'

'So that's who I met at Olive,' she said as she remembered something. 'I thought it was you. She was cosy with the actor Rohit.'

'Yeah, Rohit. I know him too.'

Samaira seemed more shocked to learn this. There had been a lot that had happened in the course of the last month but I never had a chance to sit and think about it. A tear rolled down my cheek.

Mark came over with a tissue and returned to his seat. He then sent some coffee and a drink that a waiter brought over. Both were for me but he didn't know what I needed at the time. He just sat on the couch at a distance watching me, refusing to leave for wherever he needed to go even after I told him to go. Samaira saw all of it. She took the drink and I sipped on the coffee. She ignored the pilot who was waiting in his room even though he messaged her a few times during our conversation. I was dying to ask her but thought it wasn't the time to give her a lecture. I needed to create a bond first. I needed to be vulnerable before I preached.

'I saw Abhay kiss Annie,' I said finally.

'Oh fuck. What are you going to do?' Samaira asked me. But honestly, I hadn't thought of it. I didn't know what to do. She saw my hesitation. 'Well, you have to fight for him, Didi.'

She never called me Didi. So I looked at her more intently. She seemed passionate about the topic. 'Everything has come easy for you. You've never had to fight for anything in your life. Well, here is your opportunity to fight for something you really want. If you want Jiju, that is.'

I was perplexed by her statement. 'What do you mean I didn't need to fight for anything?'

'Oh, come on. I have had to fight for everything. Attention from Mummy–Papa, good grades, any change in my life, all of it.'

'What are you talking about?' I asked.

'Mummy and Papa always praised you. Compared me to you. You got into college so easily. You got a man to marry you on your first try. I mean, hell, you even have a man waiting for you right now,' she said as she waved at Mark. How could I tell her that things had not come easily? How I had lost Mark because he hadn't chosen marriage. How I had lost my marriage because my husband chose another woman, and how I lost a job that wasn't even mine. Things hadn't come easily. But I'd let things go because I thought that was the way it was supposed to be. If things don't work out, maybe something better might come later. I'd never really understood what I needed and I'd never fought for things I wanted.

Mark came over to us, seeing Sam gesture wildly at him. He stood apart a little awkwardly while I stood up to greet him. 'Hey . . . Mark, I don't expect you to wait. You've been so sweet.'

'Are you okay, Nandy?' he asked with his hands in his pockets.

I nodded and replied, 'Thank you for staying. I'll pay . . .'

He shook his head, 'It's all taken care of. Here's the spare key to my room in case you want to rest there or you guys wanna talk there. I'm leaving now. I won't be back till much later but message if you need the room for the night and I won't come back . . . um . . . tonight. I'll just sleep in the studio. I'm here for a couple of days. . . .' He rambled on and I could see his concern for me after so many years. Even though I had given him nothing in return.

'I thought you were here for longer,' I said. I didn't want to lose him so quickly. I might need a friend in the next few months. But I guess I was destined to figure this out on my own.

'I need to head to Singapore. Work.' He said and smiled apologetically for it. 'But I'm available to talk whenever you want, Nandy. You're very special in my life. And always will be.'

I hugged him. 'You are too.'

He nodded to Sam and left. My sister sat on the couch with a smug look on her face. 'He's amazing.'

'He is . . . but he never wanted to marry me.'

'Wise. I never want to get married either,' Sam said with finality. 'It's such a boring institution and all married couples are unhappy and cribbing.'

'Don't say that. Marriage is beautiful. It's about two people who share dreams together, who want to do things for each other, make each other happy and care for each other. And they're on a journey of love, laughter and even frustration, anger and annoyance. You don't need to sync perfectly with your spouse all the time. But you have someone who cherishes you. And you're not bored or lonely. Well, sometimes you're lonely in a marriage as well but then that's just one more emotion you evolve from too. Marriage is the growth of an individual. It makes you learn so many things about yourself that you wouldn't as a single woman. And everything in life is about growth. And choosing to grow with the experiences you have. And it's better with a person you love. Always.'

She listened intently to me. Or maybe she had tuned out. One could never tell with Samaira. Her phone pinged and she looked down at it. She was already distracted. Teenagers!

But she messaged the person as I took my purse to get up. 'It's Hari,' she said as she messaged back.

'How is the shoot going? Let me talk to him?' I said excitedly. I had missed Hari's cooking and chatter in the last month.

She shook her head as she put her phone down. 'He went to the shoot location but there was no shoot there. He spent all he had earned to buy clothes and stuff to look the part but when he got there, it was just a village. There was no shooting or film or whatever you had sent him there for. He's been struggling to get out. And he has no Google Pay or bank account. So I can't even send money to him. So he's worked as a labourer to earn some money and is now taking the train back.'

My jaw dropped. 'I didn't . . .' I began to say but stopped. A sudden realization swept over me. Annie had sent Hari away purposely to get him out of the way. Or else he might have told my in-laws something about her and there would have been chaos at home. So she made up the story of a shoot for him to go away permanently.

I stood up. 'Oh my god!'

She looked at me, 'Where are you going?'

'I was so stupid.'

'What?' Sam asked, but my mind was already racing with the things I needed to do.

'I have to go,' I said as I started walking away. Then quickly turned and came back to give her a hug. I needed to say one final thing to her as well. 'I'm not judging you for being with a married man or an older man, Sam. I'm just trying to make sure you don't get hurt.'

'Don't worry about me, Didi. I'm not invested in people as much as you are. I don't get hurt by men. I just get bored.'

I raised my eyebrows in surprise.

'I won't do anything that will harm me,' she promised and smiled. 'Besides, I have you to bail me out, right?'

For the first time, I felt a camaraderie with my sister that I'd never felt before.

But she had opened up my mind to something that I hadn't seen before. I wasn't going to just fight for Abhay. I was going to fight for the job as well. I had done a much better job than Annie. And if she could try to snatch my husband away from me. It was time for me to take the most prized thing in her life from her—the managing director position.

Thirty-three

How to Overcome Any Fear

Annie

Annie stood in front of her vision board. She looked at one of the words that she had cut from a magazine and taped there a few months ago. Miracle.

She had been hoping for a miracle at work because she had been struggling to get a win, but the miracle came in life itself. The doctors gave her a clean chit of health after doing several tests. They told her they had never seen anything like her recovery. After being in a coma for a week she was able to walk, converse and have a fully functional life.

'Maybe my brain just needed a week of sleep,' she had laughed out loud to the doctor.

Dr Padmanabhan had not laughed back. 'You'll need to take rest and not get your blood pressure up.'

But how could she not get her blood pressure up? Today was the day she would give her presentation to become the next managing director of Bright Communications. She was ready. She was a walking miracle. And she would play the game.

And when the role was handed over to her, she would go to Abhay and tell him that she was pregnant. And she would have it all—a job, a designation, power, and a husband and family. Hadn't this been her dream since she was little? Nandita had no dreams, Annie scoffed as she reached for her cup of black coffee, which suddenly made her nauseous. She kept the cup down and poured herself a glass of water instead. Nandita went with the flow. Annie did not. She had chosen everything in her life. She had *manifested* each and every situation. Even her going into a coma, probably. She looked at her reflection in the hall mirror. Annie was the kind of person who took responsibility for everything and actively made changes to her life. She was focused, driven and ambitious. And all these qualities had led her to this point, a fresh new beginning. And she was ready. Because she had manifested this miracle.

★ ★ ★

Nandita

Life proves to you that if you don't make a decision, it will make one for you or someone else will. It wasn't as though I was indecisive, I just took longer to figure out what I really wanted. But everyone around me was always in a hurry so I needed to be on their wavelength, their manic energy. So I just let them take the decisions and I went along with it. But I've realized that I can also make people wait until I decide. It's not their life that they're deciding about, it's mine.

Maybe I should never have left Mark. Maybe I should never have married Abhay. Maybe I should never have done this life switch. But I knew that I wanted to fight for what I had lost. Because the time had come for me to choose what I wanted finally. Even if those decisions were made for me by someone else. Life was asking me to choose if I needed them or not. A job, Abhay, a family, my dignity.

And I was finally ready to choose.

Thirty-four

Annie

How to Win over Friends and Influence People

'Life gives us few chances to make a difference. But if we can recognize those chances and grab them with every ounce of determination we have, then we can climb to the top. Here are two people who never give up on chances. They don't think of failure as a deterrent but as a challenge to do better. Their experience in this company had been invaluable. Annie and Sahil. They've been the company's backbone, leading us from one win to another. Bright Communications today has a turnover of over two hundred crore this year because of our two brightest stars.' Ranjana spoke at the meeting where the board of directors, the team and the contenders, Annie and Sahil, were present. The board applauded Ranjana but she noticed a few team members just folded their hands. These two weren't the candidates they would have chosen.

Annie wore a dark jacket and trousers and kept her hair slicked back in a ponytail. She knew the presentation she needed to make and what she was going to say. Her tenure at the company would give her a higher edge.

Ranjana continued, 'I would like to invite them individually to the front of the room to make their presentation on who should be the next managing director of Bright Communications.'

Sahil smiled at Annie wickedly as he straightened his tie. He knew he would win. There was not an iota of doubt in his head. He had schmoozed the board of directors for a long time, having drinks with them and catering to each one. He knew for a fact that Annie had done nothing of the sort. And in this business, everything was about networking. It wasn't only based on the merit of your work. He had enough people to delegate work to, but getting the support of the board members would ensure he lasted forever in this organization and could retire with a hefty packet by doing barely anything. Looking busy was also an art.

'But before I give the floor to Annie and Sahil, I would like to introduce all of you to a new friend of mine.' Ranjana stopped for effect. Annie looked at Sahil a little worried. He shrugged. The board members seemed curious. 'Someone who has changed the dynamic of the company in a short time.'

Annie started sweating under her arms. Why wasn't the AC working correctly? What was Ranjana doing?

'A woman who didn't know anything about advertising but came in to give a fresh perspective to the clients from whom we have the next two years locked in. Not to mention that she has been a big hit with some of the team members here. I'd like you to welcome my third finalist for the spot of managing director, Mrs Nandita Patel.'

Nandita entered in a maroon sari with her hair loose, looking ravishing and confident. Her smile hid her abject terror as she sashayed into the meeting and stood next to Ranjana. The board members, the team and Sahil sat shocked as everyone noticed the uncanny resemblance to Annie. They kept turning their heads to look at Annie who sat fuming, clenching her teeth while staring at Ranjana.

'What are you doing?' Annie stood up to ask Ranjana.

'Who is this?' Sahil asked for the sake of the board members.

Nandita looked at him and smiled. He knew perfectly well who she was. But he was playing the game that everyone wanted him to. Nandita knew all about his games. How he had manipulated Rhea, how he had conspired with Shivani to get her fired. Nandita looked around and knew that corporate life was just one big game. It wasn't politics as everyone claimed it was. It was just a game of snakes and ladders. How to avoid the snakes to get to the top and the luck of the roll of the dice in getting the clients that liked you. It really had nothing to do with intelligence, merit or hard work. It had to do with how long you could play the game and no matter how many snakes kept throwing you to the bottom of the board, how resilient you were to keep trying to climb to the top. And even at the number ninety-nine on the board, there was one last snake to cross before you won the game. This was that snake—Sahil and Annie—together. Annie had ruined Nandita's home life and Sahil had got her fired. Nandita knew she needed to roll the dice with a prayer on her lips now.

'I'm Nandita,' she started to speak. 'And as Ranjana said honestly, I know nothing about advertising. I studied psychology, in fact, in college. And I'm just a housewife.'

'This is bullshit,' Annie said as she interrupted her. 'Why is she here? This is a meeting for the managing director position.

Who is interested in what she has to say right now?' She waved her hand at Nandita and looked at the board of directors. 'She has no experience. And as she said, she's a housewife.'

The room erupted in chaos as everyone started speaking. Some were nodding and agreeing with Annie shouting, 'Fraudster!' as others cupped their mouths to say, 'Let Nandita speak.'

Ranjana raised her hands and shouted at everyone to calm down. 'I know this is a sudden change but let's hear what each of them has to say. Then we decide anyway. Let's not cancel anyone just yet. Now each of you please write your name on the piece of paper in front of you and let's put it in this bowl. We'll be democratic about it,' Ranjana smiled as Annie, Nandita and Sahil wrote their names and dropped their papers in an opaque bowl Ranjana passed to them. 'Now we'll get someone neutral to select our first speaker.'

Nandita turned around to see Shivani stand up and come towards Ranjana to take out a name. Nandita hoped it wouldn't be her. She needed a little more time to gather her thoughts. She needed to see how others would be presenting and figure out her own strategy. She'd never been in a board meeting before.

'Annie Singh,' Shivani said with a wicked smile as she looked at Annie and went back to her chair.

Annie sat up boldly and loaded her presentation on to the slide projector. She knew what she wanted. She looked at Ranjana and gave her a curt nod. She couldn't believe after everything she had done for this company, her boss had been the one to betray her. She had called Nandita to give a speech for the managing director position? *The fucking gall of it all.* Well, she would show them that she was the best candidate.

'Lights off, please,' she said as she came to the front of the large boardroom, which was packed with people in chairs all the way to the entrance. Someone switched off the lights and they all looked at the screen. Annie closed her eyes and took a deep breath. She saw her vision board in her head. Miracle. She was a walking miracle. And she could manifest anything she wanted.

'Ladies and gentlemen,' she started speaking and went on to show twenty slides of her most famous campaigns, the vision she had for this company for the future, and the person she was. But her last slide was the most shocking.

She showed her MRI scan and announced. 'That was my MRI scan from when I was in a coma last week.'

There was a general buzz in the room as she said, 'Lights, please.' Someone switched on the lights and she could see everyone's faces clearly. They were in shock. Sahil looked perplexed, Nandita looked nervous, Ranjana had folded her hands and was nonchalant.

'The doctors told me I was a miracle. A miracle. I regained all my neuro faculties in a week when it normally takes months. But while that may be at this physical realm I must tell you . . .' Annie paused for dramatic effect, 'I have come back from the dead.'

A few people sucked in their breath sharply as Sahil rolled his eyes.

But Annie didn't care. She was on a roll. 'During my time in a coma I truly went to another dimension . . . and saw that I wasn't ready to die yet. There was something inside me that told me I needed to live.' She clenched her fists and spoke from a place deep within her. 'My purpose was to be on this earth. And take this company to greater heights. I needed to live . . . for all of you . . . As you all know, I'm a single woman with no attachments. I've been a pain in the ass for the last few years to several of my team members. I truly assure you

I did it because I wanted you to improve and be able to rise in this company or wherever you went. I was particularly hard on the women, I know that.' She looked at Shivani and a few others who suddenly softened up hearing Annie come close to an apology. 'But I really just meant well.' She looked around the room. 'While I was in a coma, I finally understood my purpose. And that's why I woke up. And have come back to work . . . and my sole purpose is for all of you to get what you want from this company. I assure you I will make more profits for us to take home a better salary. I will give you the growth you need. I will work with each of you individually. Because we are a team and we may be a mid-size firm now but in the next ten years, we are going to be bigger and better than any of our competitors. And that is my guarantee as your next managing director.'

She folded her hands as if in prayer as she looked around. There was thunderous applause from the team members and a few from the board members. Annie looked over at Ranjana who smiled at her and winked. She knew she had cracked the presentation. She sat down knowing that neither Sahil's presentation nor naive Nandita's speech would hold a candle to her glorious discourse.

Ranjana said, 'Let's all take a break for five minutes and reconvene.'

Everyone started getting up and heading out. Annie sighed with relief and reached for her cup of black coffee. No one saw what happened next except one person.

Annie took a sip and recoiled in disgust. She started heaving as she felt more nauseous. She got up quickly holding her mouth and ran to the bathroom where she hurled her entire coffee and breakfast. She splashed some water on her face in the sink and reapplied her make-up.

Nandita stood in the corner. She had followed Annie to the bathroom. They both stared at each other. Annie didn't say a word to her. But she didn't need to.

'You're pregnant, aren't you?' Nandita asked Annie with a look that pained her. Annie didn't reply. She pursed her lips.

'It's Abhay's, isn't it?' Nandita asked as her anger rose. 'How could you? You've destroyed everything.'

Annie tried to reach out to Nandita, but she pushed her backwards and ran out of the building.

Thirty-five

Nandita

How to Bounce

It's funny, isn't it? All your life you might hope for something but when you finally get it, you don't know what to do with it. You might not even want it any more. I had only wanted to be accepted for who I was. I didn't need recognition or appreciation for my work. I didn't need power, prestige, money or fame as most people did. I just needed Abhay to love me. There are some people who lead an active, hectic life. They're always ambitious, wanting more, restless when they don't have enough, anxious when they're doing nothing. That wasn't me. I had been an easy-going child, a studious teenager and a calm adult. All I wanted was to work if I wanted to, to be married to a man who loved me and to have an easy life.

But this life switch had thrown me into a whirlpool of politics, scams and manipulation by someone who I barely knew.

My phone rang. *Was it time to go inside already?* I didn't feel ready. I saw it was Diya.

'Hey,' I said, almost breaking down on the phone with my best friend.

'What's wrong?' she asked immediately, understanding the tone of my voice. In a few sentences, I told her everything that had happened and where I was. There was a long pause after I finished speaking my truth. I didn't know if she would judge me for being stupid, for doing this life switch or tell me to just have an affair with Mark again.

But what she said surprised me, 'Nandu, I've known you our whole life and I can tell you something about you that you don't even recognize. You are way stronger than you give yourself credit for. And you might allow others to make the decisions for you, but you are the one who puts the choice in front of them. And both choices are something you pick out for yourself. You wanted to marry Abhay. You chose to walk out on Mark. You chose to do this life switch for yourself. You might have thought in the beginning it was for Abhay to respect you, but it wasn't. It was for yourself. So you would respect yourself. So you would be more than a housewife. You needed this. Look how far you've come. What all you've gone through. What you've overcome. So you deserve to be at the board meeting. And you deserve to be heard. Now go and tell them what you are made of. And show them who you can be.'

I stayed quiet for some time, soaking in her words. I still didn't feel confident enough. Especially when I knew that Annie was pregnant with my husband's child.

'Diya . . . Annie's pregnant,' I muttered.

'I'm sorry. What did you just say?'

'You heard it. Annie's having my husband's child.'

'That bastard!'

She had blamed Abhay first. And all this while I was blaming Annie. *Why was I absolving Abhay from the whole business?* I wished I could run away from all this horror. I couldn't deal with any of it.

'Do you think if I had a child, I would need all this excitement, this job? Maybe Abhay would have been more loving and faithful?'

I could hear Diya sigh, 'No.'

'Why no?'

'No, you never wanted a child, Nandita. If you did, you would have had one. It's been four years since you've been married. But you've wanted something more. You've never understood that part of yourself. You wanted a job where people respected you and where you could make a difference. And now you have that chance. You need to think about yourself right now. Not Abhay. Not Annie. You need to focus and share your side of the story. There is a room full of people waiting to hear it. Now is the time for you to shine. You come over after your meeting. We'll figure out what to do with Abhay. One step at a time.'

I sighed, 'But what if . . . '

'Stop doubting yourself. One step, Nandu. One breath at a time.'

'Okay,' I said with more confidence. 'Okay. I'm going to do this. Thanks. Bye.'

She hung up as I went inside. Sahil had started speaking and I took a seat in the back, trying to stay inconspicuous. Ranjana saw me and gave me a nod. I nodded back. My head was swirling with the news of Annie's pregnancy and the last month of this life switch. I'd lost everything. I tried to shake off my gloom and focus on everyone there.

Sahil was bold, dynamic and spoke absolute nonsense. He spoke about the people in his team and all the good times they had making presentations over the last year. He appealed to the men about personal things he knew about each of them—from cricket to the stock market to a web series they had all loved. He said a great leader knows how to make people have fun while leading them to greatness. And this organization was not about the rat race but about building it brick by brick with each person. He spoke about the three things he planned to do in the future for which he needed the support of his team and his colleagues, including Annie. He was charming, gregarious and his personality shone in the crowd. Everyone laughed at his jokes and nodded enthusiastically at his three-point plan.

I could see Annie partly furious at his stupidity and party sick from all the coffee smell in the room. I knew she was pregnant the minute she tried to have her usual black coffee. If she could retch from that, then it wasn't just a bad stomach. If it had been a bad stomach, she would have looked unwell from the beginning of her presentation. She only felt nauseous when it came to a particular food or drink, which was one of the symptoms of pregnancy.

There was loud applause for Sahil, and he looked as pleased as punch and puffed out his chest before he sat in his chair with a contented smile.

Ranjana stood up and spoke, 'Well, that was a very impressive presentation from you, Sahil. Everyone give him another round of applause.'

Annie folded her hands as Ranjana continued, 'I would like everyone to consider my next candidate as a wild-card entry. Sometimes we have an unknown person come and really change the game. Nandita has done that for us here and

I would like to give her an opportunity to state why she deserves to be managing director.'

'That's ridiculous,' Annie spoke up. 'She doesn't have any advertising background.'

I kept quiet as I saw her venom for me rise. And then something inside me snapped. I was not the meek housewife she thought I would be. I had chosen to be here.

I got up from my chair at the back of the room and walked towards the front. My confidence was returning very slowly. I was scared of speaking and I could feel a tight knot in my stomach. But I knew that if I didn't speak now, then I would never be able to. And even if I said something that was stupid or wrong, I would always remember that I had given it my best try, I didn't need to be perfect any more. I just needed to be me.

I spoke up, 'But as you say, Annie, we manifest everything in our life, right? So if you've earned the right to be here, then maybe I have too. You spoke about a miracle, right? Well, isn't it a miracle that you met me and I changed your life around?'

Everyone was staring at me as I stood next to Ranjana.

'You didn't change my life. You only put me in a coma,' Annie said sarcastically.

'Your blood pressure put you in the coma, Annie. And I sat at your bedside for two entire weeks while you were in a coma.' I didn't add that I had tormented myself to figure out if something had happened between my husband and her. 'But you're right, I don't have an advertising background. I have a degree in psychology.'

Annie waved her hands as if to say, 'See, I made my case.'

'And frankly, I'm not here to take the managing director position from either of these two candidates who are far more qualified than me and deserve it equally,' I said. There was a gasp from Annie and Sahil who stayed quiet after hearing this.

I looked at Ranjana and said, 'Thank you for giving me the opportunity to speak here. But you and I both know I'm not qualified to be a managing director of this prestigious company. I have had the chance to work with an amazing team and it's been a privilege to spend time in this office with such incredible minds.' I walked around a little as I held on to the mic so everyone could hear me. Then I stood by Annie's seat. I continued, 'I did this life switch with someone who looks like me because I really wanted to work. I was never allowed to. People didn't think I have what it takes to get a job, stay in a job, be good at a job. Or maybe they just want women to stay at home and be around for the family rather than find what they are good at. Women aren't allowed to fail. They're supposed to be perfect at everything from the beginning. So when I got the chance to be imperfect at something, I took my chance. And I thank Annie for exchanging her life with me. It didn't work out so well for me. But I've learnt loads of lessons. And that's what I want to share with you. You may have a job that you do just for the money, or a husband who doesn't love you, or a boyfriend who isn't committed, or a client who is cranky, a manager who is bossy, or family that is judgemental, critical or overbearing. These are just external circumstances to shape who you are and where you want to be. You always have a choice. And each choice leads you to an experience that your soul desires. Respect each choice. Respect yourself. And respect each other. Wherever you go and whatever you choose, always be respectful of this time you have had together. Thank you for the time all of you have given me. And all the best to Annie and Sahil.'

I sat down and had a glass of water feeling my hands shake. I had never spoken in front of so many people and I could feel the words just tumbling out. The room was quiet.

'Wait,' Sahil said, making it clear to everyone sitting in the room. 'You guys switched lives?'

Annie looked towards Ranjana for assurance but there was no response. I spoke, 'Yes, we did. For the last month or so, I guess.'

Annie nodded in agreement.

Sahil smirked, 'Well, isn't that fraud? Impersonation? Both of you could go to jail.'

There was again confusion in the boardroom and raised voices. Someone started recording us on their phone until Ranjana told him to stop live-streaming the meeting as it was a violation of privacy and he would be fired.

Suddenly the big screen lit up and one member of the board who had been on a muted call until now switched on his microphone. It was Vijay.

'Good evening, everyone,' he said jovially. 'I'm sorry I couldn't be there in person. I was diagnosed COVID-positive just yesterday. And we didn't want to wait another week till I was well to have this meeting.'

He spoke without turning his monitor on but there was something about his voice that sounded familiar. This was the man whom Sahil had schmoozed and claimed would be on his side to give him the managing director position. This was the man whom Annie said was biased and only liked men to succeed. Vijay was the most powerful man in the organization.

His monitor came on and we finally saw his face. I looked up to see the person the entire company was afraid of. The person's vote that was crucial in choosing the next managing director.

But he looked directly at me and said, 'Hello, Nandita.'

I felt so relieved seeing him after ages. Finally, a friendly face in the sea of confused and angry people. I smiled at him and replied, 'Hello Vijay . . . Mamu.'

Thirty-six

Nandita

How to Steal a Million

I'd never told anyone I was adopted.

But it's always been something that's bothered me. I've always felt the need to do more for people who had chosen to look after me. Give myself completely to people who have shown a little bit of love. I took up psychology not to analyse others, but to understand myself better.

I resented my sister when she was young because she was the miraculous conception our mother had been trying for, for so many years. When she gave up and thought she was perimenopausal, my mother conceived at the ripe age of forty-five years. Samaira was the child they pampered because she came from a deep longing. I came from a need to keep the neighbours quiet about why my parents weren't having a child after eight years of marriage. It wasn't from love or longing like my sister's birth.

The worst part was that my parents didn't tell me I was adopted. Vijay Mamu did. When my mother got pregnant with Samaira, she was bedridden for a few months and became very religious, praying each day to every god she knew. My father became obsessed with doctors, making sure this pregnancy went through smoothly. In the process they ignored me, and I spent more time with Vijay Mamu who was already a massive part of my childhood. He used to take me out to bookstores, restaurants and my drama classes where I was encouraged to be less shy. But he told me I was too smart and quiet because I didn't find anyone on my high wavelength to talk to. It was strange because I could talk to him nonstop about practically everything and he made me laugh as no one else did.

Then one day when we were at a bookstore, I picked up a book about a woman who had lost her parents when she was very young. I had asked Mamu to buy the book for me because unwittingly it resonated with me. That's when he told me I was adopted. He needed to tell me because he said he cared about me and he couldn't hide the truth any longer. Mamu told me they had died and said he had proof from the adoption agency.

My whole world shook that day. Not because I wanted to run away or find my true parents. It was because I needed to prove that I was worth loving if a new baby came into my parents' life. Would they love her more because she was theirs and I was an outsider?

From that day onwards I did everything they asked me to even if I resented them for it. And held a grudge for them not telling me sooner. When my mother came home from the hospital to show me my new sister, I immediately asked her why she hadn't told me I was adopted. She knew then only her brother Vijay was capable of this treason and banned him from my life.

So I rarely saw him in my teenage years, becoming lonelier and quieter. Mamu reached out to me but I didn't want to do anything that went against my parents, lest they send me back to the adoption agency. Vijay Mamu and I went out for dinner before I left for college because he wanted to give me a large deposit. 'Just enjoy yourself, Nandita,' he said to me with deep affection, 'And know that whatever you need, I'm always here to look out for you.'

I knew he was part of a big organization and had built it over the years. But I never asked him for details. I loved him but didn't know him too well. But he always kept a check on me. The last time I met him was at my wedding when my mother finally forgave him properly and allowed him back into our lives. By then it was a little too late as I was going to a new family and had to find my bearings there. I didn't know how to reconnect with him. I wasn't his little niece any more. And truthfully, after a point when you're dejected, you can't meet people who know you well because they might give you advice that you just can't take. And then you can't look them in the eye to say why you're refusing to get out of a tricky situation.

When I saw his face on the screen at the board meeting, I felt I had been transported all those years ago when he used to take me to cafés, and we laughed and chatted as if I had no care in the world. I almost cried seeing him again. I wanted to pour out all that I had gone through and all that I didn't know would happen now that Annie was pregnant with Abhay's child.

Vijay Mamu laughed at me when he saw my jaw drop as did everyone else's at the board meeting.

'You're her uncle?' Sahil asked, turning to the large screen that had Vijay Mamu's face on it. He turned to Ranjana. 'You knew about this?'

'Let's all calm down,' Ranjana said as she made everyone stop buzzing around. Once the room was quiet, she said, 'Vijay, the floor is yours.'

Vijay Sampath, the founder of Bright Communications, spoke about the company he had built over the last twenty years and what it stood for. I remembered when I was young how he could go on about values, ideals and leadership. Most of the time I tuned out at age eight.

'Nandita is my niece, yes, and I knew everything about this exchange that Annie and Nandita did. What a brilliant move! I could see Nandita in action and realized she was quite capable of running campaigns. Ranjana has kept me posted about what was happening. It was lovely to see it all behind the scenes.' He looked at both Annie and Sahil to keep them shut while I wondered how he knew.

But he had seen Annie join the company six years ago and realized I looked exactly like her. I thought back to the times when he looked at me intently and wanted to say something but held himself back. He didn't want to again be the bearer of bad news and be extradited from my life by his elder sister, my mother.

My mother had married into a Gujarati family and converted herself completely into the household to be accepted. She forgot about her roots and did everything to please my father. And she believed that if a woman did that, she would be the perfect wife and mother. Those were the values she instilled in me. Except I didn't want to be a perfect wife or mother any longer. I lived by her rules for so long that I forgot to make mine.

'So let's put this to a vote,' Vijay Mamu said as I blinked myself back to the boardroom. 'Instead of chits of paper, you can log in to the Bright Communications app that all of you have on your mobile phone. I know all of you record your attendance on it and submit fake bills.' He smiled as a few nervously chattered. He was a benevolent leader whom everyone admired even if he was stern and demanded excellence. 'There's a new feature on the home page that says "MD". If you click on that, you will see three candidates. Please select the one you want. The votes will be counted and sent to me.'

'That's very democratic of you, Vijay,' Ranjana commented. 'I thought you would choose your niece.'

Vijay just smiled like the Cheshire cat as everyone took time to vote through their phones. Annie and Sahil relaxed in their chairs as they voted for themselves. I glanced at Mamu and he nodded for me to vote as well. If I needed to have anything to do with this company, I had to become an active participant in the process. I couldn't just go with the flow and hope for a miracle.

A miracle.

I remembered the night when everything switched for me. It wasn't when I met Annie. It was when Abhay refused to have sex with me, again. I was despondent, finished a bottle of wine and had hoped for a miracle. And this was it.

Now, it was my time to shine too. Sometimes we don't know if we deserve something because we feel we don't have the skills or haven't proven ourselves enough. But the universe doesn't look at grades, talent or perseverance. It looks at moments of opportunities to change your life and gives them to you whether you're ready or not. That's when your preparation comes into play. Not the skill, acumen or desire. The belief in yourself. It's the universe asking, 'Do you have enough self-worth to go through with that opportunity no matter what the world will say about you later?'

'All right,' Vijay said after everyone had a few minutes to think and vote. A lifetime passed for me in those few moments before he announced the next managing director.

I thought of all that I had lost in these last few years, in this last one month. We are all drifting through life trying to do the best we can for others and to prove something to our judgemental selves. There's no right or wrong. Holding on or letting go. It's just all of us at any point trying to understand if it's worth it. But whatever we do, we have to stop being scared of others judging us and, more importantly, judging ourselves for each thought or action taken or not taken. We need to stop overthinking. And start making more mistakes by living.

I was comfortable about letting it go. The need for approval, the job, the marriage, all of it. And to start something new.

But you know what they say about the moment you choose something with all your heart. The moment you are at peace. The universe will give you something to question it all over again or give you exactly what you need.

Vijay laughed as he saw his phone. 'This has been so much fun. So the votes are in. And truthfully there is a slim margin. I can't believe it. So we have not one but **two** managing directors instead of one managing director.'

'What?' The room said the same word out loud. Ranjana looked at Annie who seemed confused. Sahil's face lit up as he knew he still had a shot at the title.

Annie waited patiently with her eyebrows furrowed.

I know how much she needed this. How hard she had worked for it. And how happy she would be if it all went her way. She would prove to everyone that she could have a child, a husband and a designation. All the things she had plotted to get the minute she met me. Except when you do things unscrupulously, karma has the last laugh. Because, as most people think, karma isn't bad or good. It's just the universe giving you what you deserve.

Vijay smiled and said, 'And I know these two people will lead my company to great heights with their camaraderie and people relationships. Ladies and gentlemen of Bright Communications . . . Your two new managing directors are . . . Nandita Patel and Sahil Sharma.'

Thirty-seven

Annie

How to Control Your Anger

Annie slammed the door of her apartment as she entered and threw her purse on the sofa. She took the pillow from the couch and screamed into it. *How dare Vijay tell her to work under an absolute imbecile?* She couldn't believe she had lost the managing director position to a woman who knew nothing about advertising, the company or being a boss. But that was not the humiliating part. She had come third and lost to a man who was less capable than her.

Sahil had immediately conceded and agreed to work with Nandita when Vijay requested both to support each other as new managing directors. But Annie knew that Vijay would give more importance to his own niece over the next few years. Sahil was a swine. All he needed in life was a job. He didn't care who he reported to or what his designation was. He had no loyalties or dignity. He would stay in the same company for the rest of his life, hoping to please the boss and doing very little.

Vijay had told her to stay on in the company. She was a *valuable asset*. The audacity of the man. Vice president of marketing, he said. What kind of a title was that? Report to two of her least favourite people in the world? For what? Where would that lead her in a few years? Annie had earned the position of managing director. Nandita had not. But, obviously, he had given the position to his niece. The nepotism of the place sickened her.

She had almost shouted at him, 'Show the results of the votes.' But Vijay had been too clever and had asked everyone to refresh their mobile app so the results could appear on their own phones. And glaringly and disgustingly it was Nandita's name that showed even on her own phone, followed by Sahil. She knew it was rigged. *Even the damn EVMs in the country were rigged, people said. So what's the big deal about a mobile app?* She just didn't know how to prove it.

Annie had stood up and said, 'But Nandita was pretending to be me. I helped her with the campaigns. I'm the one who made the win. I should be the one who is the managing director. She's too new. Can't everyone see that?'

But the room was mute. There wasn't a single person who supported Annie. They needed to keep their jobs. This wasn't *Jerry Maguire*. She didn't have a Dorothy. Even Shivani looked away.

Annie was shocked and looked at Ranjana for support. She pleaded with her to say something for all the years she had worked late, and weekends and holidays just to sacrifice everything for this company. But Ranjana was silent as well. Annie knew that if she went against Vijay, Ranjana wouldn't get the fat payout she was promised.

Vijay spoke to her, 'Annie, let's discuss this later.'

Annie had muttered and sat down dejected. She was sure the IT people in the company had made it look as if there was only one vote that was counted. Even if Nandita had got only one vote she would have been the winner.

After Vijay had told everyone the plans for the handover, Annie had gone to her office and given in her resignation letter immediately. She refused to work in the company any longer. She didn't know if she would regret it later, but she knew this was not the place for her any more.

Nandita had come in to talk to Annie. She had stood at the cabin door and said, 'I enjoyed being in this cabin as you.'

Annie hadn't waited to see her gloat. She had other plans. She had grabbed the photo of her running her first marathon, stuffed it into her bag and stood up. As she stormed out in anger and tears she said, 'You can have it then. It's all yours.'

At home, Annie went into the kitchen and took out a bottle of whisky. She poured herself a drink and then remembered she was pregnant. 'Fuck!' she exclaimed and almost threw the glass against the window.

She went to her home office and saw the vision board that had inspired her earlier that day. Miracle, it said. She tore it down and slammed it on the floor. She stamped on it, allowing herself to feel the fury of the situation. She screamed out in pain from not having any control over her life any longer. And when she was finally done screaming, she collapsed on the floor in tears. She had never cried in front of anyone. But just because she hadn't shown her emotions didn't mean she didn't feel them.

Once the tears had run out, she picked herself up and washed her face. She would plan her next move. She would find a new job and build her life over again. She went towards her laptop when she heard a key in the door. She went out of her drawing room thinking it was Rhea.

It wasn't.

'Rohit!' she exclaimed as she opened the door to a man struggling with the key.

'I told you I needed this place on the 1st. What are you still doing here?' Rohit hissed. 'And when did you change the locks to my door?'

He barged in and she saw a petite lady with long, lustrous hair and barely any clothes standing near the elevator. 'Is she with you?' Annie asked, looking at the woman but directing the question to her ex-boyfriend.

Rohit beckoned the woman to enter but she stood still outside. Annie shut the door on her.

'What are you doing in my house?' Annie asked, folding her hands.

'This is my house. And I've asked you repeatedly to vacate it.'

'So you can get your floozies here?'

'She's not a floozy.'

'I don't care,' Annie said as she walked around and sat on her most comfortable chair in the corner. She noticed how Nandita had made slight changes to her apartment. There was a potted plant in the corner. The fucking plant lady had taken over her apartment as well. Annie's fury rose. She picked up the plant and smashed it against the wall.

Rohit took a step back. He had never seen Annie like this. She had been angry or upset but she had never been violent.

Annie allowed the wave of fury to sweep through her and put it on full display to Rohit. 'I am not leaving.'

Rohit walked around in silence before speaking, 'How about this? I'll help you find another place.'

'You think I'm stupid? You said you were selling this place. It's just a pad for you to bring that floozy.'

Rohit pointed a finger at her face. 'Let me repeat, she is not a floozy.'

Annie slapped his finger out of her face. 'Show me the sale papers then.'

Rohit fumbled. 'Okay. She is planning to buy it. She wanted to see the apartment first.'

'Bullshit,' Annie said laughing.

'Annie,' Rohit said, 'don't do this. I've let you live here for so long. You've not paid rent . . .'

'Excuse me? I've paid for the maintenance of the place. And I did offer. But you wanted something else in exchange which I wasn't willing to give.'

'But now you need to go,' Rohit insisted.

Annie sat on the sofa and looked around. For a moment she felt she had lost everything. Her job, her house, a home. But then Rohit made a cardinal mistake. And everything fell into place for her.

'You can take the sofa,' he said.

And suddenly she remembered why he didn't want it. She took out her phone and scrolled through her videos. She showed him a clip they had taped together.

'I thought you liked this sofa?' She showed him the clip, with his loud moaning and thrusting on the sofa. It was three years ago when he had first brought her home.

'Why do you still have that?' Rohit's face became ashen as he realized she had kept all the videos and photos they had taken together. She scrolled through and showed him a few more. He was young and naive. His career hadn't taken off.

'I was lonely,' Annie said sarcastically. 'I needed to hold on to them, Rohit. But I can release them now. I'm sure I'll get something from the press for this. To help me get a new place . . .'

Rohit punched the air, not forgiving himself for making sex videos. 'Annie, I swear to god, if you release those videos, I'll . . .'

'You'll what?' Annie stood up and faced him. 'I have a better suggestion. Why don't you transfer the flat to my name? Tell your wife you've sold it to me if it gives her peace. And take that floozy to a hotel.'

'You'll still have the videos,' he said. 'How do I know you won't blackmail me later?'

Annie smiled. She could see how he was scared. His entire reputation for being the family man would come crumbling down. There would be a huge scandal and Bollywood wouldn't forgive him for years, not to mention that his wife who was pregnant might walk out on him. She knew it was a small price for him to pay to keep his image, his family and his career intact.

'I'll hand over this phone to you if that's what you want. Delete the videos yourself.'

Rohit was stunned by the turn of events. He walked around the sofa and cursed himself. But he knew he had no option.

'Fine,' he muttered. 'I'll email the papers.'

'Rohit,' Annie said. 'Let's do this quickly so you're not so tense. God knows who would get my phone and see the videos. After all, I just did a life switch with a woman who looks like me. Nandita Patel. You can look her up. I believe she told you I am pregnant. Maybe the media will think it's yours!'

His eyes went wide.

She continued, Now, Rohit, please get out of my apartment. Your floozy is waiting for you.'

She slammed the door when Rohit stepped out and finally felt a sense of relief after a long day. She sat on her sofa and put her feet up on the coffee table. She had saved one thing in her life. Her home. But she needed one more thing.

She knew she was on a roll. She had one more item left on her agenda. And she knew she would win there as well. She dialled his number.

Abhay picked up after it rang a few times. 'Hello?'

'Abhay,' Annie began. 'I need to meet you . . .'

She could hear him pause and contemplate his answer so it wouldn't be incriminating later. But he took a second longer than needed.

She decided it was best to tell him immediately. 'Abhay, I'm pregnant. It's yours. Will you meet me now?'

Thirty-eight

Nandita

How to Let Go With Ease

There are many reasons people choose to stay in a bad marriage. One feels the issues won't matter as one grows older or deeper into a marriage. They see all the other qualities of a partner and leave the bad out. They begin accepting more flaws. They say, 'It's okay he cheated. At least he is a stable man.' Or, 'It's okay he lied about the finances, at least he cares for you and didn't want you to worry.' Or, 'He couldn't say anything to his mother because he's confused but he bought you jewellery, didn't he?' The excuses come naturally. At least he's intelligent or funny or a good father. At least. At least. At least.

And we let things go because we live with the 'at least' part of a relationship. We compromise when we don't want to. But compromise is the name of the marriage game. If you want a long marriage, you must compromise.

I had given four years to my marriage. So I was willing to hear Abhay out. I was angry and I wanted an explanation and justification for his actions. I could forgive him if he loved me. We would work out the details together.

'Nandita,' Abhay snapped his fingers in front of my face. 'Are you listening?'

After staying at Diya's place for the past one week, I had finally given in to meeting Abhay at our favourite Indian restaurant. But for the last half hour, he had gone on about what he had been doing and how he had been so confused about whether it was me or Annie. And when he kissed Annie in the hospital, it was to be certain that he didn't love her. So he finally said it to me. The words I had been longing for in my marriage. The sentence I needed that sparked the entire life switch.

'I love you, Nandita,' he said as he held my hand. I paused before I answered him. I looked down at the bouquet he had brought me as an apology. Orchids. I sighed. I hated orchids. They were my least favourite flowers. And they were pre-wrapped with sickly pink ribbon and metres of plastic and string choking the flowers.

'I only want you, Nandita,' he said. 'Will you come home now?'

I looked at him earnestly and replied, 'I've never liked orchids. I've told you that.'

'When?'

'When you got me orchids for my last three birthdays. I told you . . . I prefer sunflowers . . . or lilies.'

Abhay took back his hand and shook his head, 'How does that even matter? I like orchids. I got you flowers. Nandita, did you hear what I said? I want to spend my life with you.'

'Have you spoken to Annie?' I asked.

Abhay kept quiet for several seconds before he answered, weighing his words, 'She has reached out to me but I wanted to see you first.'

'First?' I asked looking around. 'First! So you're meeting her . . . second? Like if I said no, I don't want you in my life, you'd go to her?'

'Nandita, why do you twist everything? This is why it's so difficult . . .'

'To? For? It's so difficult to what? Complete the sentence, Abhay.' I folded my hands. I recognized that I would never have been able to react this way even a few months ago. I would have stayed quiet. Not provoked him. Probably apologized.

Abhay called the waiter and asked for another drink. He was stalling. A part of me wanted to know if Annie had told him. All my life I hadn't been clear about what I wanted. I expected the people I loved to know what I wanted. But I could express it now.

'Annie's pregnant . . . And you're the father.' I said bluntly. I wanted to see his reaction. He had none. He knew. I smiled, 'She told you.' It was so obvious. He wanted to see what I chose so he could get away with the responsibility of making a decision.

'I'm sorry, Nandita. I thought it was you. It had been so long . . . I didn't . . .' Abhay looked at me with pitiful eyes. 'I want you in my life. All my friends think I'll be a fool to give you up. But I need to do the right thing for Annie. So I need to support her as well, right? Do you want me to tell her to get an abortion? Is that what you want?'

How easily men shift the blame to a woman because they feel crippled to take life choices.

But I didn't have an answer to that. It had only been a day or so before my whole life had turned. Becoming managing director of a company, finding out my husband was going to be a father—it was all too much. *Annie and I had really exchanged our lives, not just for six weeks but an eternity.*

I put my head in my hands and said, 'I don't know.' I asked the waiter to get me a drink. I had wanted to stay clear for this conversation but maybe some alcohol would help ease the discomfort I felt around Abhay.

When I turned around, I saw Annie sitting at the bar. I almost did a double-take. What was she doing here? I turned back towards Abhay, 'Did you call her here?'

'Who?'

I tilted my head towards the bar where Annie was sitting sipping water. Clearly, she was careful during her pregnancy. 'Annie. Don't pretend you haven't seen her.'

Abhay shrugged. 'I was only paying attention to you.'

I ignored his answer. 'Is that why you wanted to meet her *second*? After you figured out what decision I was going to make?' Before he could reply, I got up to meet her.

I walked over to her. The waiter intercepted me before I could speak. 'Would you like your drink at the bar or at the table, ma'am?'

'At the table. I won't be at the bar for long,' I said, staring at Annie.

Annie smiled at me. 'How is it going?' she asked as if nothing was wrong.

'What are you doing here?'

Annie looked away from me towards Abhay. At that point, I knew whatever Abhay had been saying was nonsense. Something didn't feel right. My heart started racing and I was feeling sick inside. I needed to sit down. I went back to the table and sat on the sofa next to Abhay.

Annie followed me and sat on the chair opposite. 'I think it's best we discuss this together. After all, a child is involved.'

I glared at her. Annie stared at Abhay, hoping for a response that was favourable to her. I knew then that all along she had plotted to remove me from the family and stake her claim. I had been foolish enough not to recognize it. I had been naive and had put them together. Which stranger would uphold a promise? But I believed stupidly that no woman could seduce my husband. Because he was loyal to me.

Abhay didn't say anything. He was waiting for one of the women in his life to make a mistake or choose for him.

I picked up my drink. Annie said spontaneously, 'Cheers.' I replied, 'To what?'

Annie kept quiet. We were all silent at the table, unable to express what we felt and afraid to speak about a future that seemed uncertain and impossible. *Would we all be a family? Raise a child together?* People had done it in the past. But wouldn't I want my own child at some point? My child would have to compete with this firstborn who wasn't mine. Annie would be in our house constantly. She would be the mother and I would be a babysitter. The possibilities were swirling in my head.

But just then Annie said something that began to clear the clouds of confusion from my head. 'Abhay, my first night at your place . . . when we were in our room and . . .'

He scowled at her as if to tell her to keep quiet but she continued, 'We were drinking . . . I said cheers . . .'

'Yeah, so?' Abhay crossed his arms.

'You knew then,' Annie said matter-of-factly. I looked shocked.

'What?' Abhay asked nonchalantly.

I sighed before replying, 'Haven't you noticed I always say cheers with something?' He looked puzzled, 'Come on Abhay, you told me yourself that I always say cheers *to something* instead of just cheers.' If he knew that I wasn't her on the first night she was there, then all his choices were made from the viewpoint of having the affair. He didn't question her the entire time she was there. He knew she wasn't me.

But it was a small thing. Abhay barely noticed this stuff. There are lots of people who just say cheers sometimes, with a statement to something at other times. It meant nothing. Abhay himself looked confused. Men easily forget such things.

Annie looked at me with a mixture of sympathy, gloating and victory. She tilted her head to one side, 'Nandita, I didn't realize you wore your nose ring on the right side.'

'I've always worn it on this side.'

Annie looked at me and back at Abhay. 'But when I got it pierced . . . to play you . . . be you, I got it pierced on the left side.'

We stared at each other for some time. I hadn't noticed it because when I was looking at her, I felt as if I was looking in a mirror. We had got the same hairstyle, exchanged clothes and bags, and when we checked each other out before we left the resort, we agreed we looked like each other. I had specifically said, 'It's like I'm looking in the mirror.'

It hadn't occurred to us that the mirror reflects an opposite image.

But it would have occurred to Abhay. It should have.

We both looked at him. Annie didn't have her nose ring on. She had never wanted it in the first place. It was probably removed by the nurse when she was taken in for an MRI.

I looked at Abhay and spoke calmly as my heart raced. 'You knew from the beginning that it wasn't me. There were so many clues. You know what, Abhay, I don't think we should be together.'

'What?' Annie and Abhay spoke in unison.

'All I wanted for so many years was for you to love me, Abhay . . .'

'And I . . .' Abhay started before I put up my finger and shushed him. I continued, 'But I don't care any more. I just don't care.'

As soon as the words left my mouth, I knew them to be true. I looked at Annie who thought she could have my life here, but I wouldn't let that happen.

I took a sip of my drink and found more confidence. 'I'm going to figure out what I want in my life, Abhay. But I'm not going to give you a divorce. You will never be able to marry Annie. So even if she stays with you and takes my place, she'll never have anything I can't claim as your lawfully wedded wife.' I saw Annie's face fall from the corner of my eye.

'Nandita, please be reasonable,' Annie said. 'You yourself said he wasn't in love with you . . . that he never had sex . . . wouldn't it be best for everyone . . .'

Abhay interrupted, 'I didn't have sex?'

'This is not about you,' Annie said curtly to him as she looked towards me.

'Don't talk to my husband like that, Annie. He may be stupid but he's still mine. And only I get to torture him,' I smirked. 'I'm going to get Hari to collect my things . . . oh yes, he's back, Annie. After you sent him to a godforsaken place. He'll always be loyal to me. Goodbye, Abhay. I hope you enjoy the single life you deserve.'

Abhay got up as I did. He tried to protest and hold me back but I was done talking and didn't want to hear anything he had to say. Husbands rarely cherish their wives when they're with them. The minute the wife talks about leaving or having an affair, they wake up to realize what they could lose. If only they knew what they could lose without a woman threatening them, they would have a happier wife and a peaceful marriage.

Annie looked at me and smiled. 'True life switch eh, Nandita? You won. You've finally become me.'

I turned around and told her, 'But I'll never let you become me.' I knew what I was giving up. A family that allowed me to sleep when I wanted, supported me to do nothing, loved me for being nothing. A comfortable space. But I didn't want to be nothing. I wanted to be someone. And the only way one can achieve anything is to constantly leave one's comfort zone.

I was ready for my new life and I wouldn't switch it at all.

Thirty-nine

Annie

How to Get a Maternal Instinct

Abhay sat with his head in his hands as the waiter brought over some chicken tikkas for Annie as she contemplated what to do. Nandita had turned out more shrewd than she imagined. The naive housewife had turned into Shylock. It was the only Shakespeare play that Annie had read because she admired the character so much. But her life seemed to be more like *The Comedy of Errors*.

She looked at Abhay and realized she would have to be a mistress for the rest of her life if she chose to be with him. She wouldn't even be able to move into his home without people gossiping. Besides, she now already had her own home.

But what about this child? No, it wasn't a child. She needed to think of it as a foetus. She could abort it and move on with her life. But she needed him to step up and pay for everything she would have to go through.

'Well, um . . .' Annie cleared her throat to start speaking. 'That was something.'

Abhay suddenly changed tracks and looked at the flowers on the seat. He presented them to Annie. 'Do you like orchids?' he asked tenderly.

She nodded and said, 'Yes I do, actually. But didn't you get them for Nandita? Are you giving me leftover flowers? Isn't it bad enough I'm getting a leftover husband?'

Abhay sighed. 'You told me at the tennis club once when we were dining with Maria and Syed that you liked orchids. I got confused when I bought them today. Forget it.'

Annie had a twinge of sympathy for the man. She didn't know what was happening to her. Was it the hormones? She couldn't imagine a life with a man and a child. That's not who she was. She had thought she wanted a husband and a home because she was just tired. Tired of running to prove herself. Tired of trying to earn money for her family. Tired of trying to find love.

Abhay was a great man and they got along well. But she couldn't picture a future with him. Even if Nandita gave him a divorce a few years down the line, would she marry him and raise his child? She doubted it.

She had other plans already. Abhay loved his tennis and partying. Why would he stay at home to be a father? He had definitely been more attracted to Annie than Nandita. But he would go back to being the same type of husband for her as well. The one who watched Netflix in the evenings and played tennis three times a week.

But Abhay said something that surprised her. He rubbed his chin and said, 'I don't want you to get an abortion. I want to keep this child. Hold on, before you protest, hear me out.'

Annie folded her hands to hear him. He leaned across the table and spoke seriously, 'I want to be a father. No, really! I've always loved kids. But Nandita never wanted . . . never mind . . . I know it's your body and you have full right to choose what you want to do. But if you choose to have this child . . .' he hesitated before speaking the next sentence. 'If you have this child, I will raise it with my family.'

'What?'

The waiter came to ask them if they wanted to order anything and Annie glared at him as if she could've killed him. The few seconds gave Abhay a little time to think about what he had just said as the idea started concretizing in his head.

Annie turned to Abhay and said, 'I don't want a child. I can't have that responsibility for the rest of my life. I want to apply for better jobs, maybe even travel for some time, do another advertising course. There are too many things in my head right now and a baby is not one of them.'

Abhay nodded. 'I understand. But I could be with you. I would support you. We could have this child together. You could leave the child with me and go abroad.'

'What?! Wouldn't that be worse for the child? You're not making sense. It's best we abort this child.'

'What if . . .' Abhay started and stopped to take a deep breath. 'What if I paid you to have the child and give it to me? No responsibilities. I would say it's adopted.' He fell silent.

'Go on,' she said, taking a sip of water and encouraging Abhay.

'I would pay for all the medical expenses of having the child. And on delivery of a healthy baby, I would pay you . . . a crore.'

Annie almost doubled up and spit her water in his face. 'A crore?' she asked incredulously.

'Either gender.'

'But why? You can easily get remarried in a few years and have your own children with your new wife. Or you can patch up with Nandita and have kids of your own.' Annie was always logical and expected the same from others.

Abhay paused for a second and Annie said, 'Hold that thought. I need to use the ladies' room.' Annie left the table while Abhay got lost in his thoughts of marriage and his wife.

His whole marriage flashed before his eyes. From the moment Nandita had come with her parents to meet him, he had been attracted to her. But love? He had never fallen in love with her. She just wasn't interesting enough. But he went along with the whole idea that one would eventually fall in love if one spent enough time with a person. He had no chemistry with Nandita. Once they got married, he used to be eager to do things with her, to her. But when she wouldn't participate in anything, his enthusiasm waned. He couldn't explain it. He thought maybe they should have a child, but she wasn't interested in that either. She had romantic notions in her head that weren't possible to do after marriage. How many times can a man go out for a romantic dinner alone with a partner who has nothing to contribute? All conversations would end in asking each other, 'What else?'

He had supported her in getting a job in the beginning, but she would whine about her boss so much that it became tiresome and stressful for him. He encouraged her not to work and follow different hobbies instead. But even there she would get bored and leave a course or project halfway. He got her to come to the shop, look at designs, mingle with customers so she could get interested in the family business. But here again she was bored, she claimed. She didn't like sports. She didn't like politics. She didn't like thriller shows on OTT platforms. There was literally nothing he could connect with her on.

Eventually, it became a power game. A tug of war. She needed him to prove to her that he loved her. And he needed her to do more things he enjoyed. And whenever anyone brought up children, she would scoff. Maybe she had been on birth control all this while. After four years there hadn't been a hint of a pregnancy. No shout of anxiety and delight any morning of the marriage that he hoped would lead to a change in their equation.

He had found happiness in other things. He knew he was neglecting her. But wasn't she neglecting him as well? Why did he need to please her all the time? Couldn't she try to show some interest in his hobbies as well? Why did he need to initiate intimacy? Didn't she desire him?

And when Annie exchanged places with Nandita, he knew. Not at the first moment but when he had kissed her that night, he knew something was off. There was more passion, more technique, more naughtiness. And it was electric after so long. His brain had gone into overdrive. Should he remain moral and take the high ground or go with the flow? He could have been shocked and asked her where his wife was. But, by then, he wondered if Nandita really cared as well. She had sent *another woman* in her place to replace her life. Was her life so boring with him? If they could play this game, then so could he.

Eventually, it wasn't just a game. He had fallen for Annie. But he knew she wouldn't make a great wife. She had barely cared for his parents who were important to him. She had barely cared for anything except money. But when he saw her lying in a coma, it shook him. And when she woke up, he was so relieved. He couldn't lose her. Even if she remained a friend for life. Or maybe more. He hadn't thought that through. But for the first time, he wanted to be with someone and do things for her.

When she told him she was pregnant, his immediate reaction was joy. He had whooped and hooted on the phone but she had groaned and hung up. He didn't have a plan then. But he did now.

Annie asked the question again as she sat down. 'What will happen to this kid if you have other kids with another woman? I don't want you neglecting my child.'

'Do you want to be a mother?' Abhay asked directly.

Annie had thought of it and the answer had always been the same. 'No. I'm just not the mother type. I like drinking with friends, and travelling . . . and running early mornings. I can't do that with a child. I want to work abroad and study more. A baby will just hinder that.'

'Then I promise you I'll be a good father. I won't involve you if you don't want to be. I'll tell the baby he or she was adopted. But please let me have this child. Go live your life. But please don't abort this baby.'

Annie thought about it for a long time sipping her cold water. It would be forty weeks of pregnancy. She would tell others that she was just being a surrogate to a friend, technically. The money would solve all the woes of her parents. And even though they would want a grandchild, she could tell them that she'd have one eventually when she found the correct man. But not now. Not this child.

This child wouldn't be aborted. It wouldn't be abandoned. It would be raised in a home that would give it love, happiness and support. The child would have all the material benefits that she didn't have. And with her looks, the child would be stunning enough to get by in the world even if it had the father's brains.

'I'll have a lawyer draw up a contract,' Annie said. Abhay nodded as a smile spread over his face. Annie continued, 'We'll have to agree on some details.'

Abhay got up and came towards her to give her a hug. 'Thank you.'

At that moment she looked up at him and his nearness made her senses spin. He leaned down and kissed her with happiness and passion before stepping away. 'Sorry,' he muttered and went back to sit down.

'I don't mind . . . it's okay . . .' Annie said as her heart softened. *What was it? The hormones?* She knew she needed to have a plan to get out of the country as soon as the baby was born or she would be sucked into something she hadn't planned. And Annie had always been in control. She wouldn't lose that now. As soon as she delivered, she would leave. The more she was around Abhay and the child, the more her life would get domesticated.

'Would you mind if I came with you to the doctor's appointments?' Abhay asked gingerly.

Annie smiled. 'Just don't get sentimental about it. Then I'll just have to ban you until the delivery, okay?'

Abhay nodded. His life was finally looking up. And it was all because of a life switch two women had done without his knowledge.

Epilogue

One Year Later

Nandita woke up when Hari knocked gently, opened her bedroom door and set her tea on her bedside table.

She mumbled, 'Thank you' and went back to sleep for ten more minutes. She'd been working late on the presentation she needed to make today to the new clients.

She got out of bed and opened her door to call out to her sister. 'Sam, wake up. You have your job interview today.' Her sister Samaira now stayed with her in the new apartment that Nandita had bought recently.

After the whole restaurant incident, Nandita had gone back to her parents and explained the entire drama that had happened in her life. She had sobbed and apologized for doing this horrendous life switch. Her parents had been surprisingly calm and not accused her of ruining her marriage. Instead, they welcomed her back home and were supportive of her working at Bright Communications under Vijay's tutelage.

But after a few months, she realized she couldn't live with her parents because even their support was driving her crazy. Sam, who was already fed up with their parents' constant advice, begged her to find another place for both of them. With a little help from her parents, Nandita decided to buy a two-bedroom flat in a swanky apartment complex and both the sisters moved in together. This was a way Nandita could keep a close eye on the men Sam was dating and forge a bond that was missing in their childhood years.

'I'm not doing yoga with you today,' Sam said as she emerged from her room to head to the kitchen for her green tea, which she chose to make herself even though Hari was back with them. 'I've got cramps.'

'Okay, I'll cancel with Asha then. I too have to be in the office soon,' Nandita said as she chose her outfit for the day.

'Isn't it your anniversary?' Sam said, looking at her mobile phone, which had just popped up a reminder.

Nandita froze. Had she forgotten about Abhay and their anniversary? She hadn't seen him around for some time. She had not gone back ever since they met at the restaurant. She had known then that he was in love with Annie. She didn't want to be with a man who didn't want to be with her. But she was bitter then. Vengeful. She didn't give him a divorce even though he reached out to her several times to discuss the arrangements. He said he'd give her whatever she wanted. But she didn't want anything monetarily. She had wanted love and respect. And if she couldn't get that, then she would be a Mrs Patel for the rest of her life to make him feel as terrible as he had made her feel.

Samaira had asked her if it stopped her from dating other men but Nandita had just replied, 'I've had enough of men for some time, so I'm okay to just be separated for now.'

Oh, she didn't need these thoughts today. Not before the most important client meeting of all. This deal would secure her position as managing director and Sahil would be eased out. She had listened to that mediocre man for so long. Now she needed to have the managing director position all to herself and this was her chance.

She had become comfortable in the boardroom, making presentations and taking meetings in Ranjana's old office which she had filled with plants and yellow chairs to make it brighter. She had changed as a person in the last year.

She had become as ambitious as Annie.

Nandita had heard from Abhay that Annie had had a baby boy. She knew Abhay and his family must have been overjoyed. They had wanted to celebrate it with everyone they knew but the fact that their son had a child out of wedlock and from an affair had stopped them from being too vocal about it.

It made Nandita feel powerful. All those years she'd been ignored. She felt vindicated.

She shook off the feeling and left for work. It was going to be a great day.

She reached the office and set her bag down, ready to have a cup of green tea and prepare her team for the presentation that afternoon. Her new secretary, Kyna, came in to give her some mail she had received.

'Ma'am, there's someone who's been waiting for you for a while,' Kyna said as she stood waiting for instructions.

'Who?'

'I don't know. But ma'am . . .' Kyna hesitated to speak. Nandita encouraged her to go on. 'She looks exactly like you.'

Nandita froze. So . . . she had finally come. 'Send her in after five minutes.'

Nandita had spoken to Abhay a few times when he had called. At first, he had apologized and asked her if she was ready to come back to him. But she was clear. She didn't want to be with a man who didn't love her. Then he had pestered her for a divorce. She hadn't figured out the terms then. He had tried all methods of cajoling, pleading, threats and despair. But she had been bitter. After a few months, she had finally gone for therapy. It had made a world of difference to her life. She could finally open up to a person who understood her, didn't judge her and helped her deal with the resentment and unhappiness that she didn't even know she had for so long. And while she had promised herself that she would continue therapy for some more time, she felt she was at a place where she could confront an old enemy and not be ruffled.

'Hey,' Annie said as she entered. She was about ten to fifteen kilos heavier than when Nandita had last seen her at the restaurant. It was probably the baby weight which was taking time to go. She hesitated to come towards Nandita but she took a few steps and hugged her. 'It's good to see you. I like what you've done with Ranjana's office. So many plants. They're lovely.'

Nandita was taken aback. She hadn't expected kindness. She'd expected a snarky, triumphant witch who had taken over Nandita's life and had come to gloat.

Annie sat on a chair and smiled. Nandita was on her guard. The woman had stolen her life. She would use any ploy to get what she wanted.

'What can I get you? Tea, coffee, juice?' Nandita offered politely and requested Kyna to get a fresh watermelon juice and a sandwich for Annie. She felt a mixture of pity, envy, elation and sadness at the same time. She would have to talk to her therapist about it later.

She sat opposite Annie and asked, 'So, what brings you here?' She didn't want to talk about the baby, the one she had heard Abhay was keeping and had paid her a hefty sum to not abort. The boldness of the man who never exhibited a single streak of nerve when they were married . . . together . . . they were still married.

Annie looked around and sipped on some water before her juice arrived. How life had changed. She should have been here, leading the company and the employees, half of whom she didn't recognize as she sat in the waiting room which she hadn't noticed before. All the people had changed. Shivani was gone. Sahil's office opposite Nandita's was empty. He'd have been in a meeting.

'What's it like working with Sahil?' Annie asked, trying to make polite conversation before she got to the point.

Nandita nodded before answering. Annie saw her mannerisms had changed. She was more measured, less impulsive and overthought everything before answering. So corporate! 'Oh, you know . . . the same.'

An office boy brought a grilled sandwich and the juice in for Annie and placed them on the table in front of them. He had also brought a green tea for Nandita.

'Change of beverage?' Annie asked, amused.

Nandita smiled. 'Still can't have black coffee, though.'

After a long pause, Annie finally spoke her truth, 'I don't want your job or this office any more, Nandita. I have got a job offer in Canada. They want me to start immediately. They're processing my papers right now.'

Nandita felt her body relax a bit and said, 'Well, congratulations. When do you leave?' She couldn't wait for Annie to be out of the country.

'That's what I wanted to discuss.' Annie took a sip of her juice as if it was alcohol. 'God, I miss vodka,' she sighed.

'Are you . . . the baby . . .' Nandita struggled to talk about Abhay's child.

But Annie didn't talk about her child. Their child. 'It's so difficult to lose weight. I can't run any more. I'm so tired. I've just started going for walks.'

Nandita was getting impatient. 'Annie, I have a lot of . . .' She looked around to hurry the woman up.

Annie nodded understandingly. She had to rip the Band-Aid off. 'Abhay and I are planning to leave with the baby for Canada. Together. I was going to give the baby to him but then I didn't want to . . . and then he said we'll raise him together . . . even if we never got married. And then I got this offer. It's so great. I can't give up this job. Because it's what I've wanted to do.'

Nandita got up and went to her chair at her desk to sit down. She was stunned. Abhay was leaving? He hadn't told her.

'I came to say goodbye. And . . . I wish you a happy life here.' Annie got up. She couldn't say what she needed to. She couldn't beg Nandita to give Abhay a divorce. He had asked her to go meet Nandita and plead with her as his conversations had only led to arguments. But Annie couldn't beg. She was curious to see her old office and agreed to go but she wouldn't beg in front of this woman.

Annie's life was what she had manifested for herself. She understood that finally. Throughout her pregnancy, Abhay had been there for her. His parents had been shocked and thrown a massive fit. But knowing there would be a grandchild in the house was far more appealing than berating the son and a woman who was having it for them.

When Annie had told her parents, her mother had broken down sobbing. Her father was furious that she could have done something so irresponsible. But when she had given them steady instalments for running their business, they had come around only to be present during the birth and welcome their grandson into their house.

Then Abhay had made the final instalment and said, 'I'm always there to help you with anything you need later as well, Annie.' And at that moment, she knew she loved him. He was a good man. Maybe mildly boring, self-absorbed and completely oblivious but nonetheless a good father and a decent man who had been attracted to her even through the course of her pregnancy.

But Annie didn't want to give up on her dreams, her ambition or her choices. Motherhood didn't mean slowing down in her career. She had applied to different places for a job and for some time had started working at a start-up. She had turned it around in such a short time that everyone was surprised. Annie had real talent. *Not like Nandita, who got the job through her uncle.* So when she updated her CV and sent it to a few HR managers, one of them came back with an opening in Canada that was actually legitimate. She was torn then, between leaving Yuvaan and Abhay and pursuing her dreams.

'Children have their own destiny,' her mother had told her. 'This child wants to grow up in Canada and take his parents along. This child has more ambition than you do.'

Annie had pondered long about this. She wanted her child with her even more. She told Abhay that she would pay him back but to let her keep the baby. But he had refused. Instead, he had surprised her and said he'd take a hiatus from his father's company to travel with her for the next two years.

'But will you still love me if I was just Yuvaan's father and nothing more . . . for some time till I figure out what I can do in Canada . . .?' he asked, knowing that a woman that ambitious wouldn't want to be with a man who wasn't as ambitious as her.

So here was Annie saying farewell to her old life, her old office, her lookalike. But the minute she had walked in, nothing felt like hers any more. The old watchman was the same smiling, forgetful, sleepy man, the corridors were the same, the loo where she had washed her face after several meetings that had gone badly was exactly where it had been. But everything had changed. She had changed. She wasn't the person who belonged here any more. She knew this life switch had changed her in more ways than anything ever had.

Annie had come to demand that Nandita give Abhay a divorce and set him free. But she realized that everyone needed their own time to let go. And if Nandita was on the verge of letting go, Annie asking Nandita for the divorce would halt her from doing so and might go in the reverse direction and take many more years.

Annie said, 'I need to plan my departure. There's far more to do with a baby and his passport, etc. God. But it was good to see you, Nandita.' Annie reached out as Nandita came towards her. 'All the best as the managing director. Remember, Sahil is a slime!'

Nandita laughed as they shared this inside joke. 'That he still is,' Nandita said as she hugged Annie and walked her to the door, making small talk about how Shivani quit when she realized that Nandita wouldn't have any of her gossip in the company and Vijay fired Koko for sexual harassment. Annie laughed as Nandita shared details of her life, the one that Annie had given her. Neither of them spoke about the fact that Nandita was still married to Abhay.

As the elevator doors shut on Annie, Nandita breathed a sigh of relief. It was over. This life switch. This game they had played and turned their lives upside down. They had what they wanted. Or whatever they had, they had to make do with. Now their choices were their own.

Another set of elevator doors opened and a man with a visitor's pass around his neck emerged. He was small-boned, medium height, with a dazzling smile. As he smiled and nodded at her, she could see how he held her gaze with kind eyes. He must have been in his late thirties or early forties. As he stretched out his hand, she noticed he wasn't wearing a wedding ring. But she was . . . still. Somehow, she had believed it would protect her from unwanted male overtures in the corporate world. Or maybe she had hoped it would mean being back in her marriage. A marriage with Abhay. Hoping that Abhay might still love her. But for so long she hadn't thought of Abhay or loved him at all. Maybe the love had died before she switched her life with Annie. Maybe it was not a test for him to choose her. But for her to choose him.

'Hi, I'm Neil. I'm from Anything But Boring, the ABB Agency. I'm here for our ten-thirty meeting.'

'I'm Nandita.'

'I know who you are.' His eyes clung to hers, analysing her with reverence. He was soft-spoken. Completely in awe.

Nandita felt a flutter through her stomach. She turned and gulped as she escorted him to a small visitor's room cabin before responding, 'I'll just need a few minutes . . . Please make yourself comfortable. Will you have some coffee?'

He nodded, 'Thank you.'

Nandita went into her cabin and sat in her chair. She looked through the glass to the office floor. Didn't she have what Annie had wanted? Hadn't she won this life switch too? She wasn't completely successful in changing the company around but she had made an impact at this workplace. There had been several failures in the last year, but she had kept going. Nandita now knew that failure and rejection were part of life. She'd been rejected by men personally and professionally so she knew how to fight harder to be acknowledged. In some ways, she had held on to the divorce papers because it was her way of making a man's life miserable as well. But revenge wasn't who she was.

She took out the packet from the bottom drawer of her desk. The divorce papers that Abhay had sent her. They had all the terms she had asked for. Except, she had never signed them. And he had given up hope. He'd stopped meeting, calling or requesting her to sign through text messages. He'd unfollowed her and made it clear he didn't want to be part of her life any more. So why was she holding on to him?

Nandita realized she didn't need to be married any more. It was okay for her to be single. And even though the future seemed uncertain and scary as a single woman, she had been one for a whole year now. She could manage her loneliness. She could take on this new journey too.

She turned to the last page, signed her name and then put her initials on all the pages. She took off her ring and put it in the top drawer of her desk. A single tear rolled down her cheek and she brushed it away. She finally let go of the love she had been holding on to. It was the most awful and liberating moment of her life. It was the right thing to do. She called her assistant and asked her to hand-deliver it to Abhay's address.

She sent a text to Abhay. 'I've signed them. Be happy. Goodbye.' She put down her phone and breathed a sigh of relief.

'To this life switch,' she said as she picked up her cup of green tea which had become cold and took a sip. 'May it be the beginning of a brand-new adventure.'

She got up to go for her meeting.

THE END

Acknowledgements

It's been a tough few years for everyone but especially for writers. New ones popped up during the pandemic and old ones tried to find inspiration from somewhere within their homes and their memories. And we all struggled together. So this book is dedicated to all the writers out there who are trying to make a mark still and hoping to be published and read. Keep going. Your words are important. Even if you don't believe in yourself most days. There is a light. Life is long. Don't be in a hurry.

I began to believe in myself again with the help of Vaishali, my editor at Penguin, to whom I'm indebted. A friend, confidante and my inspiration. Thank you so much for allowing me to take my time to write and trusting me. You have no idea how much you mean to me.

To Ralph—who changed this book to become what it was meant to be and guided me so much. Thank you.

I'm grateful to the entire team at Penguin Random House who've known me and believed in me for over a decade. I hope I can make you proud.

I'm thankful to Maheshwari Godse who is an anchor in my life, a platform to vent and who gives me pearls of wisdom regularly. Thank you for being everything a friend can be, Mash. Always.

I'm grateful to Parikshit for knowing what I need without me expressing it and giving me all the things I want when I ask for them. I must have done something good in some lifetime to deserve you in this one.

I don't know where I would be without the help and support of my sister, Neha, who humours me with her stories, understands me and looks after me so well. Thank you for being the best sister in the world.

Ma and Dad—thank you for always going along with my decisions in life even if you've thought them strange and exhausting. And for being such cool parents.

To my friends in Aldeia de Goa Phase 5—thank you for being there for me, opening your heart and home, and welcoming me whenever I need it.

The last few years have been wilder than my entire life and through it, my baby girl, Ariaana, has stayed steadfast, strong and stable as she matured into her teenage years in the pandemic. From us watching *Schitt's Creek* and *Ted Lasso* through anxious days, to moving our house and life to Goa to vacationing in Portugal and Spain, we did it all my rani—just Anna and Mama. Thank you for being you. I don't need you to be perfect or brave or strong. You're amazing just as you are and even if you change, you'll be fabulous and I'll always love you.

And most importantly, my life is incomplete without my spouse, Bala. Thank you for believing in our love and knowing that this is forever. Cheers to us building a bright, happy, comfortable future together.